W9-AOK-103

FROM THE
VÁRDAI-DAVIDSON
LIBRARY

GREAT LIVES:

WORLD RELIGIONS

FROM THE
VÁRDAI-DAVIDSON
LIBRARY

WILLIAM JAY JACOBS

Atheneum Books for Young Readers

JOHNSTOWN
PUBLIC LIBRARY

Atheneum Books for Young Readers
An imprint of Simon & Schuster Children's Publishing Division
1230 Avenue of the Americas
New York, New York 10020

Copyright © 1996 by William Jay Jacobs

Photographs by Photosearch, Inc.

All rights reserved including the right of reproduction in whole or in part in any form.

Book design by PIXEL PRESS

The text of this book is set in ITC Century Book

First Edition

Printed in the United States of America

10 9 8 7 6 5 4 3 2 1

Library of Congress Cataloging-in-Publication Data
Jacobs, William Jay.
World religions: great lives / William Jay Jacobs.—1st ed.
p. cm.
Includes bibliographical references and index.
Summary: A collective biography of 32 founders and proponents of religions
of the Eastern and Western Worlds.
ISBN 0-689-80486-5
1. Religious biography. 2. Religions. I. Title. BL72.J29 1996
291' .092—dc20
[B]
95-23047
CIP

5—
10/23

In memory of my parents

Contents

FOREWORD
Religion and the Search for Meaning in Life

The Romans often spoke of human existence in terms of vitam agere—*"to live a life." And all of us, indeed, are born, we "live a life," and then we die.*

What then is the meaning of such a life? Why are we alive? Who are we? Will anything happen to us after death? Will we be rewarded or punished for our deeds? Is there a heaven? A hell? Is there a God?

Even before people developed written languages and written history they asked those kinds of questions. And throughout the past there have been men and women of great wisdom who devoted themselves to seeking the answers.

Their answers, preserved in books and papers, institutions and rituals, were passed from generation to genera-tion. They became guides to the basic matter of how we, as mortals, properly should try to live a life. We have come to speak of such guides to human con-duct and to the meaning of life as *religions.*

Since the very beginning of time there have been different religions, different ways of looking at ourselves and at our proper behavior. Those ideas, those sys-tems of thought, no doubt are of basic importance. Thus it is hardly surprising that believers in one religion often have found themselves in bitter conflict with believers in other religions.

In time, some of the faiths that guided people's lives disappeared, while new ones came into being. Then, too, as great leaders died, new leaders appeared to take their places. Such has certainly been the case with champions of the leading religions: Hindus and Buddhists and Muslims and Jews and Christians.

And so the story goes . . . like life itself. Today we are alive. We eat. We sleep. We laugh. We cry. And we yearn to know what life is all about. That always has been true of people. And it always will be so.

In the past, those who have lived their lives on earth often have turned to philosophers and thinkers, to men and women of religion, for answers to questions. At other times the public has rejected history's religious leaders. They have been laughed at, confined to prison cells, or, as in the case of Jesus, executed.

Still, new religious leaders have always come forward. Some of them still do. And perhaps they always will.

Who then, in the history of world religions, were the truly great figures? What did they believe? What did they say that we, too, should also believe? What is it that we ourselves can learn from them—from the lives of Zoroaster and Buddha, Confucius and Muhammad, Moses and Jesus?

Clearly, few questions can be of equal importance to us. Such matters are, in fact, what this book is all about.

PART I

Faiths of Ancient Egypt and Persia

Akhenaten (Amenhotep IV)

(1370?–1340? B.C.) Egyptian religious leader in advance of his times

*Long, long ago in ancient Egypt
lived a powerful young king named
Amenhotep IV. Today he is better
known by the title he chose for himself:
Akhenaten, meaning "one who
serves the Aten." It was, indeed, the
god Aten that he chose to worship,
a decision to be remembered and
wondered at ever since that time.*

In the eyes of some scholars, Akhenaten stands out as one of the great personalities of the past. To Sigmund Freud, the father of modern psychiatry, the Egyptian ruler was "the teacher of Moses," while historian James Breasted once described him as "the first in-dividual in human history"—a person recognized on his own.

Before Akhenaten, the Egyptians had worshiped many gods, including the supposedly supreme figures of Amon and Re. Clearly, matters of religion were important. For hundreds of years the kings of Egypt, known as pharaohs, had shared authority not only with military leaders but with priests. During those times Egyptian armies spread widely the powers of their land, conquering African and Asian neighbors on all sides. The priests, meanwhile, had given purpose to the lives of Egypt's people.

By the time that Akhenaten's father, Amenhotep III, ruled over all the empire, Egypt had become very rich and powerful. There were gold mines. There was trade. But such great success brought with it change. Conquest introduced Egyptian soldiers to neighboring countries, where they learned new

A statue of Akhenaten.
The Louvre/Giraudon/Art Resource/NY.

customs and discovered new ideas about the gods. Foreigners began to visit Egypt, spreading the ways of their native lands in trade and commerce. Eventually, even the religious ideas of the conquerors and the conquered began to come together.

One sharp break with the past came in the custom of royal marriage. Amenhotep III chose for his wife the woman Tiy, who was not a princess but a commoner. Their child was destined to rule as Amenhotep IV—Akhenaten.

When he first took on the role of pharaoh, Amenhotep was only in his teens. In the beginning he ruled just as his father had: still worshiping the same gods, still living in the city of Thebes, where Egyptian monarchs had lived for so long.

From the beginning, however, there was a difference. Young Amenhotep IV was physically weaker than many of the former kings. He could not show off his strength in games of outdoor competition, as they had done. Instead, he spent much time in thought and study, particularly in the study of religion.

Before long, the people of Egypt began to see changes about them. New statues of the gods began to appear— softer figures, more curved in their outlines. Surprisingly, too, the young monarch showed special attention to only one god: the sun god, Aten.

Formerly statues honoring Aten had been placed inside buildings. Now Amenhotep insisted that Aten properly should be worshiped outdoors—where people at the same time could see the rays of his symbol, the holy sun.

Before long, many new places of worship began to appear. Instead of huge, formal buildings made from enormous stones, the young pharaoh's temples stood closer to the ground, were covered with small pictures and statues, and conveyed a sense of action.

Drawings of the ruler himself show him as very thin, with a small neck and shoulders and a bloated belly. At times he was pictured in the act of eating animal bones. His wife, Nefertiti—said by some historians to be his sister—often is portrayed by artists as exceptionally beautiful, but also sometimes as less appealing.

The art in Amenhotep's temples probably helps to explain what the young ruler was hoping to do. Most importantly, he was trying to break with the past and work toward new goals. In part, his purpose was religious, but he had other ends in mind, too.

Probably his principal aim was to regain kingly powers lost to the powerful Egyptian clergy. In order to win such powers for himself, he first had to destroy the gods used by the priests and to put new gods in their places.

It is clear, therefore, that even so early in human history, politics and religion could become closely related. Amenhotep must have understood that religion can, in fact, be the tool—the means—for achieving political purposes.

In the sixth year of his reign Amenhotep acted with dramatic swiftness. First, he changed his name to Akhenaten (he who serves the Aten), thus turning directly to the sun god to mark the start of the new religion. Next, he moved his place of rule north some two hundred miles from Thebes, to an uninhabited location along the river Nile, naming it Akhetaten (the Horizon of Aten's Power).

At Akhetaten, despite the strong opposition of Egypt's established priests, he quickly began to build a great new city (today's Tel el Amarna) and to create a largely new group of nobles and a new group of religious figures. All of the new leaders were expected to pledge their loyalty to the royal couple, Akhenaten and Nefertiti.

Those two rulers, accompanied by their six young daughters, then proceeded to organize an almost completly new style of living. Standing alongside people of the new city, they worshiped in a temple open to the sunlight even at the altar. They arranged to house officials in gracious new buildings filled with dramatically lively new paintings.

Much of the pharaoh's art showed people shopping in busy marketplaces or running through the streets. Such portraits gave the impression of an active, exciting style of life. Similarly, instead of tombs filled with terrible figures intended to frighten away evil demons, new kinds of graves began to appear: monuments structured to remember with joy the lives of those who had passed on.

Meanwhile, statues of old gods were destroyed. So, too, were statues of former pharaohs, including even those of Akhenaten's own father.

To a remarkable extent the new religion of Akhenaten was different from anything in the past. People were asked to look to the pharaoh himself for help in whatever it was that might happen after their deaths. Statues of Nefertiti also were placed in the temples. Yet the ruling monarch and his wife made it clear that they themselves worshiped and were devoted to only *a single god*—Aten. Probably never before in all of human history had such a belief, known today as monotheism, become so prominent, so powerful.

As many scholars have pointed out, the beliefs expressed by Akhenaten in his society's religious services sound very much like those of Psalm 104 in the Old Testament, probably written more than a thousand years later. Aten,

like the God of ancient Hebrews, is praised for all He has done to bring a blessing to all living things—to lions, goats, and fish, to birds, to the grass and plants, as well as to people. All receive the blessings of Aten. It is that god, like the very God worshiped in today's world, that was said to bestow such precious gifts upon the planet Earth.

Between past and present beliefs, however, there are differences. Most importantly, the religion of Akhenaten carried with it no threats of punishment for failing to obey its moral codes. There was no kingdom of hell to face in afterlife, no penalties to pay to Aten while life still continued. Instead, there was only the beauty of Aten's sun above and the graciousness of the Egyptian pharaoh, Akhenaten, and his mate, Nefertiti.

It may well be that such rewards—without the threat of possible punishment—proved not enough to hold the respect of the people of ancient Egypt. Meanwhile, the old priests continued to attack the new religion. Before long, faith in Akhenaten's new belief began to fade, soon to disappear altogether.

At the same time, from such distant lands as Palestine and Syria, Egyptian army commanders reported attacks on their forces. Hittite armies in Asia also launched successful offensives against the Egyptians. Hundreds of clay tablets bearing appeals to the pharaoh for aid

Akhenaten with his wife, Nefertiti, and one of their daughters adore the sun.
Egyptian Museum/Giraudon/Art Resource, NY.

now have been discovered. But for some reason Akhenaten appeared unwilling to respond with supplies and troop reinforcements.

Before too long, much of the great overseas empire of Egypt was lost. The rich Egyptian treasury became empty. Still, Akhenaten continued to deal mostly with matters of religion.

It is said that the pharaoh's mother, Tiy, at last awakened him to the dangers of his situation. It also is said that in those years Akhenaten's close relationship with his beloved wife, Nefertiti, showed signs of fading.

Whatever the truth of such stories, the pharaoh began to trust more and more of his powers to young Smenkhkare, the husband of one of his young daughters. With the passage of time, Smenkhkare worked ever harder to gain unity once again with the old religious and military parties still in Thebes, the former capital.

Still, the vast Egyptian empire continued to crumble. Sensing the government's weakness, all of the remaining colonies rose up in rebellion. Soon only the small original territory of long ago continued to be under Egyptian control. Many Egyptians themselves refused to pay taxes.

Once honored and strong, Akhenaten found his former friends deserting him. His power to rule largely disappeared.

Finally, deeply discouraged at his failure as a ruler, the pharaoh Akhenaten, although still young, gave way to an early death.

For less than a year Smenkhkare ruled in Egypt, followed then by Tutankhaten, the husband of yet another of Akhenaten's daughters. Under ever greater pressure from the powerful priests and soldiers, Tutankhaten returned the capital once again to the city of Thebes. He also gave up the worship of Aten, saying he truly believed in the old god, Amon. His name became Tutankhamen, as it would have been before Akhenaten adopted the new religious faith. When Tutankhamen died, several years later, the Egyptian army took control of the government, bringing back all of the old religious practices that still had not been restored.

Meanwhile, Akhenaten the ruler had met not only with death but with discredit at the hands of those who hated him. The old Egyptian priests, once again in charge of religion, officially referred to him in their writings as "that criminal." For a time at least, his achievements faded from history.

And yet, Akhenaten undoubtedly had done much during his reign to shape events in the kingdom of Egypt and beyond. Of the pharaohs who reigned both before and after him, no others dared to declare the existence of a single, all-powerful god. In addition to his insights into religion and philosophy, he was a poet and an artist. He enjoyed painting and sculpture. He loved to hear music, including the sound of harps and the beautiful songs of a choir made up of blind singers.

There is no doubt that Akhenaten's beliefs often were too advanced for the people he was called upon to lead. Many of those beliefs, however, have stood the test of time and are very much alive today, particularly the idea of beauty in people's relations with one another and a deep respect for truth. During the reign of Akhenaten such ideals may well have reached one of the highest points in all human history.

As for Akhenaten himself, he surely stands in company with the truly remarkable personalities of the ancient world.

Zoroaster (Zarathustra)

(660?–583? B.C.) Persian who believed that human good would triumph over evil

Today, in the city of Bombay, India, visitors sometimes climb to a quiet temple raised high above the busy traffic of surrounding streets. There, more than 120,000 members of the Parsee sect come to worship the ancient god Ahura Mazda, the god of light and goodness.

It is at that temple, too, that the Parsees put out upon platforms, or "Towers of Silence," the bodies of people who have died so that birds of prey may consume them for food. According to their religion, to bury the corpses or to burn them would be destructive to the sacred elements—fire, water, earth, and air—that make up our planet.

The Parsees of India are followers of the ancient prophet Zoroaster or, as he sometimes is called, Zarathustra. They believe that Ahura Mazda eventually will triumph completely over the forces of evil led by his archenemy, Ahriman. When that victory occurs, the dead shall live again, and all people forever afterward will be free from moral corruption, from old age, and from death.

Meanwhile, Zoroastrians believe people on earth should try to live good lives, should not be warlike or angry with their neighbors, and should not worship idols or be superstitious. A wonderful new life is to come, and evil will disappear.

The religion of Zoroastrianism now includes fewer than 200,000 people around the world, most of them in the city of Bombay. Yet once it was the

ZOROASTER

सपेतयान ꠰जरथोरत्त.

A modern representation of Zoroaster. *Brown Brothers*.

major faith of ancient Persia (today's Iran), and there were great swarms of followers in classical Greece and Egypt. Zoroaster, the prophet of that ancient belief, was considered holy.

According to the legend that is part of Zoroaster's religion, even while he was still inside his mother's womb the evil leader Ahriman tried to kill him but failed. As a result, Zoroaster came into the world laughing.

In truth, however, little is known about the prophet's life. It is said that he left home at the age of twenty and joined a priestly group. He himself writes of how he studied hard to become a priest and, while still young, wrote religious poetry. According to some stories he had three wives, three sons, and three daughters.

It probably is true that as a young man Zoroaster loved to go to the mountaintops and gaze at the stars and planets. Like a modern astronomer, he felt it important to study the heavens, but he also studied such matters of science as fire and light, eager to discover why things in nature worked as they did. He was a man of intense curiosity about nature.

Legend has it that, perhaps at the age of thirty, he had a vision, much like those experienced by the Hebrew leader Moses and the Christian Paul. According to the story that lives to the present day, Zoroaster stood one morning on the bank of a river, where Ahura Mazda, accompanied by a burning flame of light, visited him and commanded that he become a prophet and spend his life preaching the truth to people of the world. Zoroaster came to believe that he, like the light and fire he claimed to have seen that day, could help bring victory to the lord of truth and light— Ahura Mazda—over the lord of evil and darkness—Ahriman.

Nevertheless, ten years passed before any other person agreed to follow Zoroaster's teachings—and then the very first convert was his own cousin. Priests became so angry at him that Zoroaster finally decided to leave the region where he had lived so long. He looked for safety—and for followers— in the land of King Vishtaspa, a mighty monarch living to the east of Persia.

For two years Zoroaster worked hard to attract Vishtaspa to his new religion. Despite strong opposition from Vishtaspa's priests, he at last succeeded. According to one story, victory came when Zoroaster remarkably cured the illness of the monarch's ailing horse. Vishtaspa, along with his queen and eighty-eight others in the royal court, agreed to adopt the prophet's new religion.

Swiftly the religion began to spread, destined only a century after Zoroaster's death to extend east to India and west as far as Greece.

Why did Zoroaster's faith succeed so greatly, at least for time? What was its appeal? Most important, perhaps, was the hope it offered people for their future. Although the devil-like Ahriman seemed highly powerful, the forces of Ahura Mazda seemed even stronger. Thus the presence of evil in people's lives, it was thought, could truly be conquered. If only people lived up to their duties, did what was expected of them by the religion, their fate—and the fate of the human race—would become glowingly bright.

Still, Zoroaster believed that people would not always triumph as they lived their lives. Individuals sometimes would fail to choose the path of good and instead might well choose evil deeds. But the decision to do good or to do evil would be *their own*. Ahura Mazda did not create evil, but much evil clearly existed in the world. It was up to each individual, said Zoroaster, to decide: good or evil. It was a matter of free choice.

Zoroaster was saying, then, that people should fight bravely against the evil around them. They should be devoted to their religion. They should be thinkers, seeking knowledge. And they should worship at the altar of Ahura Mazda—the blazing fire of goodness.

The religion of Zoroaster has always been serious but happy and joyful, as well. On holidays, believers have a good time. They are expected to be pleasant to other people and to help them. In living their lives, Zoroastrians are supposed to work hard, to act justly, and to think good thoughts. They should not be greedy, but contented; not be angry, but calm; not be warlike, but peaceful. In place of falsehood or lies, they should offer only truth.

And what of the future? Will a person who had done evil deeds spend forever in hell? Not according to Zoroastrians. With punishment after death also comes the chance for new happiness. Before passing a final judgment, Ahura Mazda may raise every person to purity and goodness. Then, when all people are good, the devil (Ahriman) will be destroyed. At that point in the future, good will have triumphed completely and everyone will live forever in what Western religions such as Christianity and Judaism speak of as Heaven.

With such balanced thinking about good and evil, Zoroaster showed his rejection of the old religious ways practiced by priests and friends. He was saying that people should face the problem of evil directly—from inside their hearts—not just through formal ceremonies and rituals or through superstition. For this if for no other reason,

A gold votive plaque, dating from the fifth century B.C., shows a priest carrying a bundle of rods used in Zoroastrian ritual. *British Museum. Photograph by C. M. Dixon.*

Zoroaster probably deserves to be ranked among the greatest figures in all the history of religion.

At the same time, Zoroaster understood that rituals and ceremonies are important. In his formal teachings, for example, he encouraged followers to give special attention to the ideas that go along with blazing fires. To him, fire was something special. It was the sign of truth and justice, but also a symbol of life itself. In every temple of Zoroaster's faith there were—and still are—sacred fires burning all the time.

Zoroastrian believers wear sacred belts and shirts throughout their lives. At the time of death their bodies are cleansed and then the belts and shirts are placed upon them once again. Next, the corpses are exposed to flesh-eating birds atop the holy temples. The bodies are given to the birds—creatures of nature—rather than, as is the practice in most other religions, mixed with fire, water, earth, and air. To Zoroastrians, those elements are holy.

In Zoroaster's time such beliefs and practices proved appealing to many people. They were dramatic, exciting. They offered hope for the future, declaring that in time evil would be destroyed and good would win out.

As Zoroaster himself grew older, he gained greater respect. Still, to some of the earlier groups of priests he stood out as the prime enemy. Finally, or so the story goes, at the age of seventy-seven he was attacked and killed by one of the rival priests while praying by himself in a temple of fire.

It is uncertain whether the great prophet's body was put out to be eaten by vultures. Nor do we know whether, after death, his wishes for a funeral service were fulfilled. There were to be no tears, no wailing to express sorrow at the passing of a fellow human being. To him, death was only a step on the way to rebirth or resurrection.

Long after Zoroaster's death, such ideas would play an important role in shaping the beliefs of other religions, including the major faiths of today: Christianity, Judaism, Islam, Hinduism, and Buddhism. All of those religions display features borrowed from Zoroastrianism.

The rite of Satan, for example, so much like that of Ahriman to the Zoroastrians, is common to later forms of worship. Zoroastrian myths, including tales of angels and archangels, were known afterward by many leaders.

From Persia, Zoroaster's beliefs spread to India and the Far East. Some historians are convinced that the idea of a personal savior, like Zoroaster himself, played an important part in the formation of the religions of those who followed the Buddha. To the West, the same could later be said about faith in the teachings of Jesus.

Scholars have written, too, about Zoroaster's influence on Judaism and early Christianity concerning such issues as the conflict between good and evil, the existence of heaven and hell, and life after death.

It was Zoroaster who first put into practice a belief that true religion should not give too much attention to prayer for material goals, including the accumulation of money. Instead, it should be far more concerned with higher spiritual purposes, along with matters inside the human head and heart. He taught that people who have good thoughts and do good deeds will share after death a good life in God's kingdom. They will live forever in "the house of song."

In centuries following the prophet Zoroaster's death, the memory of both his person and personality gradually were lost. The "wise men," or Magi— priests he had replaced with those from his own new religion—simply counted him as one of their own faith. Instead of attempting to use his searching ways, those priests often tried to read the stars in the heavens and their followers' dreams.

The Magi also are known to other religions. Among Christians it is said that the birth of Jesus was announced to "the three kings of Orient," or Magi, by a new star over the town of Bethlehem. Today, the commonly used term *magic* is drawn directly from the word—and practices—of the Magi.

Despite the passing of Zoroaster's great following, his faith lives on even today, particularly in Bombay, India, where his followers continue to practice their founder's ways. They still worship fire, water, air, and earth; still study ancient writings; and still put out their dead in Towers of Silence, just as in ancient days. They are people of high character who hold moral standards very much like those of Zoroaster himself.

PART II

ASIAN
RELIGIONS

Confucius

(551–479 B.C.) Chinese philosopher committed to humanizing the existence of people, urging "not to do to others what you would not want them to do to you"

The religion of Confucianism is one of the deepest, the most profound paths of faith the world has ever known. Yet its founder, Confucius, lived a life filled with disappointment. As a teacher, he moved from place to place in China, unhappy with the way he was received by provincial rulers. During his lifetime his ideas gained little acceptance except from a small band of loyal followers.

Then, in the centuries following his death, the beliefs he had proposed were destined to gain acceptance not only in east Asia but by people around the world. Today there are many who still champion him, while at the same time calling themselves Buddhists, Muslims, Taoists, or Christians.

In 551 B.C., when he was born in China to the K'ung family, the future hero of millions around the globe was given the personal name of Ch'iu. The word *Confucius* is really the classical Latin way of saying K'ung Fu-tzu, meaning "K'ung the philosopher," as he later became known.

Although his ancestors had been people of wealth and power, by the time of Confucius' birth the family had little money. When he was three years old his father died, but the boy's mother worked closely with him, eventually helping him to become a fine student in school.

After school hours he engaged in hunting and fishing to help support his family. He also mastered the art of driving chariots. By the time he reached the age of fifteen, Confucius was recognized as a scholar, a person who learned his lessons well and asked searching questions. While still a young man he worked for the government in the province of Lu (today's Shantung), where he then lived. His tasks were to manage stables and to keep financial records. At the age of nineteen, he married.

As is true of many famous people, little is actually known about the early years in the life of Confucius—about his family, his friends, his teachers—but the notes he left behind at the time of his death say much about his love of learning and love of the arts. Those writings tell of how he truly wished to give up his government job and to devote his time to studying poetry and music. With the birth of a son, however, he needed money to provide for his family.

Still, he managed to devote many hours outside of work not only to the subjects he always before had delighted in but also to reading history and gaining skills in mathematics.

Before long he became known throughout his district as a man of great knowledge. People of all ages came to visit, speaking with him about philosophy and the arts. It was then that he first became known as K'ung Fu-tzu, "the philosopher."

When he was twenty-three years old his mother died. Like most others of that era, Confucius spent three years in mourning while devoting most of his free time to the study of history and philosophy. After the period of mourning he left his job with the government, turning to a career in teaching.

Word spread quickly of the great knowledge that Confucius had managed to acquire. From all around the province of Lu students came to learn from him. It is said that by the time he was thirty-four years old more than three thousand pupils and interested listeners regularly studied at his side.

Even in his very early years as an educator, Confucius taught his pupils that the purpose of their learning should be more than just the mastery of specific skills. Education, he said, should help to change society—should work to improve it. When people go to school they must indeed gain knowledge, but they must also build their personal characters and learn to help others.

According to Confucius, the time a person spent in school was to be a period of personal growth having, in the long run, a much broader goal. Above all, the student had to devote himself to creating a better community—building a better society.

At the very heart of Confucius' teaching was a statement that even today is well known: "Do not do to others what you would not want them to do to you."

An eighteenth-century engraving of Confucius. *The Bettmann Archive.*

Such a philosophy is often described as *humanism*, and numerous writers have described Confucius as the first of history's great humanists.

To spread his ideas Confucius walked from place to place, followed by crowds of his students. Sometimes, in order to visit distant locations, he traveled in a slow-moving oxcart, his students walking alongside him.

Much of what he taught related to history and politics, with special attention given to how government might best be operated. Those students, whether rich or poor, who became closest to him yearned to play a lifetime role in administering governments.

Confucius himself continued to look for opportunities in political office. His interest in winning such posts was not primarily a desire for making money or gaining power. What he sought more than anything else was to show how people could live better lives if governments were organized and run in ways that would help the masses.

It is said that at one point Confucius went to visit an old man, Lao-tsu, who then possessed great fame for his views on religion and on politics. Even now, Lao-tsu's brief book, the *Tao Te Ching*, is read widely by people around the world, including students in the United States.

Yet Confucius and Lao-tsu differed in important ways. Lao-tsu, for example, believed that people should be good even to those who harmed them, an idea that Jesus was later to make popular in the Western world. Confucius disagreed, saying that kindness should be met in return with kindness, but those who injured others should be punished.

Similarly, Confucius believed that religious leaders should play an active role in government, actually working to put their ideas into practice. Lao-tsu did not think it was possible for a true father of religion to participate actively in practical matters, even if daily life was filled with such evils as robbery, murder, and greed.

According to legend, Lao-tsu eventually grew upset with his young visitor, Confucius, finding him too well dressed, too certain of his ideas. Confucius, in turn, is said to have rejected Lao-tsu as not caring enough for the problems of real life. The two wise men—undoubtedly among the greatest philosophers in all of history—thus differed greatly in their views of what human existence really is all about.

Following his visit with Lao-tsu, Confucius continued for many years to travel about China, teaching his ideas. At last he returned to his home province of Lu, serving there as minister of justice. In that role he tried to put his ideas into practice, actually helping citizens to live better lives.

As he predicted, once people had good jobs, they turned away from crime. Fewer and fewer of them were sent to prison. The jails became almost empty. For a time, the province of Lu became a model for neighboring provinces.

A few leaders close to the king of Lu became jealous of what Confucius was achieving. Along with nobles in the neighboring state of Ch'i, they plotted to get rid of the great philosopher. As a present they gave the king a gift of eighty beautiful dancers, women who took all of the ruler's time for many days and nights. Try as he could, Confucius was unable to meet with the king to discuss important problems of government.

At last, unhappy with how the province was being managed, Confucius resigned his office and took to the road once again, hoping to find a better place to organize the kind of government he had in mind.

Year followed year as the philosopher traveled from city to city. But he met with little success in gaining support from the leaders of ancient China. Finally, when he was sixty-seven years old, the government of Lu invited him to return once again, not as a political leader this time but as a scholar, to

A copper engraving depicts the wandering scholar Confucius being greeted by the prince of the province he is about to enter. *The Bettmann Archive.*

spend his time in writing and study and teaching.

Confucius agreed to accept the offer. From that time until 479 B.C., when he died at the age of seventy-three, he met with thousands of students. He also busied himself with writing; some of his literary works became so honored that they have survived to the present.

Although it has been many centuries since Confucius last walked the earth, his words still are guideposts to the lives of millions of people.

In order to remember the great philosopher's teachings, some of his followers gathered together a book, now known in the West as the Analects. That volume summarizes in a very personal way what Confucius believed, what his fears and pleasures were, and what he thought about himself.

Through the Analects it is clear that, to Confucius, learning was perhaps the most critical task in life, the act that led to self-realization and to happiness. That deep desire to learn is what he demanded most firmly of his followers: "I do not enlighten anyone who is not eager to learn, nor encourage anyone who is not anxious to put his ideas into words."

If people could be brought together in their studies, taught Confucius, perhaps the problems that so deeply divided society might be overcome. By sharing a love of learning people could overcome the seemingly great differences that set them against one another. Learning could unite society, make people aware of themselves, convince them to help their neighbors.

To achieve such goals, he said, the government had to be strong, but it also had to be devoted to helping people.

That goal—serving the people—was at the very heart of what Confucius thought education and government should be all about. Each person, therefore, needed to be taught to care about his or her family, to share in various public ceremonies, and, above all, to learn to work with the government for a better society.

Thus religion, the family, and politics should work together, through education, to build human happiness. Becoming a joyful human being was something to be achieved through a united and caring community.

Following the death of Confucius, however, life in China did not live up to his dream of happiness. There were wars between various provinces of that land and wars between religious groups. Happiness remained, indeed, something of a dream.

Still, the ideas of Confucius lived on. One of his followers, Meng-tzu (371?–289? B.C.), tried to look at such matters as politics, jobs, moneymaking in the same ways Confucius had. Like his mentor, Meng-tzu taught that human beings were basically good and should work toward improving their minds while treating other people "as you would wish to be treated yourself."

According to Meng-tzu, even such powerful leaders as kings were equal to other people in terms of their worth as individuals. What really mattered in society, he said, was education, since an educated person could find work and would not feel a need to turn to crime. Society, declared Meng-tzu, must educate everyone in order to win happiness for all.

One of the other great spreaders of the teachings of Confucius was Hsün-Tzu (300?–230? B.C.). Unlike Meng-tzu, Hsün-Tzu believed that people began their lives with a tendency toward evil conduct. Only by learning to control their minds and bodies could they turn toward goodness. Yet, like Confucius, Hsün-Tzu believed that human beings could overcome the evil in their characters and choose instead a life of high moral conduct. To do that, he taught, they had to rely on good teachers, on good leaders in government, and on a society with good laws. Such a person could then put evil into the past and live a life filled with happiness.

As the years went by in China, the ideas of Confucius more and more became recognized as the nation's official religion. Confucian writings were woven into the curriculum of the schools. Leaders in government were drawn from special academies where five Confucian classics had become the central works to be studied.

One of those great works, the *I Ching*, became especially important.

That book concerned changes that affect all living things based on the ideas of yin and yang—opposite life forces relating to everything that takes place. People, said Confucius, were required to work their very hardest to become united with all other living things—indeed, to become united with the rest of the universe. To achieve those goals people had to practice good conduct.

Other Confucian classics taught in the schools preached, for example, the idea of good faith and responsibility in politics; a community based on trust that worked for the public good; and the use of history to help people understand themselves as well as the values of both ancient and modern times.

Students in Chinese schools eventually came to offer regular sacrifices to the memory of Confucius. All across China temples were built in his honor. Along with the emperor, he became perhaps the nation's most honored person. Although Taoism and Buddhism took the lead as popular religions in that country, even followers of those faiths continued to honor Confucius.

Over time, certain changes took place in the Confucian religion. One great prophet, Chu Hsi (ca. 1130–1200), rewrote the so-called Five Classics, helping to make them the central subject of study in the schools, as well as the basis for civil service examinations. In his rewriting, Chu Hsi preserved Confucius' emphasis on the pursuit of knowledge, but in his own versions he added an even greater emphasis on devotion to formal religion.

With the Mongol conquest of China in 1279 Confucian scholars again were forced to adjust. Some tried to withdraw from the general society, devoting themselves to formal study. Others took the opposite path, becoming actively involved in practical politics in order to hold the general public close to the traditional teachings of Confucius.

One Confucian scholar, Hsü Heng, even made it a point to educate the Mongol invaders and their sons in the ways of the religion. As a result, Confucianism continued to live on in Chinese society. In time, the conquering Mongols were themselves conquered, but not by force of arms. They were won over by the philosophy of Confucius.

In the modern era, the years since 1500, the Confucian religion has played a major role not only in China but also in Korea and Japan. Some five centuries ago the Korean aristocracy made it a point to introduce the teachings of Confucius into the schools and into the process of government. Today, particularly in South Korea, the area not dominated by the communist North, the Confucian religion remains strong. In Japan, Confucianism has existed side by side with the religion of Shintoism, playing a major role in such fields as government and the schools.

In very recent times, however, Western-style industrialization in Japan, Hong Kong, Singapore, and South Korea has raised a serious challenge to the continued strength of the Confucian view of right and wrong. Nevertheless, in all of those locations, Confucian studies are currently experiencing a strong revival. Even in communist-dominated China, Confucian scholars have tried to show that their ancient religion has much in common with the highly idealistic goals of Marxist thought.

Surprisingly, too, there are religious thinkers today even in such Western locations as Europe and the United States who express a hope that the ideas of Confucius might help to restore more humane, more civilized conduct in their countries.

As was true since the time of Confucius himself, leaders who follow his teachings are quick to point out that the usual practices of life must be judged not only in terms of what may happen after death in some distant heaven or hell. Instead, those judgments must consider life in the here and now—the actions and practices of people as they pass through days and nights on earth.

In that sense, the ancient teachings of Confucius still are very much alive. The world view that bears his name, Confucianism, remains one of the most popular of religions—a faith that for over two thousand years has continued to influence more than a quarter of our planet's population.

According to some scholars the basic thoughts of Confucius now offer fruitful possibilities for helping to shape a better future. As he himself once put it:

If there be righteousness in the heart, there will be beauty in the character.

If there be beauty in the character, there will be harmony in the home.

If there be harmony in the home, there will be order in the nation.

If there be order in the nation, there will be peace in the world.

Buddha (Siddhārtha Gautama)

(563?–483? B.C.) Indian believer in the achievement of salvation and peace by the control of one's own mind and a blending into the river of life

In Asia today more than 500 million people consider themselves Buddhists. Yet the word Buddha *is not the real name of a person. It is a title of honor in the Sanskrit language meaning "one who has been awakened" or "one who knows."*

Thus the great historical figure now spoken of around the world as "the Buddha" was not generally known by that name while he lived. Instead, he was referred to by the name of the clan (or family) in India that he was born into: Gautama. And the name given to him at birth was Siddhārtha.

The child Siddhārtha was born in Nepal, India, near the Ganges River, at the foot of the Himalaya Mountains. Even now some citizens of India are Buddhists, but far more believers live in China, Japan, Korea, Mongolia, and such locations in Southeast Asia as Burma, Thailand, Laos, Cambodia, and Vietnam. Beginning in the 1960s many citizens of the United States and Western Europe began to convert to the Buddhist religion, particularly the branch of it known as Zen Buddhism.

When Siddhārtha first breathed the air of planet Earth he was the child of a provincial king and queen. In his youth, as he later recalled, "I wore garments of silk and my attendants held a white umbrella over me." Handsome and intelligent, he was blessed with an adoring father and even had silver ornaments for his very own elephants. As a small child he was known, too, for his skills with a bow and arrow.

A sculpture from the second century B.C. in an Indian museum depicts the Buddha and his disciples. *The Bettmann Archive.*

Once, while walking in the woods with his cousin, Devadattha, young Siddhārtha is said to have saved from death and then set free into the air a small pigeon that Devadattha had shot with an arrow. According to legend, therefore, even in childhood the future Buddha cared about all living things.

At the age of twelve he became confirmed in the Hindu faith, the religion of his father. He then learned the Sanskrit language and, for four years, formally studied Hinduism. By the age of sixteen, when he returned home once again, he had proved himself to be an exceptionally fine student.

While still sixteen, he married the beautiful princess Yosodhara, according to Buddhist legend a woman born on the same day he had been born. Although Siddhārtha still spent much of his time in reading and study, the two became very close.

Not until thirteen years later, when Siddhārtha had reached the age of twenty-nine, was his life dramatically transformed. It is said that he was returning home one day after riding with his servant, Channah. Suddenly they saw before them at the side of the road a very old man, bent over in pain. When Siddhārtha asked what had happened to the man, Channah responded that it was, indeed, only the story of life: the man had become ill in his old age.

The next day they encountered another old man, so weak that even with the two canes in his hands he could hardly walk. Again, Siddhārtha asked what the problem might be with him. And once more Channah answered that such difficulties simply went along with getting old.

Then, on the third day, they came upon a funeral procession for still another old man. Behind his corpse followed his wife and children, all of them deep in tears. It was, declared Channah to his troubled master, just a matter of death, something that happens to all who live.

Returning home that night, Siddhārtha could not bring himself to share in the joys of a feast that his wife had planned for him. He was much too saddened by the three old men he had seen and by his deep awareness that all life must end eventually in death. That was true, he understood, not only for the poor, who often suffered so very much, but also for those of wealth and power, like the members of his own family.

The next day, it is said, he encoun-tered in the marketplace of the city still another old man. Yet that man, in spite of his simple clothing and his obvious poverty, seemed surprisingly happy, calm, and in control of himself. The difference was that he was a monk, a man of religion who spent his time thinking about deeper questions, such as the meaning of life and how best to live it.

According to legend, it was at that time that Siddhārtha decided to leave behind him his wealth and his title as a prince and to live the life of a poor monk. Only in that way, he concluded, would he ever discover what life was really all about.

Siddhārtha's father, the king, was deeply disappointed to learn of his son's decision. Soon afterward, Siddhārtha's wife, Yosodhara, gave birth to a son, Rahula. But instead of changing his mind and staying to watch his child grow, Siddhārtha ordered his servant, Channah, to prepare at once for a journey.

Fearful that love for his wife and newborn child would prevent him from leaving to become a monk, the young prince decided not to say goodbye. Instead, he quietly gazed at Rahula and Yosodhara, both asleep in a bedroom, and then rode speedily off into the night alongside Channah.

Far from the palace grounds, Siddhārtha stopped to shave off his beard and the hair upon his head. Then, after sending his servant home, he walked alone along the road. Soon he came upon a beggar wearing tattered old clothing. In exchange for those garments he gave the beggar his beautiful princely robe.

Thus he no longer was young Prince Siddhārtha Gautama. Instead, he was truly an independent man, searching for meaning in his life. In the Buddhist religion of today that night is always spoken of as the Great Renunciation.

For the next seven years Gautama wandered from place to place, trying to learn from the great religious leaders of the time. At first he studied with Alara, a wise man whose fame was known across all of India. Yet, before long, Alara declared that he had taught Gautama everything that he had to teach. With high hopes he asked the brilliant young scholar to stay on alongside him as a teacher, an honor Alara never before had offered. But Gautama had hope for even deeper learning and, instead of staying on to teach, departed.

He studied next with Uddaka, a scholar who taught him still more about the hidden, mysterious meanings of life—things that could better be understood by feeling than by reason or logic. But once again Gautama departed, believing that there was even more that he could learn, especially about why it

is that people become old and sick and finally die.

At one point he came upon what he described as "a beautiful stretch of land" alongside a "clear flowing river." It was there that he met with five monks, one of whom remembered him from long ago as the child Siddhārtha.

The monks taught him that true wisdom could come only by giving all attention to the mind and none to the body. When the body suffers, they said, the soul grows strong.

And so, day after day, week after week, year after year, Gautama tried to gain wisdom by thinking deeply and by almost starving himself to death. As he later recalled, his arms and legs withered to almost nothing; his backbone and ribs stuck out; the pupils of his eyes sank deep into their sockets; his scalp shriveled; the hair on his head fell off; and he often collapsed, striking his face upon the ground. One time he fainted and was thought to be dead.

Yet for nearly six years Gautama continued to live such a life of suffering, hoping to find answers to his questions about the meaning of human existence—if there was meaning at all.

Finally he decided to stop torturing himself. Instead, he determined to eat and drink enough to think clearly about the world and about the deepest possible matters to be found in human life. Unhappy with his decision, the five monks he had lived with for so long departed, convinced that he was betraying them.

For a time Gautama worked to regain his health. Then once again he took to the road, eating the fruit and berries he came upon in fields, along with the rice provided to him by people on city streets.

No doubt he must have become discouraged at times, perhaps even yearning for his former home, his loving wife and child. But still he traveled on, hoping for answers to the questions he had asked for so long, yearning to know the meaning of a human life and how best it should be lived.

Already, however, he had learned a basic lesson about life: people should not eat and drink and sleep too much, nor should they have too little of those things. Instead, they should practice the Middle Path. They should seek balance in the way they lived their lives.

One evening, as Gautama traveled in northeast India, he stopped to sit beneath the branches of a wild fig tree, known since then to all of history as the Bo tree, from the Indian word *Bodhi*, meaning "enlightenment" or "wisdom." It was there, as he later told the story, that truth finally came upon him—his understanding of what life was really all about.

According to Buddhist holy books, however, before Gautama could move on to achieve his goals he was challenged, while still he sat alone, by Mara, the evil spirit. Mara appeared to him during the night and tried to tempt him to live an easy life, one without conflict. But Gautama resisted, speaking sharply against the traits he accused Mara of championing. Those traits included such weaknesses as greed, laziness, fear, doubt, praise of self, and hatred of others.

Realizing that Gautama had defeated him, Mara unhappily left the scene.

For the rest of the night Gautama remained beneath the Bo tree. He came to understand ideas he long had dealt with, and by the time morning arrived he believed that his mind at last had been freed, his ignorance had disappeared, and he had acquired new knowledge. It was the moment when he truly had achieved wisdom.

No longer, therefore, was he Siddhārtha Gautama. Instead, he had become the Buddha—the enlightened one. To the Buddha and those who later followed his beliefs, that night had been the Sacred Night and the Bo tree under which he had sat was considered the Tree of Wisdom.

It is said that for seven times seven days and nights the Buddha remained under the holy tree, deep in thought.

A statue of the Buddha in Kamakura, Japan. *Brown Brothers.*

Then he set out to teach the new religion to others. At the city of Benares he encountered the five monks who had been so angered by his decision to eat and drink. At first they would not listen to him, but finally he described to them an idea they found deeply moving: a belief in the Middle Path.

The Middle Path was a life lived in between the extremes of a life filled only with pleasure or selfishness and a life filled only with self-torture. Both of those extremes, said the Buddha, were wrong.

Instead, human beings should not lie, steal, kill, use harsh language, become involved with occupations that lead to evil things, harm living creatures, or allow one's thoughts to be ruled by either too much joy or too much sorrow. Instead, there must be *balance* in every person's life. Always remember, he told the five monks: "From Good must come Good, and from Evil must come Evil."

So impressed were the monks with the wisdom of Buddha's remarks that they decided to join with him and to become his followers. They thus became the first to begin spreading the beliefs of the new religion, the faith to become known throughout the world as Buddhism.

From the city of Benares the Buddha went on to many parts of India, every-where attracting converts to his faith. Finally he returned to his native province, the homeland he had left so many years earlier. Although his father, the ruler of the province, welcomed him warmly, his wife, Yosodhara, at first refused. But when he came to visit her in her quarters, she fell to her knees and kissed his feet in love and admiration. Soon afterward his son, Rahula, also agreed to accept the Buddhist faith.

Before long the Buddhist religion had spread widely throughout the valley of the Ganges River. Rich people and poor people, men and women alike, agreed to follow the new faith.

Among the supposed converts was Devadattha, who as a child had once quarreled with his young cousin Siddhārtha over the shooting of a pigeon. Before long, Devadattha claimed that he should become leader of the faith if Buddha were to die.

The Buddha refused to agree, however, declaring that it would be the men and women of the faith who were to make such a choice. Angered by that decision, Devadattha tried three times to kill his distinguished cousin. When those attempts at murder failed, he tried next to organize a new religious community, only to have that plan fail, too. Soon afterward he became ill and died.

The Buddha himself finally grew old

as well, eventually reaching the age of eighty. Increasingly he suffered from illness. Then, knowing at last that death was nearing for him, he gathered the monks of his religion around him. He assured them that while it was indeed true that "all that lives must die," his ideas would surely live on. After he died, said the Buddha, they must continue working to achieve the ideas of the faith they all shared.

Soon afterward Siddhārtha Gautama, the Buddha, passed on.

Although the great leader was no longer in direct command of his religion, the memory of his life did not die. His followers recalled his extraordinarily fine mind. He had been a man who could get along with kings but also with the poorest of the poor.

Even after he had become famous he still walked calmly through the streets, his alms bowl in his hands, accepting food. As he once put it himself, "Rough is the ground . . . thin is the couch of leaves . . . sharp the cutting winter wind . . . yet I live happily."

During his lifetime the Buddha tried to turn back all of those around him who wanted to transform him into a god, reminding them that he was only a human being. He admitted to suffering sometimes from fear and even terror. Yet, at the same time, he believed that throughout his life he had before him a

special responsibility—a mission. It was the purpose of his time on earth, he said, to bring happiness to people, to help them.

To achieve his purposes the Buddha acted in ways that are different from the ways of most religions. He taught people that to find proper paths in religious matters, they should come to rely on themselves, not on holy leaders. Nor did they need formal religious ceremonies and special prayers guiding them to some future after death that nobody could really predict.

Similarly, he taught that people could not depend on past lessons of history in matters of religion. Instead, they must live their lives in the present—the here and now.

Furthermore, the lessons to be learned from life, said the Buddha, could be learned only by the learners themselves, by serious and constant effort, not through preaching. Religious leaders might help to teach people about such matters as right and wrong, good and evil, but each person must eventually work hard at that task alone.

And, finally, taught the Buddha, people could not rely on supernatural, superhuman, magical forces—miracles—to save them; they had to rely on themselves and what they actually accomplished in their lives.

After the Buddha died, many of his

beliefs about religion were changed by those who followed him, people who looked upon him as truly holy and more than just human. A few of his ideas, however, lived on just as he had taught them, and were destined to become a central part of the Buddhist faith as it exists today.

Especially important among those thoughts are what are known as the Four Noble Truths. The First Noble Truth is a belief that life is filled with suffering, misery, and pain. Such experiences begin with the pain of being born. They continue with sickness during life, especially in old age, when people frequently become tired, as well as fearful of illness and of death.

The Second Noble Truth is that people are mostly concerned with their own desires: their hopes for money, for success, for personal achievement. That Truth, said the Buddha, can be overcome by the Third Noble Truth: that people can go beyond such selfishness in life, can truly free themselves from looking out only for themselves. They can achieve that triumph by the Fourth Noble Truth, perhaps the very heart of the Buddhist religion. That Truth is known as the Eightfold Path.

The Eightfold Path offers answers to the terribly serious human problems that are included in the Truths of suffering and desire. According to the Buddha, those matters can be treated and happiness can be achieved, especially when life is lived in company with others who live good lives.

There are, he said, eight steps to such happiness:

1. *Right knowledge.* Even such problems as personal suffering can be conquered if people only learn to use reason.

2. *Right aspiration.* People can achieve greatness if they set their minds on a single goal, thus giving direction to their lives.

3. *Right speech.* By words that they speak people should not hurt the feelings of others or say things against them.

4. *Right behavior.* As would later be declared in the Ten Commandments of the Bible, the Buddha said to people that in their lives they must act properly:
Do not kill.
Do not steal.
Do not lie.
Do not be unchaste. (Practice sex only in marriage.)
Do not use intoxicants. (Avoid alcohol and drugs.)

5. *Right occupation.* People should not, for example, earn their livings as slave traders, prostitutes, or drug dealers. Such ways of earning money stand against the true purposes of living a good life.

6. *Right effort.* According to the Buddha, people should behave like the ox that makes its way along even the most difficult of paths, carrying a heavy load by steadily moving ahead toward a goal.

7. *Right mindfulness.* "All we are," said the Buddha, "is the result of what we have thought." People must always be alert, therefore, to what is happening to them, what is going on around them.

8. *Right absorption.* According to the Buddha, it is of great importance to fill the mind with truly significant matters, to look at the very deepest things in life rather than to be concerned with passing desires or anger.

In the Eightfold Path, therefore, the Buddha advised people not to deal with matters relating to magic or the supernatural. Instead, he counseled them to concentrate on changing their lives, making them better. "All that lives must die," taught the Buddha. But while people still are alive they have a chance to make something good of that existence.

After the Buddha died his followers divided into two different camps, two different ways of looking at his teachings. Those approaches are known today as Mahayana, or "Big Raft" Buddhism, and Hinayana, or "Little Raft" Buddhism. The Hinayanists consider themselves to be the true followers of the Buddha's beliefs and often describe their system as Theravada, the "way of the elders."

Many differences separate the two groups. The Theravada Buddhists, for example, see people as individuals—each person dependent on himself or herself in the world, guided by the wisdom of monks. The Mahayana followers think of people as linked together in groups, reaching their beliefs through prayer and, along with priests, helping one another. The Theravadans think of the Buddha himself as a wonderful wise man who started their religion but who now is dead, is in Nirvana, and does not know what is happening on earth. To the Mahayanists, the Buddha is more of a Christ-like holy figure, one whom followers should pray to for help and guidance.

Today the Mahayana Buddhists are strongest in China, Japan, Korea, Mongolia, and Tibet, while the Theravadans practice in Burma, Thailand, Laos, Cambodia, and Ceylon. In India, once the heart of Buddhist practice, the religion faded almost completely over the years but now is beginning to gain popularity once again.

One branch of Mahayana Buddhism that in the second half of the twentieth century became very popular in Western Europe and the United States is known as Zen Buddhism. Zen gained acceptance in Japan beginning in about the twelfth century; it held a special attraction for warriors who used it for ceremonies connected with archery and swordsmanship. Its teachings also made use of Japanese poetry, gardening, flower arrangements, and tea ceremonies.

Buddhist monks pray in a temple near Phoenix, Arizona. *AP/Wide World Photos. Photograph by Jeff Robbins.*

Zen teachers in today's world try to introduce their students to practical experiences rather than just to reading. Sometimes they will even have students tear up written articles dealing with the Buddha's ideas or with the possibility of Nirvana after death. Most Zen Buddhists are far less interested in the Buddha's concern for reason and logic than they are with feeling, emotion, and the discovery of mystical secrets of existence.

Still, in Buddhist societies around the world the twentieth century has seen a return to many of the Buddha's own views of what is important in life and what is right and wrong. There has been a new emphasis on the importance of science, as well as on ideas of good and evil.

Many Buddhists, too, have given strong support to the idea of permanent world peace through some kind of new international order—a world government. They have also spoken of helping people achieve better care through forms of democracy and socialism.

Even in countries where brutal communist rulers have taken power, as in Cambodia, Buddhism has somehow managed to survive among much of the population. Believers there have suffered greatly, as they have in China, North Korea, and Vietnam. The same has been true in noncommunist dictatorial nations, such as Burma. In free countries like Thailand and Japan, however, the Buddhist religion has continued to be strong.

Now, more than two thousand years after Gautama—the Buddha—lived his life, his ideas still endure. His religion, as well as many of the political ideas that seem to go along with it, continues today to play a powerful role in the daily existence of millions of human beings on our planet.

Mahavira

(599?–527? B.C.) Founder of Jainism, a religious system deeply committed to neither hurting nor killing any living thing, even in self-defense

In ancient India, during the sixth century before the birth of Jesus, many people became upset by the religious practice of sacrificing animals to the gods. What if it were true, they asked, that animals and human beings were related and that after death some animals actually became people in their next lives? Was it just and right to kill future human beings?

They asked, too, whether it was proper for people to be thrown at birth into permanent social classes—rich or poor—with no chance ever to improve themselves.

Two religious leaders of the time spoke out strongly against the killing of animals and against permanent social classes. One was the Buddha, while another was the famed Indian, Nataputta Vardhamana, known to history as Mahavira, "the great hero."

Vardhamana was born the second son of a king named Siddhārtha, who ruled over what in modern India is the state of Bihar. As a child he learned how to use the bow and arrow, how to ride horses, and how to care for elephants. According to legend, before he even became a teenager an elephant once stormed through a garden at his father's palace, frightening away all of the boys but Prince Vardhamana.

As the elephant came closer and closer, Vardhamana still did not move. At the last minute, he grasped the animal's trunk, climbed over it to the head, and then drove it back to the stables. Workers in the stables, amazed at the royal youngster's deed, first bound the elephant with ropes and then rushed to the palace to tell what the child had done.

People throughout the land soon learned of Vardhamana's bravery. Because of that incident, he was described ever afterward by a new name: the Great Hero, Mahavira.

Beginning at the age of twelve Mahavira studied seriously the ancient Hindu religion. His teachers were a team of priests, men, it is said, that he considered far too proud of themselves and far too unfeeling toward the country's poor people.

When he was nineteen Mahavira married the beautiful Princess Yosadha and soon became a father. For nearly a decade he settled into the life of a prince, living comfortably with the rest of the royal family. But then, before he had reached the age of twenty-nine, his parents both died. They starved to death while trying to practice religious holiness by fasting.

Deeply saddened by their deaths, Mahavira determined, in their memory, to spend the next twelve years suffering and living a life of poverty. His older brother, having become king, convinced him to remain at home, at least for a while. But when he was thirty years old Mahavira departed.

At the edge of the capital city he left behind his royal clothing and took on the garb of a beggar monk. He then vowed to practice complete silence during the years of his mission.

Walking from village to village, he lived by the kindness of people who placed food in a cup that, without speaking a word, he handed to them. In the countryside he gathered for himself small portions of wild fruits and berries. Sometimes animals or insects would bite him, but he refused to hurt them in return. Because he would not speak, people sometimes struck out at him in anger. Yet even some of those who hit him grew to admire his courage, his peacefulness, his strength of character.

When his twelve years of silence finally ended, Mahavira did not return to his royal home. Instead, he continued to travel from place to place, speaking of the ideas he had gathered in his mind over so long a time. Soon, many people who listened to him—men and women alike— became his followers. They saw themselves as monks and nuns in what, before long, came to be known as a new religion.

Mahavira's religion was far from a joyous one. As he looked out at the world he saw that people seemed always to want more for themselves: more wealth, more fame, more food and drink. There appeared never to be enough for them, from birth on through death. Yet Mahavira held out to his listeners a pathway to the greatest happiness, the state of being known in the Far East as Nirvana.

According to Mahavira, the way to Nirvana was direct. It followed the Three Jewels of the Soul—right conduct, right knowledge, and right conviction. Of those, right conduct was especially important, the way to achieve it based on the Five Commandments of the Soul:

Do not kill any living thing or hurt any living thing by word thought, or deed
Do not steal
Do not lie
Do not live an unchaste life and never become weakened by drugs or alcohol
Do not covet or desire anything

If people would strive to obey those rules, said Mahavira, they could live a good life, a happy life. They did not have to spend time bowing down to idols, making sacrifices, or losing themselves in senseless prayer. Those things would not help them, would not bring them to Nirvana. Instead, he declared, they must spend their lives doing good. They must seek true happiness, true salvation, *within themselves*.

Surely, advanced Mahavira, it is difficult to conquer oneself, but when the *self* is conquered, *everything* is conquered. What else is more important in a person's life than self-control?

Like the Buddha, Mahavira continued to believe in the Hindu goal of reaching Nirvana. Like the Buddha, too, he turned against the idea that people should make sacrifices and should belong to castes (or social classes) from the very rich down to the very poor and the "untouchable."

But the two religious leaders, living in India at almost exactly the same time, differed widely in what they considered proper conduct for a person living a life of goodness.

To the Buddha, the best way was the Middle Path—the path of moderation—a life lived without extremes. By contrast, Mahavira believed that the best way to fulfillment came from self-denial, even self-torture. To him, if a person did evil deeds during life on earth, then the next life might be lived in the body of an ant, or a pig, or a lobster. Still worse, such a person could be reborn as perhaps a potato, or an apple, or a banana. All of that was caused by "desire," by a person's greed for wealth or fame.

According to Mahavira, the evil person might spend life after death in one of seven hells, suffering somewhere under the surface of our planet indefinitely into the future. The worst of sinners would sink to the very bottom—to the seventh of seven hells.

Yet there could be another path, too—the path of happiness. A good per-

A sculpture of Mahavira (right) with that of a later Jain teacher, Rishabhadeva. *British Museum.*

son could rise toward one of twenty-six heavens in the sky. And then, having reached perfection, there was a twenty-seventh heaven: Nirvana.

As year followed year Mahavira made his way through all of India, speaking to crowds of people about his beliefs. Then, when he was perhaps seventy-two years old, he became ill. With crowds of followers gathered around

him he spoke to them, preaching the importance of his first commandment, not to hurt or kill any living thing.

According to legend, he once again urged his followers that they must not go to war against other human beings, but also that they must not strike back at the bees and wasps that stung them or the mosquitoes that bit them, nor should they step upon the ants or worms they encountered while walking. All living things, he said, not just human beings, possessed souls and deserved to live their lives.

That idea—a reverence for all living things, known as *Ahisma*—is at the very heart of Mahavira's beliefs and is the central feature of the religion that he formed. According to Mahavira, nothing in religion or in all of life itself is as important as Ahisma.

It is said that Mahavira died in the year 527 B.C., and that his body was cremated in the town of Pavapuri, in the province of Bihar. Today, the town is holy ground for those who believe in his faith.

After Mahavira's death, the thousands of monks and nuns who followed his teachings continued to spread those beliefs. They wrote what they remembered of his sermons into books and then taught from those writings. According to people who spread his ideas, he was the last of twenty-four "conquerors," or Jains who held to the same values. Their religion, therefore, became known as Jainism, "the religion of the conquerors."

Clearly, however, Jainism was not for everyone. Its followers were not permitted to be soldiers, who might kill people. They could not become farmers, who would kill ants and worms as they plowed the ground. At first, they

followed the teachings of Mahavira and did not even gather together in temples for prayer.

Over the years, many things changed. Some Jains built temples, placing in them beautiful statues of Mahavira himself. Others became wealthy merchants and bankers. Yet even the richest Jains are known to give freely to charities. They are generous in supporting shelters for animals. They contribute money for the care of sick birds and even for sick insects.

In time, differences developed among the Jains. The priests of one group, known as Digambaras, or "sky clad," came to believe that the individual should have practically no possessions, not even clothing. Another group of Jainist priests, the Svetambaras, or "white clad," wear white robes and are willing to accept a wider range of lifestyles among their followers.

Jains in general are supposed to "eat little, drink little, sleep little." Like the parents of Mahavira himself, they sometimes commit suicide in old age, especially by starvation, thus passing from life in a way they consider holy.

According to Mahavira's teachings, each person is to achieve Nirvana by self-conquest, self-mastery. Everyone, therefore, shapes a life by individual choice.

A Jain ceremony in India. *Sipa Press. Photograph by François Gauthier.*

Jains believe in a personal future after death, one based on a person's actions and on the kind of life he or she has lived. The Jains say firmly that nobody else is responsible for what happens to a person—good things or bad—except the person who is living the life. Individuals are thought to shape whatever happens to them, both on earth and afterward.

Now, long after the death of Mahavira, his ideas survive. Today, about 1.5 million Jains live in India, while the beliefs of Mahavira recently have begun gaining wider attention around the world.

Mahavira taught that the world will go on and on; it never will perish. No one should kill or hurt any other living thing. It was useless, he said, for people to seek fame, glory, wealth, and honors since all of us are destined to grow old and to die. Instead, we should give up our desires for worldly goods and spend our lives practicing kindness to our fellow creatures, whether they be animals, plants, or people.

And if we do, he said, the reward could be Nirvana.

Nānak

(1469–1539) Founder of the Sikh religion, blending Hindu and Muslim beliefs

Not every great figure in history shows signs of leadership as a child. Nānak, the founder of the Sikh religion, is a good example of one who did not.

Born near the city of Lahore in what then was western India and today is Pakistan, Nānak showed little interest in being with other children of his age. Instead of playing, he spent time walking in the woods. Often he met in a cave with a hermit, where the two spoke about life and death and the meaning of existence.

In school he studied the Hindu scriptures and supposedly by the age of seven had learned the Persian language, as well as Sanskrit and Punjabi. His father, a merchant and accountant, tried to keep Nānak in school or get him to go to work, but the boy showed little interest in either pursuit.

The story is told that once, when he was supposed to be watching over a herd of cattle, he fell asleep and the powerful creatures crossed into a neighbor's wheat field. According to the tale that has survived, Nānak proudly pointed out to everyone's surprise that the cattle had caused not a blade of grass to be damaged.

Nānak's parents hoped that marriage and fatherhood might improve his attitude toward life. To that end, when he was thirteen years old they arranged for him to marry. Before long he was the father of two sons.

Having a family seemed to make little difference to Nānak, however. As a teenager he worked for his father, but

A portrait of Nānak, founder of the Sikh religion. *Courtesy Gurcharan Singh, Marymount Manhattan College.*

with little success. Stories tell of how he sometimes gave away money from the family business to beggars.

Finally his parents sent him away to another city to work as an accountant in a government office. It was there, when he was on his own for the first time, that his life began to change. A Muslim friend, Mardana, is said to have set to music several verses about religion that Nānak wrote. Singing the songs to groups of people in the community gave Nānak great pleasure. It may well be that some of the hymns used today in services of the Sikh religion first were composed at that time.

Yet it was not until Nānak was nearly thirty years old that his life was transformed. Then, according to the tale he later told, as he swam one day in a river God spoke to him directly.

The word of God, as Nānak explained it, was to make him a messenger of prayer and public service. God ordered him directly to spend his life spreading the message of charity, of service, and of praise for the Lord.

After remaining in the woods for the next three days, Nānak returned, declaring boldly to his friends, "There is no Hindu; there is no Muslim." His task, as he explained it, was to go on a lifetime journey, bringing together the rival Hindu and Muslim religions into a new faith, one pledged only to devotion to God.

With his Muslim friend Mardana at his side, playing music for him to sing by, Nānak began meeting with larger and larger audiences. He wore the style of hat usually worn by Muslims but had the yellow mark on his forehead of a Hindu. Around his shoulders he draped a yellow jacket blended with a sheet of white, causing audiences to wonder which religion he really championed. His answer to such questions was direct and simple and strong: he represented only one faith, a faith that should be shared by all people—a faith in God.

With Mardana at his side, Nānak traveled for thousands of miles, visiting such distant locations as Tamil Nadu, Sri Lanka, and the Himalayan Mountains. He journeyed to the Muslim holy places, Mecca and Medina, as well as to Basra and Baghdad. At those sites he visited with men of religion and men of politics.

Once, at the Kaaba, the holy stone of the Muslim faith, he fell asleep with his feet pointing to the stone. An angry Arab priest rudely awakened him, charging him with pointing his feet toward God. According to legend, Nānak is said to have challenged the priest to show him a direction "where God is not."

At one time, when Mardana complained of loneliness for his relatives,

A Sikh temple in India. *India Tourist Office.*

Nānak returned home with him. There, Nānak's parents urged their son to stay, offering to give him a new home, a new wife—whatever would make him happy—but Nānak refused. Instead, he sang to them of his love for God and his mission to spread the word of the new faith he had begun.

Returning again to his travels, Nānak spoke out strongly against Hindus and Muslims who had begun the practice of worshiping stone statues and idols. He worked with robbers and other crimi-

nals, trying to persuade them to change their ways and live good lives. It is said that he once preached to a woman who had become rich by practicing black magic and witchcraft, finally convincing her to give up her wealth and to become one of his followers.

Nānak sometimes offended Hindus by eating meat. His answer was that many of those who showed off by not eating meat still acted with great cruelty to other people. Muslims, too, he said, sometimes read books on religion but failed to live up to the rules of God. "Fear God and do good works," Nānak demanded of his fellow human beings as the pathway to the only true religion.

Unlike other religious leaders, Nānak did not hesitate to admit his own sins. He openly declared that he had not always been truthful, that he had sinned in sexual matters, that he had desired the property of others, had cheated, had been dishonest, had been weak. In a word, he had been *human*.

As he grew older the number of his followers grew. With their help he built a new town in India, calling it Kartarpur (home of the creator). It was there that both Hindus and Muslims came to see him, to listen to his ideas. Many became his followers or, in Punjabi, his *Sikhs*— the term that later came to mark the religion.

When Nānak's health finally began to fail, he returned to his childhood home. Lacking confidence in his two sons as possible successors, he chose instead one of his loyal disciples, Angad, to lead the faith. As he came closer to death, great crowds of people assembled to hear his final words. He is said to have forgiven his enemies and given praise to God.

Then, probably on September 22, 1539, Nānak died.

In his memory a holy temple of the Sikh religion was built on an island near Lahore. Extraordinarily beautiful, it is known today as the Golden Temple, and its location, Amritsar, is considered sacred by the Sikhs.

After Nānak's death his followers tried hard at first to hold close to his ideals. They knew how deeply he held to faith in only one God, all-powerful and all-knowing. They also understood his firm belief that the guru (wise man), like himself, should not be worshiped— as Jesus and Muhammad then were being worshiped—but should be respected only as a teacher.

The job of such a teacher, he said, was not only to help his followers know about God but also, by example, how to live a life. Nor, according to Nānak, should a person's life include self-torture or self-denial as a way to reach spiritual perfection, as other religions taught.

Similarly, Nānak's teachings rejected the Hindu belief in social classes, such as the elite Brahman upper class or the untouchable lower class. Many leaders who lived later in India, such as Mahatma Gandhi, came to agree with him that people should be able to rise or fall in society based on their own actions, not just on the social status of the family into which they were born.

In addition, Nānak refused to believe that what happened to people was decided beforehand, by fate. He taught instead that religious leaders could help human beings to discover the goodness inside of them, qualities that could make for more productive, happier lives.

To achieve those objectives they should discipline themselves—train their minds and bodies to the greatest extent possible. They should listen to holy music before sunrise and at night. And they should pray directly to God, not to someone in between.

Over the years, as Amritsar began to attract more and more visitors, many Hindus converted to Sikhism. Arjun, the fifth of eight Sikh gurus, combined the writings of the four gurus before him with those of many Hindu and Muslim leaders into the Adi Granth, a collection of holy works.

The Adi Granth includes not only religious statements but appealing poetry and music. Even today, Sikhs and non-Sikhs alike find the music particularly appealing. In all, there now are nearly six thousand hymns in the collection.

It was the guru Arjun, too, who confirmed in the Adi Granth that his people no longer were Hindus or Muslims but believers instead in "one supreme being." That statement made it crystal clear to the world that the Sikhs had broken altogether from their parent religions.

Arjun's son, Hargobind, who became guru upon his father's death, happened to enjoy both hunting and the idea of a strong military force. One result was a bitter conflict that soon followed, especially against Muslim rulers, as the Sikhs tried to use warfare to gain their religious freedom. That struggle continued through the death of Gobind Singh, the tenth and last of all the Sikh gurus.

It may indeed be one of history's great ironies that the Sikh followers of Nānak became known as a fighting people, identified by such symbols as the iron bracelet, uncut hair, the turban, and the dagger. Nānak had hoped that his new faith would succeed in uniting Hindus and Muslims, something that never happened. Instead, there has been conflict between the two faiths, with the Sikhs caught between them.

Nānak drew from the Muslims his beliefs in One God, a single creator who deserved to be obeyed. Yet never did he separate himself completely from the Hindu faith of his childhood, which holds that human beings and the human soul are tied closely to what lies beyond life on earth, and that people are reborn in some other form.

To Nānak, such beliefs were not in conflict. They were marks of faith that should bring people together and from which all humanity eventually could gain salvation.

Nānak's dream was the unity of all people on the planet Earth, both while they lived and after death.

Mohandas K. (Mahatma) Gandhi

(1869–1948) Hindu moral and spiritual leader in India's struggle for freedom from British rule; described as "the conscience of mankind"

"Who am I? What will become of me? What is life all about?"

Like young people since the beginning of human existence, young Mohandas K. Gandhi long had asked himself such questions without finding satisfactory answers. Born to a prominent family in India and educated there, Gandhi had finished a law degree in London. Then, back in India, he had been unsuccessful in his legal career and traveled to South Africa, hoping to turn his fortunes around.

One night in South Africa, an event took place that not only changed his life but also would eventually affect the lives of millions of others. Seated in the first-class compartment of a railroad train, he was asked to leave and to sit in third class with the other Indians and the black-skinned people.

When he refused, Gandhi was put off the train with his baggage and left to shiver in the cold waiting room all night. Shortly afterward, when he would not give up his seat to a white passenger on a stagecoach, the stagecoach driver beat him badly.

His experience in South Africa led Gandhi to devote himself completely to the struggle for social justice. That struggle, based on his religious beliefs, would be his personal answer to the question we all ask about our purpose in life.

Gandhi would become known throughout the world, praised by presidents and kings. He would become the single most important figure in India's successful fight for independence from British rule.

His people came to speak of him as the Mahatma, meaning "Great Soul" or "the Holy One." Sometimes they referred to him simply as Gandhiji or Bapu (father).

In the United States, Martin Luther King, Jr., declared that studying the ideas of Gandhi had inspired the strategy of nonviolence he used with such success during the civil rights movement of the 1960s.

According to Gandhi himself, his political ideas came from religious truths, particularly from the Hindu holy book, the Bhagavad Gita. Today, the name of Gandhi often is mentioned in the same breath with Moses, Buddha, Muhammad, and Jesus.

Mohandas, or "Moniya," as he was called in early childhood, was born in 1869, in the small town of Porbandar on the west coast of India. He was the last of four children born to Karamchand Gandhi, a leading government official of the province, and his fourth wife, Putlibai, a woman much younger than himself. Although not wealthy, the family belonged to the Indian merchant caste, and young Mohandas never found money a problem in his early life.

One of Gandhi's first teachers considered him "good at English, fair in arithmetic . . . bad handwriting." Writing later about himself, Gandhi said, "It was with some difficulty that I got through the multiplication tables." He cared little for the playground games of his classmates, such as cricket or soccer, but enjoyed taking long walks, a pleasure he would pursue to the end of his life.

It was not the influence of school that shaped Gandhi's formative years, but rather the beliefs of his mother, Putlibai. Although she could neither read nor write, she was deeply religious. Before every meal she would pray. Often she fasted. Once, during the rainy season, she vowed not to eat until she personally saw the sun break through the clouds. Nothing could shake her faith or her good-natured willingness to suffer for her beliefs. Young Moniya watched her and soon began to copy her religious ways.

In the busy port of Porbandar he came into contact with people of many religions: Hindus, Muslims, Zoroastrians, Christians. The Christians, he recalled later, often spoke harshly against the other religions, hoping to convert people to their faith, a practice Gandhi did not like. He very early came to believe, as he later wrote, that "all religions are true, and all religions have some error in them."

When he was thirteen, Gandhi's family arranged for him to marry, child marriages at that time being common-place in India. His bride, Kasturba, also thirteen, had not gone to school at all and could neither read nor write, but Mohandas did not mind. Even knowing that Kasturba still would spend most of her time at her parents' home, he considered himself ready for marriage.

Along with the excitement of marriage, young "Mohan," as he now was called, found himself attracted to many tempting but forbidden acts. One of his high school friends persuaded him to sneak away to a secret place and do what religious Hindus never were supposed to do: eat meat. Only a taste of goat meat proved too much for Mohan. For many nights afterward he dreamed that the goat was still alive within his stomach. He would wake up suddenly during the night, filled with fear and regret for what he had done. For the rest of his life Gandhi remained a vegetarian.

The same thing happened to him when he tried smoking cigarettes and when he toyed with the idea of becoming an atheist—not believing in any god. Each time, Gandhi learned from his experience and grew stronger as a person.

Once, young Gandhi stole money from a servant in his house. Then, feeling guilty about what he had done, he wrote a letter to his father, confessing.

Instead of punishing him, Mohan's father forgave him completely, believing that no human ever should harm another creature.

That lesson, the practice of Ahisma, or nonviolence, was one that Gandhi would follow ever afterward. It was destined to become a central feature of his life. From that time, too, young Gandhi insisted on telling the absolute truth, whatever the penalty might be for himself or for others.

While Gandhi was still a teenager, his father died. Writing about the event many years later, when he already was world famous, Gandhi still expressed guilt for having been away from his father's bedside at the moment of death in order to be with his pretty young wife. Caring for the feelings and the needs of others, sacrificing his own comforts for the sake of truth, and attacking his own weaknesses—those increasingly became the goals of young Mohandas Gandhi, growing into manhood.

At the age of eighteen, Gandhi decided to leave India for his college education. In 1888, over the protests of his mother, he set sail for England, enrolling at the Inner Temple in London to study law. Behind him in India he left his mother, his wife, and his infant son. It was a separation that was to last for three years.

Mohandas K. Gandhi with his wife. *Brown Brothers.*

During the early part of his stay in London, Gandhi found himself lonely and ill at ease. Dark skinned and very thin, he had ears that stuck out awkwardly to the sides. He found it difficult to adapt to English manners, to English clothing, and especially to English food. For a time he did not know about the city's vegetarian restaurants and tried to fill himself mostly with bread and rolls.

Gradually, he adjusted. He became a member of the London Vegetarian Society, even writing articles for the group's publications. He improved his use of the English language. He read the Christian Bible carefully, finding himself deeply moved by the deeds of Jesus. He was especially taken with the ideas of Jesus about caring for the poor and weak, as well as about nonviolence— the "turning the other cheek" when one is struck.

Through the Vegetarian Society he was thrown into contact with prominent English thinkers, including the Fabian socialist George Bernard Shaw. He began to think about his own religious views, such as nonviolence, and how they related to politics. He began to understand how the competition for profit—the very heart of capitalism— could set person against person and hurt society.

Gandhi found himself increasingly in control of his mind and body. He would not touch meat or fish of any kind, even giving up eggs. He never used tobacco or alcohol. He prayed at regular times during the day. He studied productively.

In the spring of 1891, he passed his law school examinations and was admitted to the High Court of London. The day after the ceremony he set sail for India.

A lawyer now, with an English education, he still was not sure what would become of him, what he would do with his life.

On returning to India, he was shocked to learn that his mother had died. The family had decided not to tell him, fearing that the news would interrupt his studies. Settling now in Bombay, Gandhi and his wife, no longer a child bride, became the parents of a second son. Later the couple would have two more sons.

Almost from the beginning, Gandhi's law practice in Bombay proved troublesome to him. Too often, cases were decided through bribery. Guilty people were allowed to go free, and judges traded favors with politicians. Nor was Gandhi comfortable in the courtroom. Painfully shy, he once stood to cross-examine a witness and found himself paralyzed with fright. He could not even speak.

Unhappy with life in Bombay, Gandhi leaped at an opportunity to practice law for a time in Natal, South Africa, where many Indian citizens had gone to start businesses. Once again, he left his family behind, expecting to stay for only a year. He could scarcely suspect that he would remain in Africa for twenty years, an experience that was to shape all of his later life.

Not long after his arrival in Natal, he began to understand what kind of country South Africa really was. The first judge to greet him in a courtroom demanded that Gandhi take off the Indian turban that he wore around his head. Proudly, he refused and promptly left the courtroom.

It was only one week later that the turning point came for Gandhi. While riding on a train to Pretoria, Gandhi was removed from the train for refusing to sit in third class with other Indians and blacks instead of in the first-class compartment he had paid for.

That night, sitting alone in a railroad station, shivering from the cold, Gandhi vowed to do something about prejudice in South Africa and in neighboring Transvaal, a former Dutch colony. The cause of racial justice was at stake, of course, but also at stake was what Gandhi thought of himself—and his dignity as a human being.

The more Gandhi learned about South Africa's customs, the angrier he became. Indians insultingly were called

"coolies." In the Transvaal, they could not vote in elections, could own only limited amounts of property, were not allowed on the streets after 9:00 P.M., and had to pay a special tax. Those who signed contracts as indentured servants for a five-year term were little better than slaves. Their employers could abuse them, beat them, do almost anything they pleased, while the servants had virtually no legal rights at all.

When South Africa decided, like Transvaal, to take the vote away from Indian residents, Gandhi swung into action. No longer shy, he began to play a leadership role in the politics of Indian life in South Africa.

He founded an action group, the Natal Indian Congress, to focus the energies of the Indian community, rich and poor alike. He wrote to the newspapers, organized protest meetings, spoke to officials. Although he did not gain the vote for all Indians, he won the attention of officials not only in South Africa but in England and in India.

During a visit to India to bring back his wife and children, he spoke to audiences about the brutal treatment of Indians in South Africa. On his return to Natal a furious crowd of whites, having heard about his speeches, awaited him at the dock, pelting him with stones and rotten eggs. The wife of the police commissioner shielded him with her umbrella and later urged him to take action in the courts. But Gandhi refused to sue, instead accepting an apology from some members of the mob.

During the Boer War between the Dutch and British settlers in South Africa (1899–1902), Gandhi organized an emergency medical corps of Indians to help the British cause. He and his comrades went out onto the battlefields to nurse wounded British soldiers. In the struggle of Britain against the Zulu warriors in 1906, his medical corps helped the wounded of both sides.

For those services he was awarded medals by the British authorities. It was his belief at the time that the British Empire did much to improve the life of the Empire's subject peoples. Many years later, declaring that the Empire did just the opposite, he returned the medals.

Despite the help Gandhi had given them, Britain's South African leaders passed humiliating laws against the nation's Indian population. In 1906, Transvaal passed a law requiring that all Indians, including children, be finger-printed and carry an identification paper with them at all times. Gandhi organized an enormous rally against the law at a theater in Johannesburg. He was thrown into prison for his action, the first of many jailings in his lifetime.

In August 1908, he led an even larger rally. This time, thousands of Indians openly burned their registration certificates, many of them considering it an honor to be jailed along with Gandhi.

Gandhi now determined to spend the rest of his life serving mankind. He pledged himself to *satyagraha* (the pursuit of truth), a search to be carried out by means of nonviolent action. That did not mean, he said, being "passive," just permitting someone to act against a victim. Instead, it meant working creatively, actively, toward agreement with one's opponents in finding solutions to problems.

It also meant that if a person chose to break an unjust law, that person had a duty to go to prison for the act of disobedience. While in prison in South Africa, Gandhi read the American author Henry David Thoreau's essay on civil disobedience, learning from it just as Martin Luther King, Jr., later would learn from Gandhi's writing.

In 1913, another law was passed that caused Gandhi to use massive civil disobedience. That statute declared that only Christian marriages were legal. Hindu, Muslim, and other marriages carried no legal force, so that the women involved in them were considered no better than prostitutes and the children of such marriages were seen as illegitimate. This time, even some of the Indian women, including Gandhi's wife, Kasturba, joined in the protest rallies. Many Indians, both men and women, were imprisoned as the struggle continued.

Meanwhile, Gandhi and a few friends had set up a special cooperative farming community in Natal, called Phoenix Settlement. It was based on the idea that everyone in a communal group should work together at tasks such as farming for the good of all other people in the group. Gandhi had read about such communities in the works of John Ruskin and Leo Tolstoy. At Phoenix Settlement, Gandhi also published a newspaper, *Indian Opinion*, making the case for the rights of Indians living in South Africa.

In 1910, he began a second cooperative community, Tolstoy Farm. Beginning in 1913, many Indians who had been fired from their jobs for protesting against the harsh South African laws came to work in the two communities. There they grew their own food, made their own furniture, and practiced the high moral ideas of Gandhi. Even the leaders in the community were responsible for doing their own cooking and cleaning the latrines.

Gandhi himself soon was forced to spend still more time in prison. Finally, in December 1913, he was released in order to negotiate directly with General Jan Christian Smuts, the South African military leader. Smuts had personally sent Gandhi to prison several times. The two men were opponents. But Gandhi, showing the spirit of love he considered so important, personally made a pair of sandals for the general. Smuts, in time, came to respect Gandhi greatly, considering him "a saint."

Before very long, Indian marriages were made legal. A tax placed on Indian indentured servants was removed. Indians in South Africa were given greater freedom to travel.

Gandhi had won. His use of civil disobedience—protest marches and peaceful strikes—had caused the powerful South African authorities to back down.

Now the skinny little man, Gandhi, no longer wore formal English clothing. Instead, he had begun to appear barefoot, clad in the ancient Indian *dhoti*, or loincloth, or a cape of white cloth, as he would for the rest of his life.

True, Indians in South Africa had yet to gain complete equality with whites. But Gandhi had made great strides toward that goal. And in doing so, his name had become familiar to the people of his homeland, India. Indeed, to them he was a hero, the one person who could achieve the distant dream they were beginning to share, the dream of home rule—independence from the British Crown.

In January 1915, now forty-five years old, Mohandas K. Gandhi landed in Bombay. At the dock he was greeted by a wildly cheering crowd. Gandhi knew that although their enthusiasm was great, the struggle would be both long and difficult.

He decided to begin by simply traveling around the country, meeting the people. Everywhere he found large crowds waiting for his blessings, sometimes hoping just to see him. Instead of leaping immediately into politics, he organized a religious community at Ahmedabad, similar to the ones he had begun at Phoenix Settlement and Tolstoy Farm.

Over much opposition, even that of his wife, Gandhi insisted that Untouchables—the lowest of all the Indian social castes—be admitted to the community. Some workers there even feared being polluted by water from buckets used by the Untouchables. But Gandhi persisted. The community survived.

Meanwhile, the British raj (rule) continued to have disastrous results for Indian life. The thousand or so British officials who governed the country lived in luxury while millions of Indians suffered. Many of the poorest literally starved to death in the streets while the British, unfeeling, uncaring, exported food from India for profit. Even when famine or disease struck heavily across the country, the British did nothing to help. They simply looked away.

During World War I, Indian troops had loyally served their British masters. At the war's end they expected, as promised, greater home rule in India. Instead, in March 1919, the Rowlatt Acts were passed. Those regulations allowed the jailing of Indians on mere suspicion and trial without a jury. Gandhi called for a *hartal* (a national day of fasting and prayer with no work).

When a rumor spread that Gandhi had been arrested, some Indians angrily set fires, looted stores, and destroyed British property. The city of Amritsar in Punjab province saw particularly severe violence, including the rape of an English schoolteacher.

In response, the British General Reginald E. H. Dyer ordered his Indian soldiers to shoot to kill at a crowd of men, women, and children he had trapped in a marketplace. The result was the horrible Amritsar Massacre, which took the lives of 379 persons and wounded more than 1,000 others.

After Amritsar, Gandhi led the Indian people in a program of noncooperation with the British authorities. He urged Indians not to buy British products. Students were not to attend British schools. Businessmen were not to use

British courts or offices. Neither the rich nor the poor were to pay British taxes.

In front of huge crowds of people, Gandhi himself would set afire great piles of British-made clothing contributed by his audience. Indians, he would say in his high-pitched voice, should spin and weave their own clothing. He made it a practice each day to seat himself for work in front of a spinning wheel, wearing only a white dhoti made of Indian cotton.

It was a striking image, one that soon became known around the world. Here was a man who had made himself the very image of the goodness he wished for others and of the poverty he dreamed of removing. Indians, he hoped, would come to live a simple, happy existence in small villages. Away from cruel cities and brutal machinery, they would produce for themselves whatever they needed.

Gandhi in 1921. *The Bettmann Archive.*

In March 1922, Indian civil disobedience once again turned violent. This time, Gandhi was arrested and sentenced to six years in prison. In his jail cell he read books. He wrote letters. Often he sat cross-legged and prayed. He fasted. After two years, following an operation for appendicitis, he was released.

For the next few years he tried to persuade the Indian people to develop their own cottage industries, especially spinning and weaving. He worked to bring together Hindus and Muslims as the nation's two great religions quarreled bitterly over how best to throw off British rule and how India would be organized afterward.

Then, on March 12, 1930, he set out on a mission that would change the course of India's history. Although surrounded on three sides by ocean, the Indian people were not allowed to make salt for their own use without paying a tax to Great Britain. That was true of even the poorest Indians. When British authorities refused Gandhi's gently phrased request to drop the tax, he gathered a group of his followers at Ahmedabad, where they began an incredible march of 241 miles to Dandi, on the Indian Ocean.

History would remember it as the "Salt March," one of the great symbolic acts of Gandhi's life. On arriving, said Gandhi, he would scoop a handful of seawater and make salt, despite the British law.

At every step of the way great crowds cheered Gandhi and his group. Writers and photographers sent around the globe vivid daily records of his progress. On April 5, Gandhi and his party walked slowly into the sea for a ritual bath. Then, the beloved "Gandhiji" prayerfully removed a pinch of salt.

Soon afterward Gandhi was arrested. Without even a trial he was thrown into jail. Because of the acts of civil disobedience that followed, some sixty thousand Indians also were imprisoned. But the Indian people would not give in. The salt tax no longer could be collected. Gandhi had made his point. Before long, he and the British viceroy in India reached a compromise on salt.

In the autumn of 1931, Gandhi sailed to London to deal with the British as the sole representative of India's Congress Party. Traveling there in steerage class, he walked the streets of the city where once he had studied. Now bespectacled and toothless, with a shaven head, he wore only his familiar white loincloth, a shawl, and slippers. Excited crowds followed him everywhere, warmed by his sense of humor, his wisdom, his love.

To the Western world, Mohandas K. Gandhi, the shy, unhappy, awkward Indian student, had become "the Mahatma" (a holy person).

While in England he met with virtually every important English leader, including the king and queen. The one exception proved to be Winston Churchill, who would not speak with him. Churchill openly expressed concern that the cleverness of the "half-naked fakir" could very well lead to the British Empire's loss of India. To Churchill's satisfaction, the London conference held out little hope to Gandhi of Indian independence.

On returning to India, Gandhi was shocked to find the new British viceroy there cracking down severely on the actions of his Congress Party. Before long he himself was placed in Yeravda Prison. From there, within the very walls of his jail cell, he launched a new campaign. It had as its goal greater rights for India's most helpless, hopeless people—the Untouchables.

Gandhi walks to a prayer meeting with his followers. He disliked being photographed, and his sharp look is directed to the photographer. *AP/Wide World Photos.*

To win the sympathy of other social classes in India, Gandhi began speaking of the poor Untouchables as *Harijans* (Children of God). On September 20, 1932, he announced the start of a fast. It would last, he said, until death if necessary, or until something was done to improve the life of the Harijans.

Six days later the British agreed that never again would there be a formal law that classified a person as "untouchable." Hindu religious leaders now admitted Untouchables to their temples. Some were even allowed to sit in provincial assemblies.

In the spring of 1933, Gandhi ended a twenty-one-day fast to gain still more rights for the Harijans. Many of his followers feared that he might die. "If Bapu died," declared his chosen successor, Jawaharlal Nehru, "what would India be like then?"

Gandhi did not die. He lived to see Great Britain and the other Allied nations triumph in World War II over the tyrannical forces of Germany and Japan. Twice he wrote to Hitler, hoping to reach the heart of the bloodthirsty dictator, but he received no reply.

During the war Gandhi demanded a promise from Britain to free India at the end of the war. Instead, the British imprisoned him in the luxurious palace of the Aga Khan at Poona so they could have greater control over him. Across the nation there were angry protest meetings. Violence erupted in the streets. But the British refused to change their minds.

While Gandhi was in prison his wife, Kasturba, was held there with him. She became ill. Her condition became more and more serious until, finally, it was clear that nothing could be done. She died in her husband's arms. Fearing that Gandhi, now grown old and weak himself, would also die and the world would blame them, the British released him in May 1944. It was to be his last stay in prison. In all, he had spent 2,338 days of his life behind bars—almost six and a half years.

Once free, Gandhi again began to work for Indian independence, something that now appeared possible. He tried to persuade the Muslim leader, Mohammed Ali Jinnah, that the Muslims should not try to separate from India. Jinnah, however, insisted that a new nation, Pakistan, would have to be created. If necessary, said Jinnah, he would use force to establish it.

In August 1946, the Muslims started bloody riots on the streets of Calcutta. The Hindus struck back. Soon, all across the provinces of Bengal and Bihar there were mass killings, beatings, attacks on holy places, looting. Fires left thousands homeless. Gandhi pleaded for reason and for an end to the violence. He urged Hindus and Muslims to unite to create a peaceful nation.

Finally, on August 15, 1947, Indian independence became a reality. On the same day, Pakistan also was established. Gandhi spent the day fasting and praying for peace. During that one day of happiness, Hindus and Muslims came together in brotherhood.

Then violence again erupted. Hindus fled by the millions from East and West Pakistan to India. Frightened Muslims sometimes crossed paths with them as they left the country. In Calcutta, four days and nights of violence devastated the city. Only a fast by Gandhi

Gandhi, in traditional Hindu dress, surrounded by admiring crowds in 1945. *Black Star.*

himself caused guilt-ridden Hindus to stop fighting. Muslims, too, finally became calm, concerned with the terrible vengeance that might descend upon them if Gandhi died.

In January 1948, while living at Birla house in Delhi, Gandhi again fasted for five days to put an end to violence in that city. Gandhi ended his fast with a glass of orange juice. For several days he had to be carried to his prayer meetings.

On January 30, at five o'clock in the afternoon, he walked into the garden at Birla House to address still another prayer meeting. As usual, he leaned for support on the shoulders of two young women.

Then, from the crowd stepped a young man, Nathuram V. Godse. A fanatically religious Hindu, he belonged to a group that was furious with Gandhi for permitting the division of India and the creation of Pakistan. Godse fell to his knees in front of Gandhi. Then, drawing a pistol, he fired three shots into the body of the Mahatma.

"Oh, Ram! Oh, Ram!" cried Gandhi, calling to God for help as he had from the days of his childhood. And then he was no more.

The next day his body was placed atop a pile of sandalwood logs standing near the holy Yamuna River. Millions of people, dressed in white, stood nearby. One of the Mahatma's sons touched a torch to the logs, starting the cremation fire. For fourteen hours the flames rushed upward into the sky. Some people in the crowd groaned. Others cried.

Two weeks later the ashes of Mahatma Gandhi were scattered into the seven sacred rivers of India.

Unlike many holy men, Gandhi did not spend his lifetime hiding in a cave, praying. Instead, he worked—through government and politics—to make a better world for people rich and poor. It was by means of such real tools in a real world, he believed, that human beings could truly serve God.

Caring little for material rewards, he crusaded against the evil of racism and religious bigotry, against the evil of violence, and against the evil of colonial rule—the afflictions that have so cursed our twentieth-century world.

To Viscount Louis Mountbatten, Great Britain's last viceroy of India, Gandhi was destined to "go down in history on a par with Buddha and Jesus Christ."

In speaking of the great Mahatma, physicist Albert Einstein once said, "Generations to come, it may be, will scarce believe that such a one as this ever in flesh and blood walked upon this earth."

PART III

Islam
and Its
Descendants

Muhammad

(570?–632 A.D.) Believer that people should submit themselves totally to the will of a single God and then accept what happens to them; founder of the Islamic religion

In today's world more than 970 million people consider themselves members of the Muslim faith. Every day, from places around the entire globe, they bow in reverence toward the city of Mecca, in Arabia, and declare with feeling, "There is no God but Allah, and Mohammad is his Prophet."

Muhammad. The Prophet (or "Messenger of God"). During his lifetime he was a man who loved beautiful women, fine perfume, and tasty food. He took pleasure in seeing the heads of his enemies torn from their bodies by the swords of his soldiers. He hated Christians and Jews, poets and painters, and anyone who criticized him. Once he had a Jewish prisoner tortured in order to learn the location of the man's hidden treasure. Then, having uncovered the secret, he had his victim murdered and added the dead man's wife to the collection of women in his harem.

Muhammad. One of history's great leaders in the fields of politics and religion.

His birth came probably in the year 570. He was the only child of a father he never saw—a merchant who died while on a trading mission to the city of Medina before his offspring, destined to change the course of history, was born.

In his early childhood Muhammad often was sent to live with a nurse in a nearby desert tribe because the bleak, rocky hills of Mecca, along with its climate, were considered so unpleasant. When he was six, his mother also died and he was moved to the home of his father's father. Only two years later that guardian also died, and the boy was put in the care of an uncle, Abu Talib.

Considering the insecurity of Muhammad's early years, it probably should not be surprising that the Koran, the holy book of his Muslim religion, says much about the great need of society to give proper support to young children, particularly to orphans.

The city of Mecca even then was a place of great importance to Arab peoples, going far back into history. According to the Old Testament, the biblical figure Abraham had relationships with two women, Sarah and Hagar, Sarah being his wife. It is said that Abraham, at the urging of Sarah, sent Hagar and Ishmael, the child he had conceived with her, away into the desert.

There, according to Islamic legend, the deeply unhappy young Ishmael kicked the desert sand, causing a miraculous spring of water to burst forth. Near that spring, called the Zemzem, was built a temple, a holy shrine spoken of by Arabs as the Kaaba. Ever afterward, or so the story goes, Arabs considered the city of Mecca a holy place, for it was the site of the temple of Kaaba and the well of Ishmael.

By the time of Muhammad's birth, Mecca had for many years been a prosperous center of trade. But the people living there often were unsure of themselves, worshiping many gods, bowing to many idols. Tribes often fought bitter, bloody wars against each other. In place of a shared religion, the people of the area had other interests. They spent much of their time at gambling, drinking, fortune-telling, horseback riding, and making profits from their businesses.

Because Muhammad was just a child he received no money from the estates of his father or his grandfather. To earn a living for himself he at first herded sheep, spending many days and nights alone in the desert. As he grew older he began working as a trader for his uncle, Abu Talib, traveling to Egypt, Persia, Syria, and perhaps as far as what today is Ethiopia.

One woman he served as a trader was the wealthy widow Khadijah. Before even meeting her in person he took spices and perfumes that she owned to Syria, exchanging them for precious fabrics such as silk. Returning home, he met with her to tell about his great successes.

Although she was forty years old and he only twenty-five, it is said that the two fell in love almost at once. Soon they married. From that time onward, instead of being a camel driver, Muhammad was a man of wealth, able

Worshipers at Mecca. *Sipa Press. Photograph by Aral.*

to spend time on things that fascinated him, including matters of religion.

In his travels he already had met many Christians and Jews, often speaking with them about their beliefs. Yet so busy had young Muhammad been with the business of trade that he never had learned to read and write. Following his marriage, one of Khadijah's cousins who had accepted the Jewish faith often read to him from the Old Testament.

Increasingly, too, he made it a point to learn about the life of Jesus, a leader who seemed to him a model of how people could be taught to turn away from evil habits toward lives of doing good.

Although still not mastering the skills of reading and writing, Muhammad came more and more to admire the deeds of Jesus, as well as those of Abraham and Moses. Even when he became the father of several children, he often spent time in the hills surrounding Mecca, especially in a favorite cave. There he thought about prophets who had helped those around them to find meaning—and truths—in human existence.

One night, according to the story, while he sat alone in his cave, thinking, the angel Gabriel came to visit him. Even though Muhammad could not read, Gabriel commanded that he say

aloud the words written on a golden tablet. Miraculously, he did so.

Then, rushing home to Khadijah, he told her what had happened. She is said to have believed him completely, urging him to go once again to the cave.

In the days that followed, Muhammad claimed to learn more and more from Gabriel, gradually convincing himself that he, too, could become a prophet. And when that happened, or so he believed, he could finally bring the work of Abraham, Moses, and Jesus to a conclusion, creating a new religion for all human beings to follow.

Soon he began to tell people the story of the beliefs he had come upon in the cave. At first, most of those who listened to him and believed him were members of his family and close friends in his business affairs. They encouraged him to produce a message, one that soon became summarized simply as: "There is no God but Allah, and Muhammad is his Prophet."

Before long Muhammad began to make his way onto the streets of Mecca, preaching to people who believed in idols. In the beginning most of his listeners laughed at him or simply walked away. But he refused to stop trying. Worshiping idols, he declared, was more than a mistake; it destroyed a person. Instead, said Muhammad, people should surrender themselves to Allah—

Muhammad the prophet, an engraving from a painting by Chappel. *Culver Pictures, Inc.*

the Arabic word for such submission being *islam*.

Before long, therefore, the religion Muhammad preached became known as Islam, based firmly on the idea that if people would only give themselves to the will of Allah, they then could live happy, contented lives. Those who agreed to follow the new faith were called Muslims, meaning "those who have surrendered" or "the true believers."

According to Muhammad, his ideas came to him directly from God. It was such thoughts that were destined in the years soon after his death to be collected together in a holy book, known to history as the Koran.

Although still speaking of his beliefs to his friends and family and to small groups, Muhammad soon found himself meeting with larger and larger crowds of people. He talked of the need for people to accept what happens to them and to become dependent on Allah (God), the figure who eventually would decide whether their future would be in heaven or in hell.

Such a belief can be especially helpful to poor people, causing them to accept graciously what happens in their lives. It can give them sense of peace. Sometimes, though, it also can limit the efforts of the poor to bring about change, causing them to feel there is little they can do to create better lives for themselves.

At first, Muhammad sharply criticized such popular activities as drinking, gambling, and fortune-telling. And when he did, his audiences often responded with humorous songs, finding him amusing but not taking him seriously. Soon, however, he began attacking rich merchants of Mecca for the huge profits they were gaining from the sale of supposedly sacred waters to idol worshipers.

Such merchants, probably Mecca's most powerful figures, grew more and more angry with him. They realized that if ever his ideas came to be accepted by the mass of people, their businesses could be seriously hurt. Strangely, some of the sons and younger brothers of the leading merchants became strong supporters of Muhammad, even beginning to speak of him as the "Messenger of God."

A few of them actually began to copy down the words of his speeches, saying that God himself must have supplied the words. Many of those young men also joined with the growing circle of Muhammad's followers in touching their heads to the ground to show their acceptance of God's complete power over them, a practice still followed in the Muslim world.

As the wealthy merchants of Mecca looked on with growing concern, the numbers of Muhammad's followers grew larger. At first the merchants tried to bribe the new religious leader, offering him part of the profits from trade with visitors who came to the city to worship. But he refused. His opponents also failed in their attempts to limit the business profits of Muhammad's larger clan, or family, the Hashemites.

Then, around the year 619, the tide of events began to turn against the increasingly popular religious leader. His faithful wife, Khadijah, died. So did his uncle, Abu Talib, the head of the Hashemite clan. For personal reasons, the leader who replaced Abu Talib proved far more eager to side with wealthy merchants in their campaign to put a halt to Muhammad's rapidly growing powers.

Little was done at first to stop the religious leader's preaching, his opponents limiting themselves to such acts as dumping garbage in front of his house. But as their efforts grew more bitter Muhammad began looking for another base for himself and his followers. His eventual choice was Yathrib, a town located some 250 miles north of Mecca. Since the time of Muhammad it has come to be known to history as Medina, "the city of the Prophet."

Although members of several tribes of Jews lived in Medina, most of the town's people eagerly welcomed Muhammad as Messenger of God. He himself was one of the last Muslims actually to leave Mecca, finally departing when he learned of a plot to kill him. Traveling secretly by night and following little-known paths, he finally reached Medina on September 24, in the year 622.

His journey became known as the Hegira, or "Journey of the Prophet," and now is considered holy by Muslims around the world. To Muhammad's faithful followers the date of his departure from Mecca, July 16, 622, marks the beginning of the Islamic era.

Once in Medina, the leader of the new Muslim religion began to shape the daily lives of his followers. Not only did he deal with matters of religion but also with issues of law, with the daily jobs of believers, and perhaps most importantly of all, with the organization of an army.

A major problem, of course, was where to get the money to carry out all these necessary tasks. According to Muhammad, he went out into the desert alone to think about how best to gain his ends. As he later told the story, it once again was the angel Gabriel who gave him answers to his difficult questions.

The most important answer for Muhammad was to use his soldiers to attack and then rob caravans carrying goods for sale in Mecca. As one who had led such caravans for many years as a camel driver, he knew exactly the paths that merchants would take and how best to raid them. And soon he began to do so.

Just as he expected, the leaders of Mecca decided to stop him with armies of their own. The result was war between Mecca and Medina.

In an early battle between the two armies, an enemy horseback rider came close to killing Muhammad, slashing directly at his head with a sword. But a servant of the Prophet saved his master's life by throwing his arm into the path of the descending weapon. The servant's arm was cut off, but Muhammad escaped unharmed.

The Battle of Badr, fought on March

15, 624, proved especially important to the Muslims. In that conflict some three hundred of Muhammad's followers attacked a caravan of great wealth returning to Mecca from Syria. To their surprise, a force of more than eight hundred men swooped down upon them close to the town of Badr.

Muhammad's troops, however, had come to believe their leader that to fight for the religion of Islam would bring them great rewards. Even if they were killed, their reward would be a place in heaven, where everything their bodies or minds might want would be theirs.

The result was a great victory for Muhammad and his soldiers. Not only did they kill many of the Meccans but they took still more as prisoners. That achievement, declared Muhammad, came clearly because of the will of Allah. The Prophet's followers, overjoyed by their triumph, thought even more highly of their leader and his faith.

Even before Muhammad's triumph at Badr he had turned against his former friends, the Jewish tribesmen living in Mecca. To please the Jews and convince them to follow him, he at first had ordered Muslim believers to bow down and face the city of Jerusalem when they prayed. But when the Jews still held to their older ideas, Muhammad had the Muslims turn instead to Mecca.

Following his victory at Badr, he expelled from Medina the Jews who still lived there, forcing them to leave behind all of their wealth. Only because of the strong protests of an Arab military leader did he agree not to have them killed.

To tighten his power still further Muhammad soon arranged to marry Hafsah, whose prominent husband had lost his life fighting at Badr. He did that although he already had married the nine-year-old Ayisha, daughter of one of his most powerful followers, Abu Bakr. In the years to come he is said to have had fourteen wives or other women living with him, nine of them still alive when he died.

One year after their defeat at Badr the leaders of Mecca launched a powerful attack on Medina, hoping that a great force of some three thousand soldiers could destroy Muhammad's influence forever. They did not triumph but killed so many Muslims in the Battle of Uhud that the Islamic Prophet could not regain completely the faith of his followers for many months.

Then, some two years later, the Meccans tried once more to conquer Medina, this time sending an army of ten thousand men to achieve their goal. Muhammad, however, had ordered the digging of a remarkably deep and wide trench to protect the city against his enemies' horses. For two weeks the Meccans attacked until, admitting failure, they finally withdrew. And as they did, their power to challenge Muhammad in the future virtually disappeared.

Very soon after his victory Muhammad launched a powerful attack on the Jewish clan at Qurayzah, most of whose people had sided with the Meccan invaders. All of the male Jews were murdered, the women and children sold into slavery. Jews in neighboring communities were allowed to live but each year in the future were forced to give up half the crops grown on their farms.

Muhammad could next have led his forces in winning a final triumph over the people of Mecca, but he decided not to do that. Instead, he hoped to use the merchants of that great Arab city to gain trade advantages in such places as neighboring Iraq and Syria. In that way, too, rather than by resorting to force of arms, he dreamed of expanding the religion of Islam for thousands of miles around the entire globe.

To gain his ends, he first led a peaceful religious visit to Mecca. There he won a treaty of peace meant to last for ten years, permitting Muslims to enter the city for religious purposes once a year. To win even greater support for his cause, Muhammad married two women of Mecca from important families.

The peace was not destined to last long, however; very soon the members of several neighboring tribes attacked Muslim forces. Muhammad responded by marching to Mecca with ten thousand soldiers. The result was an immediate surrender of the city with scarcely a struggle.

Muhammad, who had fled from Mecca with his very life in danger, finally had succeeded in conquering the community and becoming its leader.

Soon, many citizens of Mecca decided to become Muslims. Some of them helped Muhammad and his men destroy idols housed in temples and other holy places. In return, Muhammad made certain that poor people among his new followers were given loans to help them start new businesses. He convinced tribesmen in surrounding towns to join with him in exchange for protection by his Muslim armies.

Scarcely two months had passed after the surrender of Mecca when a group of tribesmen from the outside tried to attack the city. Muhammad's forces not only defeated them but invaded their villages, capturing wives and children. In exchange for money, he freed the family members and then divided among his soldiers all the farm animals owned by the attackers.

From that time on it was clear that Muhammad had become the strongest figure in the region. Leaders of tribes from across the Middle East came to visit him. At the same time, with the defeat of Persia by Byzantine Christians, many tribes that had looked to Persia for protection turned instead to Muhammad for help. In exchange, most of those people accepted the Muslim faith as their own.

Communities of Christians in the area sometimes agreed to pay tribute to Muhammad in exchange for his promise that they could keep their religion and would be left alone by his soldiers. In the year 630 he marched to the border of Syria with an army of thirty thousand troops, making the same kinds of arrangements with both Christians and Jews along the way. By then it was clear that he and his forces were the most powerful in the region.

Muhammad, accompanied by all of his wives and female companions, personally led a pilgrimage to Mecca in the year 632. For the first time he refused to allow non-Muslims to attend the services. He himself led the prayers and spoke to audiences.

He told his faithful listeners about the Islamic calendar that they all needed to follow. He set forth the proper duties of husbands and wives and the proper treatment of slaves. He warned against charging too much interest on loans.

That trip to Mecca, perhaps his most famous, became known in history as his Farewell Pilgrimage. Soon afterward Muhammad became ill. He suffered from pains in his head. Often he fainted. Once he appeared at a public meeting, causing his followers to think that he was regaining his health. But it was not to be.

On June 8, 632, he took to his bed, becoming steadily weaker, his speech confused and uncertain. That night, the prophet Muhammad, known as the Messenger of God, breathed for the last time.

His dearest young wife, Ayisha, by then eighteen years old, stayed by his bedside and nursed him to the very end.

Who would follow Muhammad as leader of the Muslim religion? The great Prophet had left his own choice unclear. Yet while ill he had arranged for Abu Bakr, his closest friend and the father of Ayisha, to lead the community in prayer.

Thus it was Abu Bakr who became the first caliph, or successor, to the founder of Islam. For more than two years he led the movement before the time of his death.

The Muslim he personally chose to take his place as caliph was the powerful Omar, a man who believed deeply in caring for the sick and the poor. But Omar also insisted that the laws and the faith of his society must be obeyed. For those who disobeyed he had a simple solution:

A painting depicting Muhammad's ascent to heaven. *British Library, London/Bridgeman/ Art Resource, NY.*

"Strike terror into wrongdoers and make heaps of mutilated limbs out of them."

At the time of Omar's death the Muslim religion was torn apart by a struggle for power. One group, known as Shiites, declared that the leaders of the faith should always be closest in blood to Muhammad and strict in their enforcement of religious practices.

Even today the Shiites are passionate in their beliefs, taking pride in followers who give their lives for the Muslim religion. It is Shiites who recently have been angry, even revolutionary, in their anti-Western politics. Sometimes they identify a leader, such as Ayatollah Ruholla Khomeini, the religious and political leader of Iran from 1979 to 1989, and claim that he is the Imam, or "leader of the faith" following directly in the path of Muhammad.

The other prominent Muslim group, known as the Sunnis, at present represents the mainstream of the Muslim faith around the world, including about 85 percent of all believers. Following the death of Muhammad, the Sunnis accepted the rule of the various caliphs, whoever those people might be. They refused to agree with Shiites that the leaders must inherit authority based on birth. In practice, the Sunnis usually have been more concerned with law and order, rather than passion, in shaping the life of their societies.

The vast majority of Muslims in such locations as Egypt, Syria, North Africa, and Pakistan are Sunnis. Those in Iran are Shiites. Such differences in religion sometimes have been at the heart of bitter conflicts or even wars, as in the still unsettled struggle between Iraq and Iran.

Today, the bodies of Abu Bakr and Omar lie in the city of Medina, next to that of the prophet Muhammad himself. After making a pilgrimage to the holy city of Mecca, most Islamic pilgrims go on to Medina to visit the tombs of their leaders. They know, along with historians, that although Muhammad died in the year 632, the tradition of his greatness was just then beginning and would become a reality destined to spread across the planet.

The legend of the Prophet's life led to important decisions for those who followed him. His teachings opened the way to reforms in property ownership; people were discouraged from seizing for themselves the possessions of the dead or property owned by the entire community. Another of his teachings, one not always followed, was that people should not charge large amounts of money in interest on loans.

But perhaps most important of all, he urged Muslims to expand the territories of their nations, thus spreading the practice of the Islamic religion around the world. Within months of Muhammad's death, Abu Bakr had recaptured all of Arabia. Omar conquered Damascus, Jerusalem, the Euphrates region, and Egypt. All of North Africa fell into Arab hands within a century after the great religious leader's passing.

Today there are millions of Muslims in lands as different as China, India, the former Soviet Union, and even the United States, a direct result of what Muhammad's followers have taught people about him.

The Koran, the Muslim holy book, probably was not put together until about twenty years after the Muslim Prophet's death, but it is filled with his ideas. He strongly believed in the notion of the Jihad, or "holy war" of conquest to spread religious beliefs as well as to add wealth. Yet, instead of the many kinds of religious duties common to other religions, the Koran has taught people that they should perform five very special duties:

1. They must accept a belief that "there is no God but Allah, and Muhammad is His Prophet."
2. They should try to pray five times each day, but at least three times.
3. They must give alms to the poor, especially money, food, or clothing.
4. They must fast from morning to night during the holy month of Ramadan.

5. They must, if it is at all possible, make a pilgrimage to Mecca at least once in their lifetimes.

The Koran itself is about the same length as the New Testament and contains 114 Suras, or chapters. It is a book that most Muslims read regularly or have read to them. Every day, hundreds of millions of the Prophet's followers come together in places of worship around the globe known as mosques. There they bow down toward Mecca and chant, "There is no God but Allah, and Muhammad is His Prophet."

In all, Muhammad was a complicated man, sometimes very kind, sometimes very cruel. He was known to show great courage along with great uncertainty. He could be extremely proud or could be deeply humble. He sometimes showed a burning desire for revenge—even murder—but also a gentle willingness to forgive.

Despite his many strengths and weaknesses, Muhammad was a person of astonishing achievement. And in the course of his profoundly active existence, he did much to shape the course of human history.

No wonder then that several times each day Muhammad's name still is said aloud with love by Muslims as they call out in prayer the name of their God, Allah.

Bahá'u'lláh

(1817–1892) Founder of the Bahá'í faith, based on belief in a single religion for all of humanity, as well as in education, equality for all people, and world peace

From the Islamic faith of Muhammad there grew in modern times a new religion, one pledged to uniting all the people of the world into one religion and all the nations of the world into one government. It is the faith now known everywhere as Bahá'í, and its followers, including people in America, are known as Bahá'ís.

The leader who catapulted that belief out of its Islamic base and into world prominence was known as Bahá'u'lláh. He taught that everyone should be brought together into a single civilization. When that occurs, he said, wars will end forever, as will struggles based on race, class, and religion. People will live always in peace and joy.

And what of Bahá'u'lláh himself? He is thought by his followers—more than two million of them around the globe, in 340 countries—to be the latest in a series of divine prophets, including Zoroaster, Moses, Jesus, the Buddha, and Muhammad. It is he, they believe, whose teachings have set the stage for a future of true human fulfillment and happiness.

The Bahá'í faith did not start with Bahá'u'lláh, but rather with another religious leader. It began in Muslim-dominated Persia (today's Iran) in the middle of the nineteenth century. There, one evening in May 1844, a young man named Siyyid Ali-Muhammed declared in a Persian city that he was the messenger of God, the Bāb (or gate) through which future events could pass.

Both the Bāb's mother and father were descended directly from Muhammad. Not surprisingly, then, as a child he showed intense interest in religion. His decision in 1844 to proclaim a new faith was seen as a threat by both major Islamic branches, the Sunnis and Shiites. They both opposed the Bābīs or followers of the Bāb, finally arranging for the ruler of Persia to have the religious leaders arrested.

While a prisoner, the Bāb was wickedly caned across the soles of his feet. At his command, however, none of his followers struck back, believing that their religion would always survive since it was the will of God.

During the months that followed, many Bābīs were killed outright while others were tortured or sold into slavery. Most leaders of the new faith were executed. Finally, on July 9, 1850, the Bāb himself was formally shot to death by a squad of Muslim soldiers.

In reaction to that killing, some Bābīs angrily fought back, although the Bāb had urged them never to be violent. When two of the movement's young people attempted to kill the Persian monarch, the response was a reign of terror against the new religious group, marked by bloody cruelty and numerous executions.

The Bāb himself had eagerly looked forward to a time of new studies in science, to widespread scholarship, indeed to the creation of a whole new society that would work for the good of its people. He spoke confidently of the coming of a new leader— "the Promised One"—who would achieve those ends and make that holy vision come true. Yet, with his own death and the massacre of thousands of his followers, it appeared that his immediate goals, along with his broader dreams, would never come to pass.

One young leader of the Bābī movement who managed to escape execution was the nobleman Mírzá Husayn Alí, a member of one of Persia's richest and most prominent families. It was he who was destined to become known to history as Bahá'u'lláh—the founder of the Bahá'í faith.

Born in 1817, Mírzá Husayn Alí had been twenty-two years old when his wealthy father died. For the next five years he spent much time helping with charities, doing his best to educate and otherwise serve poor people.

At the age of twenty-seven he became a personal friend of the Bāb, traveling widely with him to win new converts and raise money to help support the holy cause. The two men worked closely together, even cooperating in the choice of a new name—Bahá'u'lláh, or "glory of God"— for the enthusiastic young believer.

When the Bāb was assassinated, Bahá'u'lláh tried hard to prevent believers in the new faith from turning in revenge to bloody violence. But when

Mirzá Buzurg-i-Núrí, the father of Bahá'u'lláh. The only photograph of Bahá'u'lláh—a pass-
port photo taken in 1868—is on display at the Bahá'í World Centre in Haifa. *Office of Public
Information, Bahá'ís of the U.S.*

the two young Bābīs attempted to kill the Persian shah, Bahá'u'lláh himself was arrested and placed in an underground dungeon known as the Black Pit.

Every day a prisoner was taken upstairs from the dungeon into the light outside and then murdered, sometimes by having a spike hammered into his throat. Following his death, he would be chained for many days afterward to prisoners still living below in the Black Pit. An executioner dug holes with knives into one prisoner's body and then lighted candles and left them to burn away in the holes.

Possibly because of his family's wealth and outstanding reputation in neighboring countries, Bahá'u'lláh somehow managed to survive. Instead of killing him, the shah had his home burned down, after having it looted of its fine furniture and precious works of art. Then, without even a trial, Bahá'u'lláh was thrown out of Persia. He took refuge in nearby Baghdad, the capital city of Mesopotamia (today's Iraq).

Along with him to Baghdad came many loyal members of the Bābī faith, people still looking to him for leadership. Among them was his younger half-brother, Mírzá Yahyá, who himself soon claimed to be the religion's true leader. To avoid a conflict over control, Bahá'u'lláh went into exile in the mountains for nearly two years, spending the time in prayer and the writing of poetry.

In 1856, when it became clear that Mírzá Yahyá's leadership was not succeeding, Bahá'u'lláh agreed to return to Baghdad. For the next seven years he worked to pull the religious community back together and to spread its ideas throughout the region. Scholars, men of religion, and government officials came often to meet with him.

Meanwhile, he began to write a book, the so-called Book of Certitude, that described his view of God and his sense of human responsibilities. Filled with new ideas, it later would become the basis for what today is known as the Bahá'í faith.

So great was the new religious leader's reputation becoming that the neighboring shah of Persia grew deeply concerned. Eventually the shah convinced officials in Baghdad to expel Bahá'u'lláh and his closest followers to Constantinople (today's Istanbul, Turkey).

It was before moving to Constantinople that Bahá'u'lláh declared to his closest followers that he truly was a prophet of God, like the prophets of earlier religions. The formal announcement received little attention at the time, but that event presently is celebrated as the most important festival of the Bahá'í religion.

After living in Constantinople only from August to December of 1863, Bahá'u'lláh and his group were forced to settle in a far less populated Turkish city, one then known as Adrianople. It was there, before long, that he publicly announced his role as a prophet.

Soon, followers of his religion stopped describing themselves as Bābīs but, instead, as Bahá'ís—members of a new faith whose practices could change the way that people on planet Earth would live.

In September 1867 Bahá'u'lláh began writing directly to the ruling figures in most countries. He described himself as the religious figure promised in such books as the Torah, the New Testament Gospels, and the Koran. He claimed to be the leader whose faith eventually would unite the human race, bringing all people together into one nation. When that happened, he said, there would be lasting peace, social justice, and a united world.

Faced with such a statement, the leaders of Ottoman Turkey reacted sharply. They issued an imperial order condemning Bahá'u'lláh and some eighty of his close followers to imprisonment for life in the Turkish penal colony located in Acre, Palestine.

Under force of arms they quickly arrested all of the Bahá'ís and shipped them to Acre. It was believed that in the prison city, known for its damp alleys, crumbling buildings, and criminal population, Bahá'u'lláh and his followers would be unable to survive. They would die and so, too, would their religious movement.

At first, just as those who imprisoned them had hoped, some of the Bahá'ís died from the severe conditions of their life in captivity. In time, however, Bahá'u'lláh won better treatment for himself and his comrades. Fewer and fewer guards were left to oversee the group of new believers. Even when some angry Bahá'ís struck back at people of the city who had attacked them, a court decided to punish only those few prisoners involved in the counterviolence.

Bahá'u'lláh, meanwhile, had begun writing once again to heads of state, including such prominent leaders as Queen Victoria of England, Emperor Louis Napoleon of France, and Emperor Franz Joseph of Austria. To each of those monarchs he asked for help in forming a world government to settle disputes among nations. He presented ideas for an educational system that would guarantee learning for every person on earth. He proposed a universal standard of weights and measures for all countries, as well as an economic system structured to break down trade barriers and to unite nations. He suggested, too, the development of a new language that would help bring together all people living on the planet.

Writing to leaders of other religions around the world, he urged them to join

The Bahá'í House of Worship in Wilmette, Illinois, the first Bahá'í temple in the Western world. *Office of Public Information, Bahá'ís of the U.S.*

with him in helping to find answers to those disputes that always before in history had caused competition among religious groups. Instead, he argued, there should be cooperation in working to bring all people together.

For his own Bahá'í followers, Bahá'u'lláh rejected many of the old Islamic laws that the Báb had simply accepted. He also refused to support the Muslim idea of a Jihad, or holy war. At the same time, he urged his followers to welcome ideas that were right, no matter which religion held to them, including those of the Islamic believers who had tried so hard to destroy his new faith.

In the years that followed, Bahá'u'lláh

Entrance to the house in which Bahá'u'lláh's remains are buried, a place of pilgrimage to all Bahá'ís. *Office of Public Information, Bahá'ís of the U.S.*

succeeded in converting many famous leaders then living in Palestine and in other places around the world. He won the support of local Palestinian people through such deeds as the construction of an aqueduct to bring fresh water to Acre.

As he grew older he spoke increasingly of the need for the world's people to come together into one family. He urged that instead of just loving the country they lived in, they should love other people, everywhere on earth.

On Mount Carmel, across the bay from Acre, he chose a site for burying the remains of the Bāb. Since then, many new office buildings and religious shrines of the Bahá'í faith have been constructed there in what today is the city of Haifa, Israel.

With the passage of years Bahá'u'lláh became even more involved in writing, as well as in meetings with Bahá'í visitors from around the world. As he grew older it became clear to him that his time on earth was nearing an end.

On May 29, 1892, at the age of seventy-five, after a brief illness, he died.

Today the Bahá'í faith has become one of the world's fastest growing religions. It has attracted members from virtually every race, nation, and social class. In the United States, with its headquarters in Wilmette, Illinois, the group's converts usually have been well-educated people, including doctors, lawyers, college professors, and schoolteachers—usually seekers of a better way of life for all humanity.

In 1963 an assembly of Bahá'ís from around the world elected a new nine-member governing board: the Universal House of Justice. Including members from several countries—people who had been Christians, Jews, and Muslims—the leadership group presently is dedicated to the goal of spreading the faith of Bahá'u'lláh widely. Eventually, the Bahá'ís hope, it will include *everyone*.

What will happen is, of course, uncertain. When the Muslim leader Ayatollah Khomeini returned from Paris in 1979 to rule Iran (Persia), he made a special point of terrorizing the Bahá'ís. He arrested more than a hundred of the group's officials while thousands of other members of the faith were made homeless or forced to flee the country.

But to devoted followers of Bahá'u'lláh, the founder of the movement, such events in human history seem only temporary. They continue to believe, as he had, that a better time—a time of unity and happiness—is certain to lie ahead for all people.

Ayatollah Ruholla Khomeini

(1900?–1989) Fanatical Muslim religious leader who tried to show how religion and politics could be united to achieve popular goals

It was sometime in the late 1950s that a middle-aged scholar, Ruholla Khomeini, was honored with the title of ayatollah, *a word that in Arabic means "mirror image of God." For most of his lifetime, the Ayatollah Khomeini was a man of religious faith. He was also destined to become a political leader of Muslims in the land of Persia, the country known for much of our present century as Iran.*

Living in an old one-story house in the Iranian holy city of Qom, Khomeini wore a black turban on his head, a symbol to show that he was a descendant of the prophet Muhammad. He ate only cheese, toast, fruit, rice, and yogurt. Every day he spent many hours alone in prayer and meditation.

Yet for ten years, the Ayatollah Ruholla Khomeini ruled Iran with an iron fist. His every word could mean life or death for citizens of that land or for other people—including Americans—who came under his unchallenged power.

At his command thousands of Iranians were executed. He fought a bloody war with neighboring Iraq in which young children and teenagers sometimes made suicide attacks on the enemy lines. Sometimes, too, such young people were sent running barefoot into minefields to blow up explosives, clearing the way for advancing Iranian soldiers.

Meanwhile, in Khomeini's own nation the ayatollahs would not allow men and women—or boys and girls—to swim together. Nor could boys and girls go to school together. In the name of religion, people caught drinking alcoholic beverages sometimes were executed. Couples showing affection in public—even just holding hands—were severely beaten. No music could be broadcast on Iranian radio or television because, said the Ayatollah Khomeini, music dulls the minds of those who hear it and makes them silly and lazy.

During the years of his rule, Khomeini poured words of abuse onto the United States, a superpower, and managed to humiliate two American presidents, Jimmy Carter and Ronald Reagan. He used acts of terror against his enemies in other countries. Iran, a huge exporter of oil, became isolated from much of the world, including the other superpower of the 1980s, the Soviet Union.

Claiming to be the great champion of the Islamic religion, Khomeini earned the hatred of most other leaders in the Muslim Middle East. Those leaders—if not their people—united in opposition to the Islamic Republic of Iran, which Khomeini himself had founded.

And what of the Iranian people themselves? Ten years—an entire decade—under such a ruler! Yet, when he died, despite all the suffering he had brought to his nation, his funeral was a scene of passionate sorrow and grief. In the streets of Tehran, the Iranian people wept openly. Wailing, they stretched their arms toward the heavens. They fought one another for the honor of touching his corpse, an object they were certain was sacred, holy. The memory of his reign, they were certain, would last forever.

Who really was this man Khomeini? What did he stand for that made him one of the most loved—and most hated—figures of modern times? What can we learn from his remarkable life about the world's people—and what it is they may be searching for in their religious leaders?

The child who one day would lead his nation "in the name of God" probably was born in the small town of Khomein on May 27, 1900. But the date, even the year, is uncertain. His parents, Hajar and Mustafa—last names seldom were used by Muslims in those days—chose to call him Ruholla, or "soul of God." He was the last of their six children.

Although not wealthy, Ruholla's father and his grandfather both were mullahs (religious leaders) and were held in much respect by the community. When Ruholla was only five months old, his father was murdered for reasons that even now remain unclear. Eventually, the killer was brought to trial, convicted, and executed, mostly because of testimony given in court by

Ruholla's mother, something unusual for a woman to do in the ancient land then known as Persia.

It was his mother who brought him up, along with an iron-willed sister of his murdered father. The two women first taught him to be unbending, rigid, in defending the sacred Muslim religion against competing faiths.

Like the other boys in Ruholla's town of Khomein who were to receive an education, he was sent to a religious school. Each day he would read aloud a portion of the Muslim holy book, the Koran. By the age of seven he had completed it, for what would be the first of many readings during his long lifetime. Bright and quick-witted, he was an excellent student. He also enjoyed playing soccer.

When he was fifteen, both Ruholla's mother and his aunt died. He continued in school, however, with the family now directed by his oldest brother.

By the age of nineteen it was clear that he would be a religious scholar. With such a purpose in mind, he arranged to study with the Ayatollah Abdul Karim Haeri, one of the country's leading students of the Koran. Soon he became Haeri's prize pupil.

In 1922 Haeri moved to the city of Qom. There he began to organize a national center for Islamic studies. Ruholla, too, wanted to live in Qom, and it was in that city he would remain, as student and as teacher, for most of his career.

As the years went by, Ruholla's life slowly began to take shape. He took on the surname Khomeini, from the city of his birth. He studied logic and law, as well as Islamic philosophy. He learned to live simply, eating little and furnishing his quarters with only a few Persian rugs on which he both ate and slept. He wrote poetry about nature and about his religious faith. At the age of twenty-seven he went on a pilgrimage to the holy city of Mecca in Saudi Arabia, the journey expected of all devout Muslims.

When Khomeini was twenty-eight, he was married, by arrangement, to the daughter of an ayatollah from the city of Tehran. According to some accounts, she was only thirteen years old at the time. Khomeini's first son died. His second son, named Ahmed, would one day become his chief political assistant. He also had three daughters who lived to adulthood and as many as fourteen grandchildren.

Gradually, Ruholla Khomeini's reputation as a religious scholar began to grow. He wrote book after book, eventually producing twenty-one. In his writing and in his teaching he was greatly influenced by the ancient Greek philosophers, particularly Aristotle and Plato. From his reading of Plato's

Republic he began to think seriously about the ideal state—the perfect government—ruled, as Plato believed, by a philosopher king. But, to Khomeini, the philosopher had to be first of all a man of religion, a person finding his vision of life—his sense of purpose—in God.

Religion, he came to believe, was not just a matter of ceremonies. It was to be a way of life, lived day by day. The religious person must fight passionately against evil wherever it existed, even in the government of his own country. Nothing could be more holy, said Khomeini, than to give up one's life fighting against tyranny and injustice. And, given the chance, men of religion had a duty to enter politics in order to create a more perfect society.

As he grew older, Ruholla Khomeini worked ever harder at disciplining himself to serve the Islamic religion. His life became regimented, orderly. Three times a day he walked rigorously for exactly the same length of time, twenty minutes. Every day he ate his meals at exactly the same time. Every evening he went to bed and every morning he arose at exactly the same time. He never missed the proper moments for saying his prayers. He fasted even when nobody else was fasting.

Gradually, Khomeini became a person of indomitable strength and willpower. His eyes carried a fierce and piercing gaze. Tall and thin, clothed always in formal robes, he soon became a famous scholar and a man many already had grown to fear.

During the years of Khomeini's youth and his development as a religious leader, great changes had begun to take place in the land of Persia. Most importantly, a new line of rulers, the Pahlavi dynasty, took power. From the beginning, the Pahlavi shahs (kings) set out to transform Persia—to modernize it and to break down the ancient social and religious customs that they believed were holding the country back.

The religion of Islam proved a special target for Reza Shah, the first Pahlavi monarch. He had mosques torn down. He transformed religious schools into government-run schools that forbade religious teaching. Like Kemal Atatürk in Turkey, he had women remove their veils and urged people to dress in Western style, like the British, French, and American tourists he encouraged to visit.

The shah also refused to support religious leaders with public tax money, thereby taking income away from such men as Khomeini. The old Arab calendar, based on the moon, was replaced by a calendar based on the sun, like that of the Western nations.

As in Western countries, too, people were expected to choose family names. Ruholla was registered by the government as Ruholla Mustafavi, taken from his father's name, Mustafa.

Finally, the very name of the country was changed. No longer was it to be known as Persia, but as Iran, to call attention to the ancient Aryan race from which most of the nation's people were descended, in contrast to the people of the neighboring Arabic states.

To Ruholla (Mustafavi) Khomeini, the dramatic changes pushed through by the shah were a betrayal of everything he stood for—everything to which he had devoted his life. At first Khomeini said little. Then, in 1941, he published a book, *Unveiling the Mysteries*.

In that book, he declared that the shah's government was without value. All of the new laws that had been passed, he said, should be burned. The only true government, stated Khomeini, must be based on Islam. It must take a form decided by the religious leaders. And religious leaders must supervise all of the government's activities. They should be the real power behind the throne.

Because the shah believed the Aryan race was superior to all other races, he strongly supported Adolf Hitler's Nazis, who claimed to be pure Aryans. Great Britain, then at war with Nazi Germany, toppled the shah from power and replaced him with his son, Muhammad Riza Shah.

Once, in 1953, Muhammad Riza Shah visited the Muslim holy city of Qom. When he appeared before the religious leaders there, all but one of them rose to greet him. That one cleric was Ruholla Khomeini.

All across Iran, Khomeini's name was becoming well known. Young Muslims, in particular, came to admire his courage, his defiance. Like him, they believed that Islam should be not only a religion but a way of life.

Before the 1950s ended, Khomeini had been honored with the title ayatollah, shared with fewer than a thousand other Muslim leaders of Iran. In 1962 he was named grand ayatollah, a title held by only six other clerics.

It was also in 1962 that Khomeini led a general strike to protest the shah's order that witnesses in courts of law no longer were to swear an oath upon the Koran, the Muslim holy book.

Tension rose even higher in 1963 when the shah, with the encouragement of the United States, announced his White Revolution. According to the shah, the time already was overdue for Iran to modernize itself, to leap into the twentieth century alongside the Western nations. Now, women were to have equal rights. Lands owned by the

The Ayatollah Khomeini in exile in France. *UPI/Bettmann.*

clergy were to be seized. Iran would cast its lot with the West.

The Ayatollah Khomeini proceeded to launch a fierce attack on the White Revolution. On the campus of Tehran University, students joined in support of Khomeini. They held marches and distributed pamphlets. When the ayatollah was thrown into prison for demanding that the army remove the shah, rioting broke out in the streets.

For several months Khomeini remained in jail. Then he was released but required to remain in his house. Still, his verbal attacks against the shah continued. In 1964 he spoke strongly against a new agreement with the United States, one that exempted American soldiers stationed in Iran from trial by Iranian courts.

The Iranian government responded by expelling Khomeini from the country. He fled first to Turkey, then to a Muslim holy site in Iraq. Even from his place of exile he attacked the shah, sending tape-recorded sermons to be played in Iranian mosques.

As the years passed, Iran became prosperous, mostly because of the sale of oil to Western countries. But the prosperity did not filter down to the great mass of Iranians—and almost never to the poor. If anything, they were even poorer than before.

Increasingly, those who hated the shah turned to the clergy for support, and especially to the exiled Ayatollah Khomeini.

In 1978, when Iraq expelled Khomeini at the shah's urging, he took up residence in France, on the outskirts of Paris. From there, he stayed in close touch with his Iranian followers. At his command there were work stoppages, enormous public rallies, days of silent prayer. None of the shah's many efforts succeeded in stopping Khomeini.

Meanwhile, the economic situation inside Iran grew more serious. Because oil workers stayed away from their jobs, the economy ground slowly to a halt. The country soon was in desperate straits.

In January 1979 the shah left the country for a trip to Egypt, saying it was only a vacation. But the Iranian people knew that he would never return.

Millions of people jammed the streets of Tehran and other Iranian cities, calling for the Ayatollah Khomeini to return from France, loudly demanding that he take over the reins of power.

On February 1, 1979, to thunderous applause, Khomeini entered Tehran. Never again, he promised, would he allow the United States to force the rule of the shah upon them.

Soon Khomeini proclaimed an Islamic republic in Iran. Now at last, he said, the nation had a "government of God."

Within days, the executions began. Supporters of the shah were killed, as were those who offended traditional Muslim values, such as homosexuals, prostitutes, and adulterers, as well as users of drugs and alcohol. Newspapers that dared even to question "the Imam" (Khomeini) were shut down. Many Iranians convicted of criticizing their new leader discovered that the price of that act was death. Within a few months, thousands of people had been shot, hanged, or stoned to death.

Khomeini attempted almost at once to export his revolution. His agents tried to stir up trouble in Egypt, Saudi Arabia, Kuwait, Bahrain—all across the Arab world. The ayatollah's picture began to appear on the walls of shops in cities of the Soviet Union with large Muslim populations, such as Baku, and even in Jerusalem, the capital of the Jewish nation, Israel.

In November 1979, after President Jimmy Carter allowed the shah of Iran to enter the United States for medical treatment, Iranians exploded in rage. Many of them climbed the walls of the United States embassy in Tehran. Once inside, they made hostages of American diplomats and soldiers.

Khomeini's followers reach out to touch him after his return to Iran in 1979. *UPI/Bettmann.*

For 444 days, until the day that Jimmy Carter left office and Ronald Reagan was inaugurated as president of the United States, the Americans were held captive, often blindfolded and publicly insulted by the Iranians. Again and again the ayatollah spoke of his hatred for the United States—the enemy of the Islamic world.

Despite that hatred, President Reagan secretly sent diplomats to Iran. Their mission was to offer military supplies in exchange for the freedom of Americans then held hostage by the ayatollah's supporters in such Middle Eastern countries as Lebanon. Eventually, an arrangement was worked out.

When word of the "arms for hostages" deal at last became public, President Reagan—who often had spoken with passion against Khomeini's cruelty—was deeply embarrassed.

Some of the arms supplied by the United States were used by Iran in its eight-year-long war with neighboring Iraq. Although Iran had far more soldiers, Iraq, led by Saddam Hussein, had a powerful air force and guided missiles. Nor did Saddam Hussein hesitate to use such inhumane weapons as poison gas against his Muslim brother, Khomeini. Finally, in 1988, both sides, by then exhausted by the terrible and costly years of bloodletting, agreed to a truce.

The Ayatollah Khomeini had long been in ill health. When first he took power in 1979, he had promised the Iranian people that "the remaining one or two years of my life I will devote to you to keep this movement alive." Ten years later he still had not won victory for his movement—the struggle to make belief in Allah (God) a way of life for the world.

What he had done, however, was to transform his country. Where before Iran had been a busy crossroads of trade between East and West, it had become isolated.

By the time of his death, on June 3, 1989, the once-prosperous land was a place of poverty and devastation. Veterans of the ferocious war with Iraq, many of them blind and crippled, begged for bread on the streets of Tehran.

Yet many of Khomeini's followers still revered him, still loved him. They continued to believe firmly, like the Ayatollah himself, that Islam must be not just a faith—a religion—but must be a way of life for all the world.

To such people, governments are merely tools to achieve a much broader, more universal goal—the goal that someday everyone on the planet would finally join them in becoming "true believers."

PART IV

JUDAISM

Moses

(Thirteenth century B.C.) Religious prophet and founder of the Jewish faith; today his ideas of law and government still exercise enormous influence

Like the lives of such profound leaders as Buddha, Jesus, and Muhammad, the life of Moses set a tone—a direction—for believers in one of the great religions of humankind, in his case the religion known as Judaism.

It was Moses who led the Jews out of a life of slavery at the hands of the Egyptian pharaohs. Then, from the peak of Mount Sinai, or so it is told, he brought to his people the Ten Commandments. Those holy laws set a direction for the future life of Jewish society and became a starting point for the two faiths destined to branch off from Judaism: Christianity and Islam.

Like the life stories of so many of history's great leaders, there is much that is uncertain about Moses. How many years did he really live, and when? What truly were the events of his childhood, his marriage, his journeys? How well was he accepted by the Jewish tribal people he is supposed to have led?

Not all of the answers to such questions are known. Still, the story of Moses as told in the Bible is one that has survived for more than three thousand years. Of all the great personalities in history, very few have had such enormous importance in shaping the beliefs of other human beings. Muhammad praised him. Jesus claimed that "I came not to destroy the law (of Moses) but to fulfill it."

Although Jesus taught otherwise, many nations still have laws to punish murderers with the death penalty.

Businessmen, too, find it hard to follow such Christian practices as giving to all who beg and forgiving people who attack them or steal from them. Instead, most people still believe in severe punishment for those who break the Ten Commandments delivered by Moses, containing such firm guideposts as "Thou shalt not steal; thou shalt not kill."

Some historians have argued that Moses never lived at all, that the Bible story of his life is really the combined story of several leaders' lives. Recently, however, there has been growing support for his actual existence and for the truth of the Bible in telling his deeds.

He is seen as a person of many faults: an impatient man with a short and fiery temper, who once killed an Egyptian with a single blow. But he also is considered a person of enormous administrative skill and an exceptionally talented leader with deep faith in his God. Perhaps more than anyone else in history, he may be the one who transformed religion from magical and superstitious practices into a matter of deep belief in a single God.

According to Hebrew tradition, the early life of Moses was shaped by the decision of an Egyptian pharaoh to put an end to the growth of the Jewish population in that country. It supposedly was that leader's plan to have all new-born Hebrew boys killed at the time of their birth. It is said that to prevent that from happening to their child, Amram and Jochebed, the parents of Moses, tried for three months to hide him. Then, fearing he was about to be discovered, they carefully placed him in a reed basket and set him afloat in the river Nile.

According to tradition, it was Thermutis, the daughter of the Egyptian pharaoh, who came upon the child and decided to adopt him. And it was she who named him Moses, meaning "he who was drawn out," since he was drawn from the river.

Many legends have survived about the childhood of Moses. Perhaps the best-known tale concerns the time that the pharaoh was playing with him and Moses took the crown from the monarch's head and placed it on his own.

Furious, some of the pharaoh's advisers urged him to kill the ambitious child at once. But one adviser suggested a test: that two platters be placed before the boy, one containing a golden crown and the other filled with brightly burning pieces of coal. If he took the crown, then he was to be killed.

As the story goes, Moses first reached for the crown. But the angel Gabriel appeared to him, pushing the child's hand instead to the coals. Moses placed his painfully burned fingers into his mouth to ease the pain. That act, it is said, explains why the Bible describes Moses as "slow of speech and of a slow tongue" (Exodus 4:10).

Little is know about the education of Moses, but it seems likely that in his youth he learned about government, military matters, and the religions of the time. Some historians think he also found out about his own background—the fact that he had been born a Jew.

On one visit among Hebrew workers in Egypt he is said to have come upon an Egyptian guard beating a Hebrew slave to death. Young and strong, he did not hesitate to strike at the attacker, killing him. Very quickly, however, the story of his deed began to spread. Soon afterward, when he saw two Hebrews fighting, they questioned whether he would kill them, too, and what right he had to criticize them.

Supposedly out of fear that the pharaoh would prosecute him as a Jew for murdering the guard and possibly even put an end to his life, Moses departed from Egypt. He fled to the land of Midian, on the Sinai Peninsula.

It is said that while resting one day near a well he saw shepherds frightening from the well the seven beautiful daughters of Jethro, a close religious adviser to the Egyptian pharaoh. Rising to the defense of the young women, he drove the shepherds away.

Gustave Doré's etching depicts the finding of the infant Moses by Pharaoh's daughter. *Brown Brothers.*

In time he came to marry one of Jethro's daughters, the strong-willed young Zipporah. Gershom, the first of their children, was raised as a Hebrew while, at least in the beginning, the second child, Eliezar, was not. But the Bible tells how Zipporah eventually came to treat Eliezar as a Jew, thus saving him, as well as Moses, from a murder plot to be carried out by the Devil.

Moses is said to have lived for a time as a farmer in Midian, caring for the lands of Jethro. Yet while working in the fields, he thought about the Hebrews he had left behind in Egypt. He also thought about the ancient Egyptian king, Amenhotep IV (Akhenaten), who had believed in only one god, the powerful sun god Aten. Such a single, strong god might well be able to free the Hebrews from their many years of slavery in Egypt.

It was then, as told in the Bible's story, that a remarkable event took place. As Moses led his flock one day near the Mountain of God (Sinai), he came upon a burning bush—a bush that although covered by fire miraculously was not destroyed. From that bush God spoke to him, urging him to free the Jewish people from their slavery in Egypt and then lead them back to the land of Israel, where they had lived more than four hundred years earlier.

At first, it is said, Moses hesitated, thinking that he did not have the ability to perform so great a task. But the Bible tells how God assured him that he truly had the strength to achieve a victory.

The Bible also recounts that Moses asked the name of the holy figure commanding him to do such a deed. The answer was Yahweh (Jehovah), meaning "he who creates" (or brings into being). In the Hebrew tradition of the time, Yahweh would eventually come to be seen as the supreme Lord over everything on the planet Earth and in the heavens.

It is told that even after a detailed discussion with God, Moses still hesitated to go ahead, describing to God his problem with speaking aloud ever since his childhood. Although displeased with Moses for his self-doubts, Yahweh agreed to allow Aaron, the prophet's smooth-speaking brother, to make the needed formal presentations to the pharaoh of Egypt.

With some uncertainty but with a deep sense of mission, Moses is said to have agreed to do the will of God. He then returned to his wife, Zipporah, and to her father, Jethro, informing them only that he intended to visit with his people in Egypt. Zipporah and the couple's two young sons, he said, should go along with him.

In Egypt, says the Bible, Moses and Aaron directly confronted the pharaoh, Ramses II. To him, the two Hebrew brothers passed on the word of the Lord to "let my people go!"

But the pharaoh claimed not even to know about their God. Instead, he declared that he himself was the true lord of the universe. He was determined not to let the Israelites depart.

The biblical account tells next of ten plagues sent by God against the Egyptians. In the first, all the waters of the Nile were turned into blood. In the second, thousands of frogs were sent into the homes of the Egyptian people.

In the third, the dust of the land was transformed into lice, covering both people and animals. Later there came hail, locusts, and thick darkness.

After each plague began, the pharaoh pleaded with Moses and Aaron to end it, promising to let the Hebrews leave. Yet each time after the problem was removed, the pharaoh "hardened his heart" and refused to let them go.

Finally, as the story is told in the Book of Exodus, God had the Hebrews kill a lamb and sprinkle its blood on the doorposts of their houses. That night, God passed over the houses marked in that way but killed all the firstborn sons in the homes of the Egyptians, including the son of the pharaoh. It was at that point that Ramses at last told the Jews to leave.

Just before their departure they celebrated the passing over of the Lord (or Passover) for the first time. That holiday, marking the Hebrew liberation from slavery in Egypt, still is observed every year by members of the Jewish faith. Some rabbis consider it the most important of all events on the calendar.

So quickly did the Hebrews leave Egypt that even the dough for the bread they were preparing did not have time to rise. Thus they ate unleavened bread, known today as matzo, a tradition still followed by many Jews to mark the beginning of their freedom as a people.

Yet before they could escape completely, the pharaoh decided to pursue them with his soldiers and kill them. Just as they were about to cross a body of water (the Red Sea in some accounts),the Egyptian soldiers had almost caught up with them.

As the Egyptians approached, Moses led his followers directly into the water where, at God's command, a path of safety appeared before them, leading to the other side. Then, when the soldiers tried to follow, the tide rushed in, drowning almost all of the pharaoh's men.

Having brought his people to safety, Moses is said in the Book of Exodus to have joined with his sister Miriam in a prayer of thanks to God. Some time later, finding themselves in a great desert, they came upon a lake but were disappointed to find the water bitter. Moses then threw wood into the water, supposedly causing salt to form and making the water sweet enough to drink.

At other times, when they were hungry he led them to a breadlike food called manna and then to a flock of birds they could eat. When they once again were thirsty for water, he struck a rock, causing a beautiful stream of water to gush out for his followers.

Finally, the Hebrews reached Mount Sinai, where God first had spoken to Moses from the burning bush. The Bible tells how the visitors were greeted there by thunder and lightning along with the sound of a trumpet. Moses then climbed to the peak of Mount Sinai and remained there for forty days and forty nights.

When he descended from the mountain he carried with him two stone tablets on which were engraved the Ten Commandments. Those commandments could be summarized as follows:

1. I am the Lord thy God which have brought thee out of the land of Egypt, out of the house of bondage. Thou shalt have no other gods before me.

2. Thou shalt not make unto thee any graven image.

3. Thou shalt not take the name of the Lord thy God in vain.

4. Remember the Sabbath day to keep it holy.

5. Honor thy father and thy mother.

6. Thou shalt not commit murder.

7. Thou shalt not commit adultery.

8. Thou shalt not commit theft.

9. Thou shalt not bear false witness against thy neighbor.

10. Thou shalt not covet thy neighbor's wife . . . nor anything that is thy neighbor's.

As Moses, carrying the Ten Commandments in his hands, approached his people at the base of the mountain, he was shocked to see them, with the help of Aaron, worshiping a golden calf. Furious, he smashed the tablets against the rocky mountainside. He then threw the golden calf into the fire. At that point, the people realized what they had done wrong, and they believed once more in Yahweh, the God of Israel.

In the biblical account, Moses climbed again to the peak of Mount Sinai and then returned with a second set of tablets, ones he himself had made at God's command. This time, as he approached his people he smiled, and rays of light came from his skin. He believed that God had forgiven the Jewish people for worshiping the golden calf. Despite all of the unreligious things his fellow Hebrews had done, Moses still had faith in them, still intended to help them.

While in the wilderness, the Jews constructed what is known as the Tabernacle, intended to protect the stone tablets of the law, which were housed in a beautiful box known as the Holy Ark. The Ark was thought to be divine—so holy, in fact, that God himself was in it. In today's world virtually every Hebrew synagogue has an Ark, and inside it are kept a set of sacred scrolls—the first five books of the Bible, known as the Torah.

In the story of the Bible, the ancient Hebrews wandered for forty years before they finally entered the Promised Land, Israel. One reason it took so long was that scouts sent out by Moses had

An undated woodcut shows Moses destroying the stone tablets bearing the Ten Commandments. *The Bettmann Archive.*

Michelangelo's statue of Moses. *S. Pietro in Vincoli, Rome/Alinari/Art Resource, NY.*

brought back stories of how dangerous their former homeland had become. Although still a "land of milk and honey," it was inhabited by giant people of great strength.

To avoid conflict with some of those people, like the powerful Midianites, Moses chose other pathways. Nevertheless, he found it necessary to fight with the Amonites and the people of Bashan, led by the giant ruler Og. In the land known today as Jordan, some of Moses' peopled decided to settle, putting them into conflict with the Moabites and the Midianites. In those struggles it was the leadership of Moses that enabled the Hebrews to triumph.

During the years of their wandering, the Jews encountered many problems. One of those was the lack of water following the death of Miriam, Moses' sister. It is said that once the Hebrews left Egypt, God rewarded Miriam for her loyalty by the presence of clear, sweet water. But when she died, the waters disappeared.

Faced with the unhappiness of his people without water, Moses, helped by God, brought water forth from a rock. Yet when the water finally appeared once again, neither Moses nor his brother, Aaron, gave credit to the Lord. For that, it is said, both he and Aaron were condemned to die before ever entering the Holy Land. Some religious leaders argue, however, that the true reason for Moses' punishment was that when he first arrived in Midian and rescued the seven daughters of Jethro, he had claimed to be an Egyptian and not a Hebrew.

Of the two brothers, it was Aaron who died first. Legends describe how, at the time of his death, Aaron was so loved that both the men and the women of the Jewish faith cried deeply for him. (Because Moses was so firm and so often angry it is said that after his death only the men shed tears for him.)

Although Moses himself was growing old, he continued to work hard to prepare his people for a life in Israel. He organized an army and taught his soldiers how to fight. He trained military leaders. He made every possible effort to unite the Hebrews and to make them strong. Still, he and his people remained in the wilderness.

To remember those years, a time of preparation for life in Israel, many modern Jews still celebrate the holiday of Sukkoth, some of them even praying in simple little huts of that name. The holiday is a reminder of time in the ancient world spent in wandering.

When it became clear to Moses that he, too, like Aaron and Miriam, was close to death, he is said to have expressed to God a desire to live still longer. For the sake of his people, however, he prepared his closest follower, Joshua, for a leadership role.

He spoke to Joshua about the holy words of what later would become the Torah (the first five books of the Bible). And he spoke of the religious wisdom so crucial for a man he hoped would be a model for the Hebrew people, bringing them at last into Israel.

The Bible tells that as the end of his life came near, Moses climbed from the plains of Moab near the city of Jericho to the peak of a mountain. There, as he looked out into the distance, he was met by the Lord who, in the Old Testament version, ended the life of Moses with a kiss.

It is, of course, impossible for us to know how large a portion of the Torah actually was written by Moses. Almost certainly, however, he did much to aid in its creation, especially in such matters as the Ten Commandments. Moses, a man who stuttered as he spoke and who had killed a soldier in his youth, went on to play a dominant role in establishing the kingdom of Israel. Far more than his successor, Joshua, it was Moses who truly made possible the creation of that community.

It was he who took a group of clans and shaped them into a great nation. In his lifetime he served as a prophet, a reformer, a lawmaker, a judge. He transformed believers in a variety of gods into believers in one God.

In all of human history, few leaders can be said to equal him in their influence, an impact that continues even today for millions of people, including not only Jews but Muslims and Christians as well.

Jesus spoke well of Moses. Such groups in America as the Puritans of New England and the Mormons of Utah have followed his ideas closely. In the field of government, the laws of Christian nations probably hold more closely to the techniques of Moses than of Jesus. They still cling to the notion of severe punishment—"an eye for an eye and a tooth for a tooth"—rather than to the simple forgiveness of criminals. In matters of daily business, people in the industrialized world may speak of Christian virtues, but they live by the practical ways of Moses.

To his own people, the Jews, his reputation has stood alone through all the centuries. For, as is perhaps said best in the Bible (Deuteronomy 34:10), "There arose not a prophet since in Israel like unto Moses, whom the Lord knew face to face."

Jeremiah

(640?–575? B.C.) Leading Jewish teacher and prophet whose spiritual ideas have much in common with those of Jesus

To some scholars, Jeremiah stands out as the greatest of all the Old Testament prophets, a personality whose ideas came very close to those of Jesus, who freely quoted from him. One historian, Charles Francis Potter, has gone so far as to say that if members of Christian churches and Jewish synagogues could regularly compare the teachings of Jeremiah with those of Moses and Jesus, the two religions could not help but come closer together.

As Potter dramatically put it, "Jeremiah was the Jesus of the Old Testament and Jesus the Jeremiah of the New."

It is said that some of the disciples of Jesus even thought their leader was really Jeremiah come back to life. Strangely, the deaths of both Jesus and Jeremiah eventually were brought about by members of faiths that the two men were defending.

One reason that Jeremiah is unique among personalities in the Bible is that we know so much about his inner thoughts—probably more than about those of any other figure in all the Scriptures. In the Old Testament book that bears his name, Jeremiah prays openly for the death of his own relatives. He bitterly curses the day he was born. He charges that God used him unfairly, wrongly. He laments that he has been deprived of the pleasures of family life, left only with the word of God for comfort.

Despite all such complaints that emerge in Jeremiah's writings, he still holds out high hope for the Jewish people today—faith that if they accept God and worship Him only, their futures will be bright and the land of Israel will be theirs forever. During his own lifetime Jeremiah saw his country lose its freedom, saw it become a colony of Babylon. Yet eventually he was destined to stand out as the leading teacher of ways for Jews to start anew and, holding firmly to their religion, to survive.

Jeremiah was born in the tiny village of Anathoth, only one hour's walk from the Temple of Jerusalem. Although members of his family involved themselves deeply in religious matters, some of them serving as members of the clergy, Jeremiah himself never became a rabbi. Instead, he was fated to struggle often against synagogue authorities, living his life as a prophet—a person inspired by God to speak in His name about future events.

It is said that Jeremiah received his call to become a prophet during his early twenties, an age that he worried was too young for so serious a task. But as he later described the experience, the Lord firmly commanded him to speak out, leaving him no choice but to obey. His mission, he said, was to "root out, pull down, and destroy" the ways of worship then being practiced.

Jeremiah's early days as a prophet did not go well. He predicted an invasion by the Scythians, something that never

happened. He then argued for giving special authority to religious leaders of the Temple of Jerusalem, a position that angered many people in his own town, even though it was close to the city.

Finally, when Jehoiakim became king, Jeremiah took a strong stand against that monarch's acceptance of customs from nearby Babylon and Canaan. He was especially angered at the way Jehoiakim honored the proud display of wealth and his open support of free conduct by men and women in matters of sex. He was upset, too, by the use in Temple ceremonies of sacred cakes, carved and eaten in honor of the Queen of Heaven, a goddess of the neighboring Philistines.

But what most infuriated Jeremiah was a practice of the king involving the sacrifice of children. Their living bodies sometimes were thrown into blazing fires in honor of the god Molech—a ceremony Jeremiah considered against all that the Hebrew religion had ever taught. It, too, was a practice brought in from neighboring countries.

The deeply disturbed Jeremiah finally gathered together a great crowd of people in a valley outside of Jerusalem. There he delivered a bitter speech condemning the practices of Jehoiakim. In conclusion, he raised an earthen jar toward the sky before crashing it to the ground. It was, he said, what God would do to people who followed such terrible practices.

When he returned to Jerusalem, Jeremiah was struck viciously by a representative of the king and thrown into prison for a day and two nights. While there, the young prophet became deeply discouraged. He cursed the day of his own birth and wished that he had never been born.

On his release, however, he immediately spoke out in public against those he charged with breaking the laws of God. As a result, he was arrested once again and put on trial. This time the government demanded his death. But when Jeremiah declared in court that he had been sent by God to speak to the Hebrew people, a group of older men rose to his defense. They declared that prophets such as he had a responsibility to speak out openly and should not be punished for what they said.

To the surprise of nearly everyone, Jeremiah was freed. He had the right, it was said, to free speech. Nor did the king himself choose to punish the daring young prophet, even after Jeremiah angrily predicted in public that when the monarch finally died, because of his cruelty his body would be dragged about the city like that of an animal and never be buried.

Not long afterward Jeremiah wrote a book. In it he declared that the Babylonian king, Nebuchadnezzar, would one day invade the land of the Jews, just as he already had invaded and conquered Egypt. After the book was read aloud to King Jehoiakim, the monarch personally slashed it to pieces with a knife and threw the remains into a fireplace. He angrily sent officers to arrest Jeremiah and Baruch, his aide, but the two men escaped. Baruch soon made new copies of the book and had it distributed widely.

Before Nebuchadnezzar and his army managed to reach Jerusalem, Jehoiakim died. On the advice of Jeremiah, the Hebrews than surrendered to the Babylonian leader without a struggle. As a result, many of the Jewish people, including members of the royal family, were taken to Babylon in captivity. Jeremiah, however, was allowed to remain.

About one year later he wrote to the captives, having heard that they expected to return soon to Jerusalem. In his letter he urged them instead to build houses, to plant gardens, and to raise families. That, he said, would be best for them since, or so he predicted, they would be forced to remain in Babylon for seventy years. When a leader of the captives responded to Jeremiah in an angry letter, the prophet strongly replied to him that the Israelites must not "rebel" against the will of the Lord God.

Those Hebrews who had remained

behind in Jerusalem became increasingly unhappy. Some of them deserted the Judaic faith and turned to worship of the sun or the gods of the Syrians. So displeased did Jeremiah become with such people that he once displayed in public two baskets of figs. One basket contained good figs, the other rotten ones. The good figs, he said, represented Jews who had been exiled to Babylon; the bad ones were those Jews who remained behind but were questioning their religious heritage.

Not long after that, the kings of five countries along the Mediterranean coast broke out in open rebellion against Nebuchadnezzar. Appearing before representatives from those lands, Jeremiah wore a yoke, or harness for animals, made of wood. He urged that, for the time at least, the Babylonian leader should be obeyed since he was really the servant of God.

Jeremiah wore the wooden yoke for several days until one of the Hebrews broke it, demanding freedom for Israel. In response, Jeremiah began to wear a yoke made of iron, urging his people to be patient.

Five years later a rebellion broke out. As Nebuchadnezzar's forces rapidly approached the walls of Jerusalem, the city's leaders freed the slaves of the region, hoping for their help. But then, when the Babylonian troops pulled back, the slaves—both men and women—were once again taken into captivity. Meanwhile, Jeremiah was put into prison for warning the public that Nebuchadnezzar would return and demand revenge.

The new king, Zedekiah, freed Jeremiah, but when the prophet's warnings continued, the monarch agreed to his arrest once again. This time he was secretly thrown into a deep and filthy pit, a place where it seemed certain that before long he would die.

In what must have appeared miraculous to Jeremiah, one of the workers at the royal palace, an enormous Ethiopian slave named Ebedmelek, found him there. With the help of three workers sent by King Zedekiah, Ebedmelek managed to rescue him.

The king then went secretly to meet with the still-imprisoned Jeremiah. In their conference Jeremiah strongly urged the monarch to surrender to the Babylonians. Zedekiah, however, expressed fear that he then would be seen as the enemy of those Jews who already had stood out against Babylon. Still, the king promised not to allow the Jewish nobles to kill Jeremiah. As to the fate of the prophet's rescuer, Ebedmelek, some legends declare that he survived for as many as sixty-six more years.

To the surprise of many Jews, Nebuchadnezzar's forces soon returned

Jeremiah lamenting over Jerusalem, an engraving by J. Rogers from Bendeman's painting. *Culver Pictures, Inc.*

to Jerusalem, crashing through the city's protective walls. They killed all of Zedekiah's children and then blinded the king himself. Next they looted and burned down the city, executing many of its people. In return for his support, Jeremiah was invited to come to Babylon, but he chose instead to remain among the ruins of Jerusalem.

Only a few weeks later an open rebellion broke out against the Jewish leader left in charge of the battered capital city. Eventually the revolt was crushed, but those newly in charge decided to take refuge in Egypt, insisting that Jeremiah go along with them.

What became of the great prophet when once he arrived in Egypt is uncertain. It is known that he continued to support Nebuchadnezzar, claiming that the Babylonian was an agent of God. Such statements may well have contributed to Jeremiah's death. According to the accounts of some writers,

The prophet Jeremiah, a detail from Michelangelo's painting in the Sistine Chapel, Rome. *The Bettmann Archive.*

including two early Christian historians, he was stoned to death by his Jewish enemies, people made angry by his sermons. It is sometimes said that it was the Egyptians who finally provided him with an honorable burial.

To most religious scholars Jeremiah is seen as a man of enormous importance. Like Jesus, he sometimes gave himself over to weeping. But like Jesus, too, he remained a person of great courage. Often he became impatient and angry with the Hebrew people, demanding that those who were tormenting him should be punished by God. Sometimes he would become impatient with the Lord, even shaking a fist toward his master. Yet in every instance he returned to loyalty—to faith. He then would express sorrow, regret, or "repentance" for his deeds, much as Christian leaders did in the New Testament.

Despite the way Jeremiah spoke of God's power in controlling the events of history, he was especially aware of a "God of love." To him, although people would be punished for their evil deeds, they also would receive rewards for their good deeds. As Jeremiah saw it, human beings behaved the way they did—for good or for evil—less because of their minds than because of their hearts. Thus if they searched for God with love, they truly would find Him.

Nor when things went badly should people give up. Through the centuries many Jews used the writings of Jeremiah to help them believe that, despite Israel's loss of land and nationhood, they should not give up. For such people the rebirth of Israel in 1948—after Hitler's failure to destroy all Jews—was proof that Jeremiah truly had been correct.

Similarly, Jeremiah did not believe that people were born to be corrupt and evil. It is true that once he angrily compared Israel's chance of doing good to the possibility of an Ethiopian lightening the blackness of his skin color or of a leopard changing its spots. But, time and again, Jeremiah declared firmly that people had the power to repent for their sins, and God most certainly had the power to forgive them.

Jeremiah taught that despite all the weaknesses of people, they eventually could find their way to God. They could be reborn. Their hearts could be purified. They could be saved.

Thus, as a prophet Jeremiah deserves to be remembered not only for his personal greatness but for the positive faith he shares in common with major figures in the world's other great religions.

It well may be that because of such faith and hope people continue to seek out religion as a proper guide as to how best to "live a life."

Golda Meir

(1898–1978) As prime minister of Israel, she played a critical role in achieving the Zionist goal of return to Israel, homeland of the world's Jews

To be a child. To be a Jewish child. To be a Jewish child in Russia at the dawn of the twentieth century.

Those three experiences were to shape the life of Golda Meir, a woman destined to become the leader of Israel—the Jewish homeland she helped to establish.

As a child she knew cold and hunger. She knew fear. And she was determined that other Jewish children should not have to endure what she had endured. Because of her achievements in working toward that goal, she is remembered as one of the truly outstanding leaders of modern history.

Today, while many Jews do not follow their religion closely, they, like Golda Meir, identify themselves firmly as being

Jewish. Also like her, they are deeply committed to the survival of Israel.

One of Golda Meir's earliest memories was that of being hungry, yet having her mother sorrowfully take food from her plate to feed her younger sister, Zipke. Even more frightening was the vivid memory of her father trying to nail a board across the door, fearing a pogrom—one of the frequent attacks against the Jews by crowds of angry Russians.

She knew that in many pogroms the Russians, shouting "Christ killers," had stormed into the Jewish quarter of a city or village. They stole what they wanted from the homes. Some of them drove nails into the heads of Jews. They threw Jewish children from upper-story windows onto the streets below. Women were raped and their stomachs were ripped open. Some had their breasts cut off with knives.

Meanwhile, the police usually stood by, refusing to help the victims. Only if the Jews dared to fight back would the police step in, arresting not the attacking rioters but the Jews who dared to defend themselves.

Sometimes the Russian monarchs, the czars, would personally order the beginning of a pogrom. By blaming the Jews for the nation's problems, a czar could divert popular attention from his own failings.

Some Jews thought the violence would end if, by revolution, the czars were overthrown and a new kind of government established. Other Jews had little hope for such a change. Instead, they argued that the terror, the hunger, the beatings, would end only when Jews had a country of their own in Palestine, the ancient Zion of biblical times.

Golda Meir was born in 1898 in the Russian city of Kiev. Her parents, Moshe and Bluma Mabovitch, had eight children in all, four boys and four girls. All of the boys and one of the girls died in childhood. Only Golda, her younger sister, Zipke, and an older sister, Shana, managed to survive the poverty and dis-ease that was then the lot of Jewish children in Russia.

Moshe Mabovitch later moved his family to the city of Pinsk, hoping that in that city there would be more work to be done by a skilled carpenter such as himself. Day after day he went out looking for jobs, but there were none. The family, living together in a tiny room, was hungry. Their situation grew desperate.

At last Golda's father made a decision. He would take his family to the *goldene medina* (land of gold)—America. There, it was said, there was work for everyone. Even poor people from Russia could become rich. Furthermore, in America there would be no need to live in fear. In America there were no pogroms.

They came to live in a poor section of Milwaukee. Golda's father took whatever carpentry work he could find to support his family, and to add to their income, his wife opened a small grocery store in the neighborhood. Shana, the older daughter, found work in a tailor shop, sewing buttonholes by hand.

By the time the Mobavitches arrived in America, Golda was eight years old and immediately began attending school. At dawn every morning, however, her mother had to buy items to sell in her store. She would leave Golda in

Golda Meir as a young woman. *The Golda Meir Library, University of Wisconsin—Milwaukee.*

charge of opening the store and running it until she returned with her purchases.

Golda hated working in the store. Sometimes she cried. But, as in most matters, once Bluma Mabovitch made up her mind about something, nothing could convince her to change it. Later in life that would be true, too, of Golda.

Golda worked in the store not only in the morning but until ten o'clock every evening, as well as all day on Sunday. Somehow, however, she still managed to make straight As in all of her subjects and was recognized as one of the brightest children in the school.

At the age of fourteen Golda moved on her own to Denver, where her older sister, Shana, married by then, had gone to live. Many of Shana's friends were Jews, who, like the Mabovitches, had come to America hoping for a better life. Most of them were socialists— people who believed that all workers had the right to live in a democratic society and to have decent jobs.

Many of them, too, hoped that someday there might be a national homeland for Jews in Palestine: a place where Jews from around the world could set up a nation of their own. Those people were known as Zionists.

One evening a quiet young man named Morris Meyerson joined the usual discussion group at Shana's house. He and Golda soon came to enjoy each other's company. Before long, the two were in love.

Golda attended high school classes in Denver. She spent time with Morris. And she talked politics, becoming more and more interested in the idea of Zionism. Although she could not accept the communist beliefs of Karl Marx, she did become a follower of the American Eugene V. Debs, who believed that "democratic socialism" was the way to build a better society.

After about a year, Golda returned to Milwaukee to be with her mother, who missed her greatly. She enrolled once again in the high school there, becoming vice president of the graduating class. Next she attended a college in Milwaukee, preparing to become a teacher. She also worked at a school that taught Jewish folk culture to young children.

Most important of all to her, however, was her involvement with the movement to free Palestine from Turkish rule. Because there was an active, energetic Jewish community in Milwaukee, many Jews from Palestine came there to speak. Golda learned from them about the new city of Tel Aviv, which had just been founded in desert sands along the Mediterranean coast. She learned about the agricultural settlements (kibbutzim), where Jews were trying to set up model communities based on sharing and caring for one another. She learned about the Labor Zionist Party in Palestine that was working to make the dream of a Jewish homeland a reality.

As Golda later put it, "Zionism was beginning to fill my mind and my life." She still attended college. She still corresponded with Morris and intended to marry him, even though he did not share her great enthusiasm for a Jewish homeland in Palestine. Yet, for Golda, both her academic studies at school and her love for Morris were becoming less important than her passion for Zionism.

In 1917, Golda finally married Morris Meyerson. Not until 1921, however, did she finally persuade Morris to leave America and to sail with her to Palestine to start a new life.

Once there, Golda and Morris applied for membership in Kibbutz Mechavia— a communal farm located ten miles south of Nazareth. For Golda, living in a kibbutz was important. People who lived in such communities owned no personal property and made no individual profits. Instead, people were to work together, sharing their faith as Jews and—as a group—meeting the needs of the community.

As a member of the kibbutz, Golda busily plunged into its work. During the day she picked almonds, worked in the kitchen, took care of children, raised chickens. In the evening she learned Hebrew and Arabic. As hard as it all was, she loved farmwork, believed in the ideals of the kibbutz. Morris, on the other hand, simply hated the situation at Mechavia.

Finally, to please Morris, Golda agreed to move to Tel Aviv. She became a secretary in the office of Histadrut (the Israel Labor Federation).

Next they moved to Jerusalem, where Golda gave birth to a son, Menachem. Then came a daughter, Sarah. To support the family, Morris brought in a small salary as a bookkeeper while Golda took in laundry.

For four years, from 1924 to 1928, the couple struggled to make ends meet. For Golda, it was the hardest time in her entire life. She later admitted to wondering whether this was all that life was about.

Then one day, just when she was feeling at her lowest, she visited the Wailing Wall, all that remained of Solomon's Temple from ancient biblical times. There she saw people on their knees, praying, and she determined that her life did indeed have meaning after all.

The Wall had uplifted her sights and made her want to keep working for the high ideals of a homeland in Palestine for the world's Jews.

In their married life, Morris and Golda began to drift apart, although

Golda Meir with Israeli young people celebrate the birth of the state of Israel in 1948. *Karel/Sygma.*

they were not formally divorced until 1945. To divert her mind from such personal problems, Golda took on more and more work on behalf of Jewish causes.

She once again began working for Histadrut. There, people began to notice her, to recognize her great ability. In time, she was chosen as a delegate to the World Zionist Congress.

In 1939, when war with Germany began to seem probable, the British rulers of Palestine feared that the nation's Arab population might side with Hitler. To assure Arab support, Great Britain issued what was known as a White Paper, sharply limiting the immigration of European Jews into Palestine.

That single act cut off the escape of thousands of Jews from the bloodthirsty Nazis. Golda joined with the Jewish leader David Ben-Gurion in trying to fight the White Paper. But nothing could be done. As a result, many lives were needlessly lost.

When World War II finally ended in 1945, the Zionist leaders decided to act as if a Jewish nation already existed. In response, the British government arrested many leading Jews, including Ben-Gurion. With almost all the other major figures of the nationalist movement in prison, Golda took over the leading position in Palestine's Jewish community.

Meanwhile, a committee of the United Nations had been investigating the situation. On its recommendation, the United Nations voted to divide Palestine into two nations, one for Arabs, the other an independent homeland for the Jews.

The Arabs of the Middle East refused to permit such an arrangement and immediately began to prepare for war.

The Jews, without money to buy arms, turned desperately to the outside world, especially to America, for help. David Ben-Gurion, freed from prison, sent Golda to America to do whatever she could, but with little hope for her success.

Remarkably, in a whirlwind tour of the United States she quickly raised a total of $50 million. Then, almost immediately after returning to Palestine, she set out at Ben-Gurion's request on a highly daring secret mission. Her purpose was to assure King Abdullah of Jordan that a Jewish nation, when it was finally formed, would not harm his country.

Wearing black robes to pass as an Arab woman, she crossed the Jordan River and anxiously made her way by car to the Jordanian capital, Amman, passing safely through several military checkpoints.

Once she had arrived in Amman, King Abdullah asked her, among other questions, why the Jews were in such a hurry to have a nation of their own.

"We've been waiting for two thousand years," Golda Meir later remembered answering him. "Is that really a *hurry?*"

Jordan, it soon became clear to her, would certainly join Egypt, Syria, Lebanon, and Iraq in making war on the new Jewish nation. Still, Golda believed that the time for independence had come, and David Ben-Gurion agreed with her.

On May 14, 1948, Golda and twenty-four other Jewish leaders declared the formation of the nation of Israel. Meeting together, they signed a declaration of independence, much like that of the United States of America.

In the bloody war that soon followed, the Israelis, although badly outnumbered, surprised the world by defeating the attacking Arab armies. Israel had won its independence.

After the war, Golda served first as Israel's minister to the Soviet Union. Next she was elected to the Knesset, the Israeli parliament. Then, from 1949 to 1956, she served as Minister of Labor and Social Insurance. In that position she organized Israel's generous housing program for refugees flocking to the country from around the world.

In 1956 David Ben-Gurion chose her to be his Minister for Foreign Affairs. At Ben-Gurion's suggestion, she began to call herself Golda Meir, the Hebrew version of Meyerson. Because of her strong will and firm character, Ben-Gurion once described her as "the only man in my Cabinet." During Israel's spectacular victory over the Arab nations in the war of 1956, it was Golda who, along with Moshe Dayan and Shimon Peres, was mostly responsible for winning the cooperation of France and Britain.

In January 1966, ill and growing old, she resigned her position in the Cabinet.

By then she had become a grandmother with five grandchildren and, like any other Israeli citizen, proudly would push a baby carriage along the crowded streets of Tel Aviv. She did her own cooking and laundry and went from place to place without a guard, often riding on the city buses. Yet, although semiretired, she stayed active in the affairs of the Labor Party.

In 1967, the Arabs once again tried to destroy Israel, only to be spectacularly defeated in the Six Day War. To protect itself against further Arab attacks, Israel occupied the Gaza Strip, the Golan Heights of Syria, and the West Bank of the Jordan River, as well as East Jerusalem and the Sinai Peninsula.

Two years later, when the prime minister of Israel was stricken with a heart attack, Golda Meir was chosen to replace him.

Seventy years old, she had become the leader of the Jewish nation.

What Meir wanted most was peace with Israel's neighbors. She offered to speak with Arab leaders in their capital cities, at the United Nations, in neutral countries such as Switzerland— anywhere. But they would not meet with her.

Meanwhile, because Golda Meir refused to give back Arab lands taken in the Six Day War, enemies of Israel— even in such supposedly friendly countries as the United States—spoke of her as "intransigent," meaning that she would not change her mind.

Once she met in Rome with the Pope, who also asked why she did not give in to some of the Arab demands. Her answer may have surprised him.

"Your Holiness," she said, "do you know what my earliest memory is? It is waiting for a pogrom in Kiev. Let me assure you that my people know all about 'harshness' and also that we learned all about real mercy when we were being led to the gas chambers of the Nazis."

Similarly, as Golda Meir was asked many times, what would happen if the Jews simply went back to the pre-1967 boundary lines? But that, she reminded people, is exactly where things stood when the Arabs last attacked them. The Arabs, she pointed out, keep on trying to wipe out the Jews. "But do they really expect us to cooperate?"

In 1973, on Yom Kippur, the holiest of Jewish holy days, the Arabs launched a massive surprise attack on Israel. Caught off guard at first, the Israeli armies were thrown back with heavy losses.

Eventually they rallied and once again went on to win a spectacular victory. Still, Meir never forgave herself for accepting the advice of those military commanders who, on the eve of the war, had assured her that no attack was coming.

By then seventy-six years old, she finally retired from office. But she continued to speak out, continued to defend the right of Israel to exist. Her private life was given over to her children and her grandchildren. She loved to read, to listen to classical music, and to cook traditional Jewish foods, such as gefilte fish.

Golda Meir had accomplished much in her lifetime. And if Israel still had not persuaded its Arab neighbors to make a just and lasting peace, it was not because she had failed to try. President Anwar el Sadat of Egypt, her foe in the Yom Kippur War of 1973, praised her as "a first-class political leader." It was Meir, declared Sadat, who deserved credit for starting the peace talks that ended the conflict between Israel and Egypt over the Sinai Peninsula.

On December 8, 1978, at the age of eighty, Golda Meir died.

World leaders, including former enemies like Sadat, expressed sorrow at her passing. She was, they said, an "extraordinary woman," an "extraordinary human being."

To those who knew her, Jews and non-Jews alike, Golda was, as they so often put it, "unforgettable." And truly, that is the way she is remembered.

Even today, not every Jew living in Israel is deeply religious. Nor are all the Jews who come to visit from around the world. But people in that land cannot help but identify with the difficult history of the Judaic faith over thousands of years.

That struggle is central to what Israel is all about and why the life of Golda Meir stands out so prominently.

PART V

JESUS AND THE CHRISTIAN EXPERIENCE

Jesus

(7–6? B.C.–30? A.D.) Founder of the Christian religion; seen by
followers as Son of God

"Merry Christmas!"
"Happy Easter!"
"Happy New Year!"

Around our world today perhaps a third
of the planet's population celebrates
at Christmastime the birth of a child,
Jesus of Nazareth. Every spring there is
another holiday, one marking the crucifixion of Jesus and the story of his holy
rebirth. Throughout our own lives, whenever we write or speak about the date,
the year we mention is based on the coming of a single person—Jesus.

Jesus, a Jew, was born in Palestine
during the reign of the Roman Emperor
Augustus, at a time when the Romans
ruled that land. He died during the reign
of Emperor Tiberius, condemned by
personal order of Pontius Pilate, a

Roman leader then in command of the
territory.

Different parts of the Bible tell differing stories of Jesus' ancestry. Some
speak of him as the child of Joseph and
Mary (Miriam), with King David as his
ancestor. Others speak of a miraculous
birth, with Mary as his mother but God
as the true father. The actual place of
his birth is uncertain, although the best-
known story is that told in the Bible's
Gospel of Luke, one of the four
accounts of Jesus' life. It speaks of his
family's visit to Jerusalem, and of their
child's arrival in nearby Bethlehem. His
name, Jesus, is a Greek version of
the Hebrew name Joshua, meaning
"Yahweh (God) helps."

According to Luke, Mary and Joseph
made the journey from Nazareth to

Bethlehem for the sake of a census count, part of the required taxing process. At the time, as Luke describes it, Mary already was "great with child." And so it was, he says, "that while they were there . . . she brought forth her firstborn son, and wrapped him in swaddling clothes, and laid him in a manger; because there was no room for them in the inn" (Luke 2:6–7).

Fully six centuries later, a Christian monk tried to fix the time of Jesus' birth so that calendars ever afterward could be dated from that event. His mistake was to choose a date several years after the actual appearance of the holy child. The Gospel of Matthew declares that Jesus was born in Palestine during the reign of King Herod. But since Herod died in 4 B.C., most modern scholars place the actual birth of Jesus in 7 B.C., or even more probably in 6 B.C.

The New Testament says that the baby Jesus was circumcised eight days after his birth. Several days later Mary and Joseph are supposed to have taken him to the Temple in Jerusalem. There, in the story told by Luke, an old man named Simeon took Jesus in his arms and prayed for him. Simeon had been told that before dying, he was destined to see the child who one day would be the Savior of all the human race. Giving thanks to God, Simeon declared that he himself at last was ready to depart in peace.

The Gospel of Matthew tells how three Magi, or Wise Men, came to Bethlehem, possibly from such eastern lands as Persia or Babylonia. Supposedly they were followers of Zoroaster (Zarathustra) but came to worship the newborn child as King of the Jews. Today the feast of the Epiphany celebrates the visit of the Magi. They are said to have brought gifts to the child, including gold (since he was to be a king); resin from a tree known as frankincense (since he was divine); and myrrh, or gum from a small shrub, to show that he also was human and someday would die.

Matthew also declares that King Herod learned of the three Wise Men's visit and, worried, tried to find out from them where Jesus might be. Mary and Joseph, however, are supposed to have escaped to Egypt, remaining there until the death of Herod, when they returned to their home in Nazareth, a village in Galilee some thirty miles from the Mediterranean Sea.

It is thought that the boy Jesus grew up in Nazareth, learning from his father, Joseph, the skills of a carpenter, while being deeply involved in Bible reading and prayer. According to scholars, Jews from all over Palestine tried to travel to Jerusalem for three religious festivals each year, particularly for the Passover, celebrating the escape from Egypt of Hebrews under the leadership of

Lorenzo di Crédi's painting "The Adoration of the Shepherds" depicts the infant Jesus soon after birth. *Uffizi, Florence/Alinari/Art Resource, NY.*

Moses. In Jerusalem they would worship at the Temple.

As described in the Bible by Luke, Mary and Joseph frequently visited Jerusalem for the Passover holiday, for the first time bringing young Jesus along with them when he was twelve years old.

Somehow, Jesus became separated from his parents there. When at last they found him, he was in the Temple, deeply involved in discussion with learned teachers and rabbis. According to Luke, "all that heard him were astonished at his understanding and answers" (Luke 2:47). Amazed as his parents were at his knowledge, Mary still is said to have been upset, declaring that they had looked everywhere for him. Jesus then replied impatiently that they should have known his responsibility to be "about my Father's business" (meaning "the business of God").

Some later Christian writers therefore claim that even at an early age he thought of God as his father. Still, in his later preaching Jesus spoke of *all* people as his brothers, since they, too, were the children of God. In any event, for the time being Jesus returned to what Luke describes as "obedience" to his parents, as the family returned home once again to Nazareth.

To many scholars the next eighteen years in the life of Jesus, until he reached the age of thirty, are "a time of silence." Virtually nothing is said in the Bible about those years. Nor is much known about his family. The Gospel of Matthew mentions four sisters: Tamar, Rahab, Ruth, and Bathsheba. The Gospel of Mark lists four brothers, all with typical Jewish names: Joseph, Judas, Simon, and Jacob (James). But it is not clear how many of them actually were the children of both Mary and Joseph.

Scholars sometimes point out that

loyalty to his family meant little to Jesus. In one biblical passage he speaks of love for family as interfering with true devotion to a great cause. At another time, some of his brothers are said to have openly scoffed at his sense of mission. Not surprisingly, then, Jesus appears far more concerned with matters of religion than with members of his family.

For the next eighteen years after the important visit to Jerusalem, Jesus probably spent much of his time in study. He appears to have been influenced greatly by his reading of the Bible, not only the Torah (Genesis, Exodus, Leviticus, Numbers, and Deuteronomy) but also by the Psalms, Jeremiah, Hosea, and Malachi—sources he quoted often. During his boyhood and then as a young adult he read widely, too, in the Jewish literature of the time. Like other Jewish children, he must have been expected to memorize and then to repeat the words of the Torah and the laws of the society.

Jewish religious groups that already were active before the birth of Jesus, for example the Essenes, appear to have influenced him greatly. Some of his most famous statements such as "thy kingdom come" have recently been traced directly to the Essenes through the Dead Sea Scrolls, discovered in 1947 in Palestine. Similarly, the Lord's Prayer, now part of services wherever there are Christians, was commonly used more than two thousand years ago by the Essenes—and then absorbed by Jesus.

Such groups as the Essenes also believed that, before long, a Messiah would appear, a Savior who would lead the Jewish people far closer to God the Father. Such an idea was spoken of in community worship services. It was a force that during the childhood and adulthood of Jesus deeply moved many believers in the Jewish religion.

Not only did groups such as the Essenes exert great influence in that exciting time in history, so, too, did religious individuals, single figures whose impact could be enormous. For Jesus, perhaps the person who did most to shape his thinking was John the Baptist.

Although probably not much older than thirty, John, it is said, attracted great crowds of people. Alone in the desert much of the time, he covered his body with a camel's hair garment and allowed his hair and beard to grow wildly around his head. Speaking to audiences, he declared that the day of God's final judgment was close at hand, hoping that his listeners would change their lives for the better. "Repent," he said, "for the kingdom of heaven is at hand."

Some who listened to John the Baptist thought he must be the Messiah or Savior—the Christ. But he denied that. He was, he declared, "crying in the wilderness" in hopes that people still would manage to save themselves. Many of his listeners still longed for a savior: a religious figure like Moses, or a military hero who would free them at last from Roman rule. Some even hoped that God himself would appear, liberating them from the evil of the present world and establishing a new order on the planet, one that would bring with it a permanent justice and everlasting peace.

Other deep believers sometimes would appear in public, causing people to think one of them might perhaps be the coming savior. The Hebrew scholar Hillel is a good example. According to a story about that leader, a nonbeliever once approached him, declaring his intention to stand on just one leg. If, while he did that, Hillel could explain to him the meaning of the entire Torah, he then would convert to Judaism. Hillel, it is said, responded to him: "Do not do unto your neighbor what is hateful to you," a saying that Jesus later changed slightly to make into the Golden Rule: "So whatever you wish that men would do to you, do so unto them" (Matthew 7:12).

Like so many other scholars, Hillel

did not satisfy the Essenes since he would not agree with them that the world was about to end. Thus, many religious Jews still continued to await the coming of the true savior. They found themselves unhappy with the Pharisees and other conventional leaders of the Temple, calling them "seekers of smooth things." The result was deep and even bitter disagreement among Jews about what their beliefs should be.

It was during that continuing disagreement, perhaps in the year A.D. 27, that Jesus is said to have appeared before John the Baptist alongside the Jordan River, asking to be baptized. Jesus of course had been born a Jew. He had been circumcised and then confirmed according to Jewish custom. He had preached and taught as a wandering rabbi.

With his baptism, the way may well have opened to a new direction in his life. For many years he had spoken of God as "Father." But, as the Bible's Gospel of Mark declares, when his baptism by John was complete and he came forth from the waters of the Jordan, Jesus is said to have heard the voice of God declaring to him, "Thou art my beloved Son; with thee I am well pleased."

If, indeed, he was the Son of God, then he truly had before him a vital mission to perform in helping other people.

Following his baptism, Jesus is said to have gone off to be alone with God in the wilderness. There he had an experience not unlike those of other great religious figures. Stories tell of Zoroaster encountering the angel Ahura Mazda while alone by a river; of Buddha having his own deeply moving awakening beneath the branches of the Bo tree; of Moses meeting with God while in front of the burning bush. In the case of Jesus, the four Gospels tell of how, while he was alone, he was tempted by Satan—the Devil.

According to the Gospel of Matthew, after Jesus spent forty days by himself, just as Moses had done, the Devil offered to turn rocks into bread so he at least could have food. But Jesus refused. He also refused the temptation to leap, supposedly in safety, from a mountain that was a symbol of the Temple in Jerusalem. Finally, when offered a chance to rule "all the kingdoms of the world" if only he would bow down to the Devil, he is supposed to have responded, "Begone, Satan!"

The incidents of temptation by the Devil are said to show, most of all, that Jesus had little ambition to glorify himself or to achieve power. Instead, he trusted God and was dedicated to spreading the word of the Lord to others. After temptations, therefore, he set out for the cities and villages of Palestine to perform a mission.

His task was, first of all, to renew the message told in the Bible and to spread word of it to the people. To do that he gathered around him four followers who had been fishermen, now to become "fishers of men." One of them was named Simon, whom Jesus renamed Peter, meaning "rock," just as heroes of the Old Testament supposedly had been renamed by God in light of their special missions.

Together, Jesus and his disciples set out to declare that "the kingdom of heaven is at hand," meaning that the bondage of human life soon would end.

The dedicated travelers stopped first of all in the town of Capernaum, speaking in the synagogues there. But Jesus did more than simply speak to people. He quickly became known as one who could heal the sick. As a result, by evening of the first day, great crowds had gathered to see him.

He is said to have helped people who were seriously ill, not only with physical diseases but mental ones as well, supposedly caused by demons. Included among those he helped was the mother-in-law of his disciple Simon Peter.

Jesus remained in Capernaum for only that one day. For all the cures he

Bellini's interpretation of the face of Jesus. *Academia di S. Fernando, Madrid/Alinari/Art Resource, NY.*

performed he accepted no pay. Nor did he pray openly to God for help. Instead, he urged those who were ill to gain faith in themselves and in what God could do for them.

Yet since healing the sick was not the principal mission he had in mind, by daybreak of the next morning he had departed, going off into the wilderness once again.

Jesus then chose to visit many towns, and was assisted by a group of twelve followers known as Apostles. Since there also were twelve tribes in Israel at the time, it often is said that Jesus intended to bring new faith and meaning to the lives of all the Jewish people.

Clearly, he had little interest in simply explaining the Bible in a formal way. Instead, he hoped that he and his Apostles would spread to people an understanding of how God intended them to live their lives. Along with the twelve chosen teachers, he also received strong support as well as financial help from a group of women including the highly devoted Mary Magdalene.

In the beginning Jesus concentrated his work in the province of Galilee, including Nazareth, where he had lived his early life. It is said, however, that he visited Nazareth only once. People there could scarcely believe how famous the young carpenter they once knew had become. The Gospel of Luke even declares that some of the disrespectful townspeople tried to throw him off a cliff.

Little is known about the brothers and sisters of Jesus and how they responded to his rapidly growing fame. Even Mary, his mother, is not spoken of in the Bible during the years of his ministry, appearing once again only at the time of his death.

Whatever may have gone on with his family, Jesus busied himself with the messages he so often delivered in the synagogues. Perhaps the most famous of them all is the Sermon on the Mount, possibly presented on a hillside overlooking the Sea of Galilee. Much of what is known today as Christianity may be summarized in that address, undoubtedly one of the greatest, the most profound of speeches ever delivered in human history.

"Blessed are the meek," said Jesus, "for they shall inherit the earth" (Matthew 5:5).

"Love your enemies,"' he declared, "do good to them which hate you. Bless them that curse you, and pray for them which despitefully use you" (Luke 6:27–28).

"Judge not, that ye be not judged," advanced Jesus (Matthew 7:1). "Ye have heard [it] . . . said, An eye for an eye, and a tooth for a tooth: But I say unto you, That ye resist not evil: but whosoever shall smite thee on thy right cheek, turn to him the other also" (Matthew 5:38–39).

Such ideas set apart the thinking of Jesus and his followers from much that had been said before they began to preach. Perhaps most famous of all is the statement in the Sermon on the Mount known as the Golden Rule, based, as noted earlier, on the words of Hillel: "So whatever you wish that men would do to you, do so to them" (Matthew 7:12). Jesus thus was suggesting to people that by treating others the way they themselves would like to be treated, they could live happier lives.

Yet Jesus did not want listeners to think he was speaking against the ways of the Jewish religion or that he was some kind of rebel. Instead, he claimed only to be asking his listeners to live up to God's rules: "Think not that I am come to destroy the law, or the prophets: I am not come to destroy but to fulfil them" (Matthew 5:17).

Finally, Jesus urged that people not show off in public prayers to God. Instead, they should pray from behind closed doors, directly to the Lord, who surely would hear them. The private message he suggested for their use has ever since been known simply as the Lord's Prayer (Matthew 6:9–13):

Our Father which art in heaven, Hallowed be thy name. Thy kingdom come. Thy will be done in earth, as it is in heaven. Give us this day our daily bread. And forgive us our debts, as we forgive our debtors. And lead us not into temptation, but deliver us from evil: For thine is the kingdom, and the power, and the glory, for ever. Amen.

It is almost certain that the Sermon on the Mount by Jesus was not a call to political or social revolution. He did not ask in it for the redistribution of property to bring about the economic equality of all people. But he did call on people to truly live their lives according to the high principles of God, as already set forth in the Bible.

Not long after Jesus began his ministry, John the Baptist, who had launched him on his career, was arrested by Herod Antipas, then in command of that part of Israel for the Roman rulers. The brilliant John, who usually lived in the wilderness, did not approve of Jesus' being always in crowds of people. Jesus still deeply admired John, but he felt that his own way of preaching could achieve greater results.

"Go and tell John," he said, "what you have seen and heard: the blind receive sight, the lame walk, lepers are cleansed, and the deaf hear, the dead are raised up, the poor have good news preached to them. And blessed is he who takes no offense at me" (Luke 7:22–23).

After keeping John the Baptist in prison for ten months, Herod Antipas had him killed, describing him as a dangerous rebel. Before long, however, Herod heard of the preachings of Jesus and feared that perhaps John the Baptist somehow had returned from the dead to punish him. For Jesus, like John, told his audiences to repent from their sins and to seek their futures as part of God's kingdom, not the kingdom of Herod Antipas.

Fra Angelico's painting of Jesus transfigured. *Museo di S. Marco, Florence/Art Resource, NY.*

At the time, even some of Jesus' own close followers believed he really was John the Baptist, restored to life. Others saw him as a newly emerging prophet, like such great Hebrew religious leaders of the past as Moses, Jeremiah, and Elijah.

At one point, Jesus asked his Apostles who they thought he really was. One of them, Peter, declared: "You are the Christ, the Son of the living God" (Matthew 16:16).

In response, Jesus praised Peter for speaking of him as "the Christ" (or in

Hebrew, the Messiah). Yet he also made it clear that, in his own mind, it was certain that death was coming to him soon. It would come, he said, in the city of Jerusalem.

According to the New Testament Gospels of Matthew, Mark, and Luke, only one week after predicting the approach of his death to the Apostles, Jesus stood with Peter and two other Apostles, James and John, on a mountaintop in Galilee. There, they suddenly saw before them the figures of Moses and Elijah, who joined in conversation with Jesus until a bright cloud surrounded them. Then the voice of God is said to have declared about Jesus: "This is my beloved Son, with whom I am pleased; listen to him" (Matthew 17:5).

In accordance with his promise to the Apostles about traveling to Jerusalem, Jesus is described as leaving the region of Galilee for that city, knowing he was destined to perish there. Along the way, great crowds, especially including many children, gathered around him, listening to his teachings.

Rich people and poor people expressed their devotion to him. As always, however, Jesus predicted that in the future God would give special rewards to the poor and to the unknown, so that "in the age to come . . . many that are first shall be last, and the last shall be first" (Matthew 19:30).

Finally, Jesus and his followers reached Jerusalem. There he met with much criticism. Such religious groups as the Pharisees and the Sadducees were angry that some people described him as the Christ, or the Messiah. Unlike most religious leaders, he had not spent many years of study with a famous scholar. Also, he often worked on the Sabbath day, helping the poor, even though working on the Sabbath was considered wrong.

Once, it is said, Temple guards were sent to arrest him but, impressed by his words, they returned to the Temple without taking him prisoner. Still, the words he spoke in the Temple so angered some listeners that they threatened to stone him.

At another time, the religious leaders brought to him a woman who was accused of making love with a man other than her own husband. The scribes asked Jesus what should be done with her, since Moses had demanded that such people be stoned. It is said that Jesus, known to be warmhearted toward sinners, understood that the scribes were trying to embarrass him.

According to the Bible, after pausing briefly with his head down, he turned to them and said, "Let him who is without sin among you be the first to throw a stone at her." When the embarrassed scribes all left, Jesus is said to have looked at the woman and advised gently, "Go and sin no more" (John 8:1–11).

The Gospel of John tells how, shortly afterward, Jesus traveled to the town of Bethany, near the Judean desert. There he was told that his friend Lazarus had died. Weeping, he visited the tomb. Over the objections of friends, Jesus demanded that a large stone blocking the entrance to the tomb be removed. He then cried loudly, "Lazarus, come out!"

To the astonishment of all who were watching, the supposedly dead man, Lazarus, stumbled into the daylight, wearing the clothing of a corpse.

When news of what had happened reached leaders of the Jewish community in Jerusalem, it is said they became deeply concerned. They feared that many Jews would choose to follow Jesus as a leader and that the Romans, expecting an open rebellion, might choose to crush the entire society. To prevent that, they declared, something had to be done.

The Gospels of Matthew and Luke suggest that Jesus, knowing he might well die, nevertheless prepared to return to Jerusalem. Riding on the back of a donkey, he arrived in the holy city a few days before the Jewish holiday of Passover. Once there, he soon began speaking to large crowds of people, describing himself as the Son of Man.

Entering the holy Temple itself, however, he became deeply disturbed. To his shock, many merchants were gathered inside the building, selling their products to people. Money changers traded Jewish shekels to visitors, making great profits. In a fury, Jesus finally turned on crowds of buyers and sellers, a whip in his hand. He overturned the tables of the money changers. Angrily he declared that God described the Temple as "a house of prayer for all people," which, instead, they had turned into "a den of robbers."

In the days that followed, some leaders tried to trick Jesus either into opposing the Roman government or into speaking against the Jewish people. Once, he was asked whether it was proper for Jews to pay tribute money to the Romans.

Jesus insisted that before answering he first must see a coin. The one he was given had upon it a picture of the Roman emperor, Tiberius Caesar. Then, it is said, Jesus replied to the question by saying, "Render therefore unto Caesar the things which are Caesar's; and unto God the things that are God's" (Matthew 22:21). His response thus avoided conflict between the Roman authorities and his fellow Hebrews. The statement is used even today as proof that church and state need not be in conflict.

Still, as Passover grew closer, Jesus is said to have felt ever more certain that the time of his death was coming near. The Gospels of Matthew, Mark, and Luke say that at a Passover seder (the traditional form of dinner for that Jewish holiday), Jesus took a piece of matzo and gave pieces of it to his followers, declaring, "This is my body."

He then took a cup of wine and, after expressing thanks to God, said, "This is my blood," just as always had been done in Jewish services since the Exodus of Moses from Egypt. But now it took on a different meaning.

In speaking at length to his followers that evening, Jesus urged them, regardless of what happened to him, to continue as leaders in helping people who were in need. He told them they should always serve one another and "be of good cheer."

Then, he and his group descended from the Mount of Olives into the garden of Gethsemane. Briefly alone, Jesus prayed. Unexpectedly, a group of armed men led by the Apostle Judas suddenly entered the garden. Judas approached Jesus and, supposedly as a show of respect, kissed him. When he did that, the authorities turned to Jesus and arrested him.

Accounts in the Bible differ as to what happened next. But it is said that Caiaphas, the foremost Jewish religious figure, questioned Jesus, trying to find out whether he really had claimed to be the Son of God. That incident may never have happened, since such a title was not claimed for Jesus until many years after his death. Nevertheless, Caiaphas turned him over to the leader of the Roman government in Jerusalem, Pontius Pilate.

Pilate was a man known for his hatred of Jews and for his violence in dealing with them. To him, Jesus easily might have appeared to be a political rebel.

Pilate is said to have asked Jesus directly whether he was king of the Jews. Jesus responded only by declaring that "You have said so," and then refused to answer to other charges. Although the Bible describes Pilate's uncertainty about what to do, he eventually condemned Jesus to execution.

It was to be done by crucifixion—hanging from a cross—a particularly slow and painful way for a convicted criminal to die. Prisoners sentenced to such a death first were beaten with a whip and then nailed to the cross.

According to the Bible, in the case of Jesus he was commanded to carry his own cross to a hill known as Golgotha, outside the city. Already weakened and bleeding, he could not do so, but a Jewish spectator named Simon leaped to his assistance, carrying the cross for him.

At Golgotha the hands and feet of Jesus were nailed to the cross and then it was raised upright. Above his head, it is said, was attached a sign saying, JESUS OF NAZARETH, THE KING OF THE JEWS.

Roman soldiers, it is said, gambled for his clothes at the foot of the cross. Later the soldiers placed a crown of thorns on his head and scornfully called him "King of the Jews." Then they spat upon him and, bowing upon their knees, pretended to worship him. On each side of Jesus hung another prisoner, men condemned like him to crucifixion.

Coming closer and closer to death, Jesus called out in prayer, "Father, forgive them, for they know not what they do."

Yet even he must have experienced doubts, since later he shouted, "My God, my God, why hast Thou forsaken me?" a statement that had appeared in Psalm 22 of the Bible.

Finally, at the very edge of death, he declared in peaceful but triumphant prayer, "Father, into Thy hands I commend my spirit!"

And then he "gave up the ghost" (Luke 23:46).

It is written that a Roman soldier who had watched the execution soon spoke softly in words destined to survive to the present: "Truly this man was the Son of God" (Mark 15:39).

Joseph of Arimathea, a member of the Sanhedrin—the Jewish group that had brought about the crucifixion— won permission from Pontius Pilate to bury Jesus in land he owned very close to Golgotha. Followers then wrapped the body in linen and spices, placing it in a large chamber whose entrance was sealed by a heavy rock.

What happened next is unclear, but the New Testament accounts say that Jesus arose from the dead. He spoke to the Apostles. And then, one day, he is said to have led his followers to the Mount of Olives in Bethany, where he blessed them and then was "carried up into heaven." As the Gospel of Luke puts it, by then they had become utterly certain they worshiped him, "and returned to Jerusalem with great joy" (Luke 24:52).

Once Jesus died, his followers began to spread the message he had taught them, first to other Jews like themselves and then to outsiders, or Gentiles. Throughout the Roman Empire they founded Christian communities. In time, even the powerful leaders of countries became converts to the religion whose founder had once been an unknown personality and who finally had been executed as a criminal.

For a time his closest believers, the Apostles, continued to use Jerusalem as the center of their teaching, closely following the practices of Judaism. Yet whenever possible they told stories about the man they described as the

Messiah. Meanwhile, many Greek-speaking or Hellenistic Jews spread the story of Jesus to synagogues throughout the Middle East and the Mediterranean world. Before long the word had reached such cities as Alexandria, Damascus, Athens, and Rome.

In Antioch, the capital of Syria, the followers of Jesus began to be called Christians, from the Greek word Christos, or "anointed one," similar to the Hebrew word Messiah.

At the same time, in various cities of the Roman Empire, followers of Jesus reached out more and more actively to non-Jews, teaching them about the ideas of Jesus. Still, at least for a century after the crucifixion, the worship of Christians followed closely upon the roots of Judaism, as had the teachings of Jesus himself.

By the year A.D. 100, however, the Christian religion had become a reality in itself, despite the opposition to it by some Jews as well as by the rulers of imperial Rome. Particularly after the failure of two major Jewish rebellions against the Romans, thousands of Hebrews began speaking of themselves as Christians, at least in part for the sake of greater safety. Meanwhile, many nonbelievers came to find the teachings of Jesus satisfying and appealing.

Two centuries later, in A.D. 312, the emperor Constantine is said to have prayed for God's help in a battle then taking place near Rome. According to his own story, he saw a flaming Christian cross in the sky with the words written on it, IN HOC SIGNO VINCES (in this sign you shall conquer).

Constantine declared afterward that it was Christ who inspired him to victory and to whom he was deeply grateful. He then proceeded to have many Christian churches built. Years later, in his new capital city of Constantinople (today's Istanbul), he formally became a Christian.

Thus, three centuries after the birth of Jesus, the ideas of the once unknown Jewish child had become a central element in the civilization of the Roman Empire and of the world. As the child Jesus had grown, his character had become ever stronger. His personality had become ever more attractive and inspiring. He had taught people the good news that, like himself, they too could move ever closer to God.

Knowledgeable in the beliefs and practices of Judaism, Jesus had explained the ideas of that religion in a beautiful way, a way people could understand and remember. By his own existence he also had given them an example of how to "live a life."

Now, many centuries later, it is virtually certain that the example of his life will continue to live on always in human memory.

Paul

(10?–62 A.D.) Most important leader in spreading the faith of Jesus to other lands

Like Jesus, Paul was born a Jew. He remained a Jew for much of his life. But probably because of Paul, most of the followers of Jesus stopped considering themselves to be only a branch of the Jewish religion. Instead, they expanded to become one of the great independent faiths in world history—Christianity.

Paul came to believe that by accepting Jesus as the savior—"the Christ"—all people in the world could be united. Or as he put it, "There is neither Jew nor Greek, there is neither slave nor free, there is neither male nor female; for you are all one in Christ Jesus" (Galatians 3:28).

That was the revolutionary message he personally spread in travels throughout much of the ancient world, including places ranging from Jerusalem and Damascus to much of what today are well-known locations in Greece and Turkey. His own life probably ended in a prison in Rome.

Later in history, such Christian leaders as Saint Augustine, Martin Luther, and John Calvin drew heavily on the teachings of Paul. Indeed, over the centuries his thinking did much to shape the character and direction of the Christian religion. It was Paul, for example, who first spoke of Jesus as "Jesus Christ," meaning that he was the Christos or Messiah— the king and savior so long awaited by the Jews.

How could the life of any one person such as Paul have had so dramatic an impact? What events took place that make him stand out so vividly? Why is

144

he considered by many to be one of the most important personalities in the entire history of the world?

Paul was born in the highly populated city of Tarsus, located in what today is Turkey. Although his family was deeply committed to the Jewish religion, Paul was fascinated even very early in his life by the mystery religions and cults of people who lived near to him. Still, as a child he studied the Hebrew language and closely followed the heritage of the Old Testament. When speaking to people in the Greek language, he was known as Paul; in Hebrew his name was Saul.

Paul's parents appear to have been prosperous—indeed, so successful they were entitled to the privilege (and advantage) of Roman citizenship. As a young man Paul became skilled at tent making, a task that put him in contact with people of many different backgrounds. It is said that from those people he learned much about the ceremonies of other religions, including the special joy of celebrating the rebirth of a god who had died. It was a lesson he would never forget.

At some point in his youth, Paul was sent to Jerusalem for formal study in preparation for becoming a rabbi. Probably he was not in Jerusalem when Jesus was crucified, but soon afterward

he joined with the strong-willed Jewish sect of Pharisees in condemning the followers of Jesus. Indeed, if he had been present at the time of the crucifixion, he probably would have supported it.

One reference in the New Testament even describes the presence of a young man named Saul when Stephen, a supporter of Jesus, was stoned to death. Whether he actually contributed to Stephen's execution is unclear. But the evidence is almost certain that Paul persecuted the early Christians, working hard to put an end to the Christian movement before it could spread.

Then, almost overnight, Paul changed his mind and became a convert to the cause of Jesus. According to one account, while traveling to Damascus he saw a great light in the sky and then suddenly heard Jesus speaking to him, asking why he was doing such terrible things. Once a bitter enemy of the Christian cause, he quickly became one of its strongest supporters.

Remaining in Damascus, he learned all that he could about the life and the teachings of Jesus. Then, in Jerusalem once again, he spoke with two men: James, the brother of Jesus, and Peter, a fervent believer in the Christian cause. So angry were the Jewish Pharisees to learn of Paul's conversion that he decided it would be safer to leave the holy city altogether.

Raphael's "The Conversion of St. Paul." *The Bettmann Archive.*

His place of refuge was Antioch, the capital city of Syria. It was there that he became known as a major leader in the rapidly spreading faith of Christianity. In that city, Jews who believed in the mission of Jesus were even willing to eat with the Gentiles, something not done by Jewish followers of Christ in Jerusalem. Paul found such a practice easy to live with, a solid step along the way to the kind of religion he had in mind.

To Paul, it was far more important that people should believe in the Holy Christ than in the life experiences of Jesus, a Jewish man. Thus, year after year he tried harder to preach to Gentiles, not just to Jews. As a result, when he traveled to cities in Asia Minor and other locations, Jews became increasingly angry with him, still holding strongly against the idea of Christ as a Savior and not just a highly gifted teacher. Some of the Jewish Christians became furious with Paul for the great attention he was giving to the Gentiles.

In one important visit to Jerusalem Paul argued that believers in Christ did not have to eat only kosher meat. They did not have to follow special Jewish rules regarding the circumcision of newly born baby boys. To Paul, Gentiles did not first have to become Jews before truly being received as followers of Jesus. Instead, they could simply become known as Christians.

The result of Paul's teaching was an increasing break between followers of Christ and the organized Jewish religion. Despite that, he set out on his second major journey as a missionary, working hard to spread his ideas to *all* people. He traveled to such distant locations as Athens, Macedonia, and Corinth, as well as to Syria. Accompanying him was the talented young Timothy, son of a Jewish mother and a Greek father. Timothy was destined from that time onward to appear in Paul's letters, an important part of the New Testament Bible.

As a result of his travels, Paul succeeded in founding several new churches committed to the teachings of Jesus. Sometimes, as in Thessalonica, Greece, he had to move on after angering Jews and others who did not accept his views. Especially annoying to them was his claim that Jesus was the Son of God and had been raised from the dead after crucifixion. Sometimes, too, as in Athens, Paul failed completely to establish a new church. But by about the year A.D. 50 he had done well in many population centers across Greece and Asia Minor.

On his third great missionary journey Paul probably remained for as long as three years in the important city of Ephesus, located on the Aegean coastline of today's Turkey. From there, he and his followers managed to win converts to Christianity both inland and in cities all along the coast.

Their success, however, caused a major problem for the Christian missionaries. Worshipers from older religions long had come to Ephesus to buy silver or marble statues of their gods. Merchants, angered by the sharp decline in their business, caused Paul and his supporters to be brought to trial in a beautiful open-air stadium along the shore, one seating twenty-four thousand spectators.

Although the Christians escaped punishment, Paul determined to move on. He and his group proceeded northward along the Aegean coast and then to Corinth in southern Greece. In Corinth he was shocked to learn that his own teachings about people's freedom from the laws of the Old Testament Bible had led many to become disorderly in their lifestyles. They had, for example, begun to have love affairs with men and women outside of their own marriages.

Paul's visit to Corinth succeeded in bringing some citizens back to more traditional conduct. Nevertheless, many of his opponents warned that Gentiles won over to the Judeo-Christian religion would become too free in their habits.

The writings of Paul are preserved in the New Testament. During the trip that later was described in the biblical book of 2 Corinthians and Galatians, he spoke often of the need for unity between Jews and Gentiles in a single church. He firmly declared, too, that salvation—getting to heaven—was not largely dependent on old-fashioned religious practices, such as circumcising newborn boys. Instead, it depended, above all, on *faith*. That view may well be Paul's most important contribution to Christian thought.

Many of his followers warned Paul not to return to Jerusalem because of anger against him there for favoring the Gentiles. He insisted on going to the city, hoping to present money he had collected for church purposes and to argue that Jews and Christians should work together.

Soon after his arrival in the ancient capital city, a struggle broke out between Paul's supporters and his opponents. At least in part to save him from harm, Roman soldiers arrested Paul and placed him in their military prison located in nearby Caesarea. There he remained for two years until a new Roman governor, Festus, arrived.

When Festus threatened to send him back to Jerusalem for a formal trial, Paul refused. He declared that as a Roman citizen, as his parents had been,

he had a right to be tried directly in the city of Rome. "I appeal to Caesar," said Paul, soon winning approval of his request.

His journey to the Roman capital was marked by severe thunderstorms. While docking at Malta, along the way, the ship that carried him was broken apart upon rocks in the harbor; Paul and some of his close followers barely managed to survive. For three months they remained in Malta, finally arriving in Rome in the springtime of A.D. 60.

What happened next is unclear. From Paul's own writings, it appears that during the next two years he was given freedom in Rome, often preaching the Christian gospel in the city despite being accompanied constantly by guards.

According to some accounts, he was freed and proceeded to travel to Spain, hoping to convert the people of that country to the teachings of Christ, and then managed to visit Greece and Asia Minor once again. After that, supposedly, he returned to Rome, was put in prison, and then was beheaded.

Other stories, however, are quite different. One of them declares that Paul never was released but that, instead, he was tried and put to death by the emperor Nero in the year A.D. 64 as part of that ruler's general effort to destroy all possible opposition.

Benjamin West's painting of Paul preaching to the Corinthians. *The Bettmann Archive.*

Whatever the truth about Paul's death, his life clearly was one of the most important ever lived. He personally transformed Christianity from a mere branch of Judaism to one of history's greatest independent religions. Because of his background as a Jew, along with his broad experience in the Gentile world, he understood what ideas might be accepted by most people. His letters were destined to become a guidepost, setting the tone of Christian practices for nearly the next two thousand years.

Later church leaders, particularly Saint Augustine, made much of Paul's words. The Protestant movement's principal figures, including Martin Luther and John Calvin, emphasized Paul's belief that a Christian's *faith*—even more than *works*—determined whether that person would achieve salvation and a place in heaven.

Yet what probably survives more than all else in Paul's thinking is his confidence that through a belief in Christ, the barriers between people could somehow be broken down. In his own life, although born a Jew, he later became a "Christian Jew," a man who eventually made Christianity a dominant religion. Still, he always believed that religion would someday succeed in uniting all of those who lived a life on planet Earth.

Augustine

(354–430 A.D.) Following a youth filled with wildness and sin, converted to Christianity and wrote books later to prove crucial in spreading the ideas of Jesus

As a boy and then as a young man, Aurelius Augustinus— known to history as Augustine—was primarily a sinner. He preferred playing to studying, sometimes stole from a neighbor's orchard, and later lived with a mistress for fifteen years without the benefit of marriage, even fathering a son. In his famous book of Confessions, *Augustine points out that at first he found places like the city of Carthage, with its great palaces and rich public baths, deeply unholy yet extremely interesting.*

The very same young Augustine eventually became one of the great leaders in Christian history. He grew highly skilled at explaining to others the meaning of the Bible. He worked out a system of religious practices that were followed not only by Catholics but later by many Protestants and still are in use today. But perhaps most important, his life has lived on as a vivid example of how a sinner could transform himself into a saint.

For more than fifteen hundred years people have been inspired by Augustine's writings about Christianity and by the story of his life experience. Among those who followed in the path of Jesus, few others have stood out to such an extent as Augustine.

He was born in the North African town of Tagaste in the year A.D. 354, the son of a deeply religious Christian mother, Monica, and a nonbelieving father,

Patricius. Because he avoided study in order to play, he often was beaten. It was to avoid such beatings that he first began to pray, turning to the God his mother worshiped.

Some of his teachers encouraged him to learn Latin, and it was from authors writing in the Latin language that he read many stories openly discussing sinfulness, especially relating to sex. He later declared that the influence of helpful, kind teachers truly could lead young people toward fine sources of knowledge.

At the age of sixteen, Augustine was forced to leave school because of lack of money. After a year, however, he was sent to Carthage, where he studied, attended many theater performances, and experienced a wild social life. It was during that time that he met a woman he was destined to live with for fifteen years but never to marry. Early in their relationship the couple had a son, Adeodatus (the gift of God). He was a child Augustine came to love deeply.

Although writing later of his many social pleasures in Carthage, Augustine also describes much progress in his studies. He greatly improved his personal skills in public speaking while becoming particularly devoted to philosophy and to such Roman scholars as Cicero. He worked, too, at the Bible, but at that time found its simple style far less attractive than some of his other readings.

What most appealed to him in Carthage was the Manichean religion, a faith he formally joined. For nine years he remained a Manichean, most of those years spent as the head of his own school. As a teacher, he worked with young people to influence their knowledge of literature and philosophy while both teaching them public speaking and competing successfully himself in speech contests.

In the year 383, when he was nearly thirty years old, Augustine gathered his lover and his son and left Carthage to teach in Rome. There he continued to study such ancient philosophers as Aristotle while working on his skills as a speaker. It was after only a few months in Rome that the Manicheans offered him a leadership position in the Italian city of Milan.

Living in Milan became a turning point in Augustine's life. It was there that he went to visit Ambrose, the city's Christian bishop, having heard much about the Catholic leader's speaking skills. Instead of concentrating on oratory, however, Augustine was deeply moved by Ambrose's comments on Christianity as a religion. Before long, the Manichean decided to leave the religion he had been preaching and to become a Christian.

While his conversion was taking shape, Augustine's mother, Monica, came to Milan to be with him. Joyful because of his decision, she demanded that he also send the mother of his son back to Africa and marry a religious Christian woman. But since the mate that Monica selected from a wealthy family was legally too young for marriage, Augustine simply substituted another woman to serve as his lover. His young son, Adeodatus, remained with him in Milan, and Augustine openly admitted how very much he missed the companionship of the woman he had dismissed.

Augustine's decision to become a Christian had not come easily to him. The teachings of Ambrose, along with the efforts of his mother, had made a difference. At the same time, the ideas of Faustus, a leader of the Manicheans then living in Milan, struck him as childish, even foolish, compared to the content of his readings in Christian philosophy.

Then, while walking with friends one day through the streets of Milan, he came upon a beggar, a poor man who although eager for money still seemed happy, even "joking and joyous," as Augustine later remembered the scene. From that experience he came to believe that despite all of his worries, he truly could find happiness in religion.

Some days afterward, when he was once again depressed, he suddenly heard a child singing a song, "Tolle, lege. Tolle, lege" (Take up and read). Augustine immediately opened a copy of the apostle Paul's letter to the Romans that he happened to be carrying. The reading declared firmly that instead of satisfying the lusts of the flesh, people should turn to Jesus Christ (Romans 13:13–14).

At that moment, Augustine later wrote in his book *Confessions*, "all the darkness of doubt vanished away." From then on he saw Christ as his personal savior.

On Easter in the year 387, Augustine was baptized as a Christian alongside his son, Adeodatus, in the public square of the city of Milan. Performing the ceremony was Ambrose, later to become a saint, while in the audience stood Monica, Augustine's mother, who also was destined to be honored with sainthood.

Augustine planned next to return to Africa, where he could live a life of prayer. But before he could leave, his mother died. Postponing his departure, he spent a year in Rome, writing sharply against his former religious partners, the Manicheans.

In the year 388 he arrived in Carthage before traveling on to his home city, Tagaste. There he sold all of his possessions, gave the proceeds to charity, and, along with a small group of friends, settled into an intensive life of Christian study and writing. Before long, however, he was especially saddened when his sixteen-year-old son, Adeodatus, suddenly became ill and died.

Augustine hoped to remain a monk, devoting himself primarily to study. On one occasion, however, an enthusiastic audience he addressed at Hippo insisted that he stay on with them as a priest. Valerius, the bishop of Hippo, convinced Augustine to spend part of his time in the priesthood there but promised him a life that he could give over mostly to scholarship.

Thus, in the year 395 Augustine officially became a priest, studying Christian religious matters more closely than ever before. He especially identified with the works of Paul, who had chosen to become a Christian after spending his youth as a loyal believer in Judaism.

Valerius soon died and Augustine became bishop of Hippo, a position in which he was remarkably productive. He was destined to continue as bishop until his death in 430, thirty-five years later.

As bishop of Hippo, Augustine had far less time for study and writing. Instead, he had to preach; he had to travel and to lead formal meetings; and he had to face major challenges to the way he thought Christians should live their lives. Yet, despite all of those responsibilities, he managed to publish more than five hundred of his sermons, as well as hundreds of letters and learned papers.

His first major struggle at Hippo was against the Manichean leader, Felix. In that case, his triumph was so clear that Felix himself decided to give up his religion and convert to Christianity. Another Manichean, Fortunatus, lost so badly in two public debates against Augustine that for a scheduled third day of debate he refused to appear.

One popular Christian group in Africa, the Donatists, accused other Christians of having too many priests who had been sinners. To them, Augustine responded that Christianity was not a religion of priests but of Christ himself, or as he put it, "I believe not in the minister by whom I was baptized, but in Christ, who alone justifies the sinner and can forgive guilt."

After many years of struggle the Christian church banned Donatist priests from leading religious ceremonies, even threatening them with the possibility of death, to be enforced by soldiers of the Roman government. It was a decision that Augustine agreed with completely and applauded with pleasure.

In still another conflict, Augustine took sharp issue with the Celtic monk Pelagius. According to Pelagius, the

A painting of Augustine by Botticelli. *Uffizi, Florence/Alinari/Art Resource, NY.*

world was filled both with good deeds and evil deeds, and for doing those deeds, individual people should receive either praise or punishment. Augustine responded that it was the grace of God that made it possible for people to achieve successes, but human beings themselves were responsible for their sins. As to which people would gain salvation and go to heaven and which were to be punished in hell, Augustine looked to the will of God for such decisions—decisions that remained a matter of deep mystery to human beings.

While Pelagius spoke of "free will" as the very heart of human existence, Augustine stood strongly in favor of *God's will* as the basis of human nature. Although the Catholic Church eventually sided with Augustine's position, the matter continues to be debated even now.

A more immediate problem greatly troubled Augustine: the invasion and looting of the city of Rome in the year 410 by the Visigoth military leader Alaric. According to many Romans, the once-powerful empire had been badly weakened because of Christianity's supremacy. In response to that charge, Augustine worked from 413 to 427, finally producing his most famous study, *De Civitate Dei (City of God)*.

He argued in his book that Rome had been weakened by the moral decay and bad conduct of its people. While Roman civilization was deeply corrupt, he said, the Christian religion there remained healthy, clean, and strong. Roman people in the "City of Earth" were busy with loving themselves, but true Christians in the "City of God" should join together in trusting the will of God.

Augustine's *City of God* was, in many ways, a summary of his own life experience. In it, he rejected the sinful pleasures he had experienced in youth and expressed supreme confidence in a just and moral God. His lifestyle after converting to Christianity stood out as a model for future generations—a way that devoted followers of Jesus ought to live.

Faced with serious signs of aging, Augustine began in the year 426 to prepare the way for others to take over his leadership role at Hippo. He appointed Eraclius to follow him as head of the monastery there. Another monk, Possidius, began writing a gentle biography of Augustine, describing the priest's great efforts for poor people and the simplicity of his lifestyle. Meanwhile, Augustine's *City of God* was gaining ever wider attention, a book the Catholic Church of today still honors at a level surpassed only by that of the Bible.

On August 28 in the year 430, as invading Vandal soldiers closed in on Hippo, the gravely ill Augustine gave himself over to prayer and to the reading of psalms. It was on that date, still honored by Roman Catholics, that at last he died.

In the years that followed, the fame of Augustine continued to grow. For the first thousand years after his death the Christian Church treated him with respect and high honor. So, too, did the humanistic leaders of the Renaissance. Martin Luther and John Calvin, the major figures of the Protestant Reformation, studied the ideas of Augustine carefully, Calvin in particular quoting him at great length.

Today, as the twentieth century comes to a close, noted scholars give high honors to Augustine's qualities of soaring intelligence and religious faith, as well as to his capacity for reaching out to human beings in need of help.

According to some historians, it well may be true that with the fall of Rome and the enormous difficulties of the Middle Ages, Christianity itself might never have survived if not for the great teachings of one man—Augustine. Surely, he ranks in religious history alongside such dominant Christian figures as Saint Paul and Martin Luther.

Patrick

(389?–461? A.D.) Taken from Britain to Ireland as a slave in his youth, he eventually turned that land to Christianity

Saint Patrick's Day! In much of Ireland and America the seventeenth of March is a day given over to celebration and parades in honor of an Irish Roman Catholic saint.

Surprisingly, Patrick himself was not Irish. He was a boy named Succat born in a Roman-ruled Britain whose Roman name, Cothrigge, was Latinized into Patricius (Patrick) well along in his lifetime. Nor was he honored with the title of saint until many centuries after his death.

Patrick's father, Calpurnius, owned much land in Britain and served both as a tax collector and a member of his district council. Within the Christian church he held the title of deacon. The father of Calpurnius also had been active in the church, holding the title of presbyter, or priest.

Although little is known of Patrick's youth, he probably showed only slight interest in affairs of the church during his early years. Writing later about himself, he spoke of a youngster who "knew not the true God, and kept not His commandments."

In the year 406, when Patrick probably was sixteen years old, everything suddenly changed. Irish tribesmen raided the western coast of Britain in search of slaves. Along with hundreds of other British young people, the well-to-do Patrick was carried off to Ireland and put into forced labor as a shepherd.

Day after day, season after season, he tended the herds of an Irish chieftain. As he later described that part of his life

158

in his book, *Confession*, it was a time of great change, when he more and more gave himself over to prayer. According to Patrick, he usually would pray a hundred times each day, out of fear of God as well as love of Him. In his words, "I felt no hurt . . . because of the spirit . . . within me."

It was one night, he says, some six years after his captivity began, that he heard the voice of God declaring to him, "Blessed youth, thou art soon to go to thy fatherland." Almost immediately he departed for the Irish seacoast where, with some difficulty, he finally persuaded a shipmaster to take him aboard as a crew member.

The ship later was wrecked, probably on the coast of Gaul (today's France). For many days thereafter the crew went hungry until, as Patrick tells it, he prayed to God at the angry captain's urging. Soon afterward a group of wild hogs appeared. The Irish crewmen fell upon the animals, providing themselves with enough food to survive. It is said that after that incident, the sailors became much kinder to Patrick, thinking that his God had actually saved them.

Because Patrick's *Confession* says little about what happened next, historians differ in their accounts. Some declare that he stayed for several years in Gaul. Others argue that he soon returned to Britain and to his parents.

An unattributed engraving shows Patrick journeying to Tara, seat of the Irish kings. *Culver Pictures, Inc.*

In any event, after several years he decided to visit Ireland once again, hoping this time to carry the word of God to the Irish people. As Patrick later told the story in his *Confession*, he dreamed that his former captors had strongly urged him to come back, declaring, "We ask thee, boy, come and walk among us once more."

Although he already had learned the Irish language while a captive, Patrick had little education in formal religion. Still, British church leaders thought he

Traditionally Saint Patrick has been honored in countries to which the Irish people emigrated, especially in cities of the United States. This Saint Patrick's Day parade took place in New York City in 1874. *The J. Clarence Davies Collection, Museum of the City of New York.*

could be helpful to the cause of Christianity there. Other missionaries had gone to Ireland before, but with little success. Thus, in about the year 431 they sent Patrick to that land, giving him the title of bishop. At the time of his departure he was perhaps forty years old.

When Patrick first set out on his mission, he had serious doubts about his own knowledge of religion and his skills as a missionary. Yet once he arrived

in Ireland, he immediately became absorbed in the task. He traveled widely in order to meet with tribal leaders. Whenever possible, he attempted to introduce them to Christian practices while still preserving traditional Irish ceremonies.

Patrick's visits took him across northern Ireland to such well-known places as County Down, Ulster, Connaught, and Armagh. It is said that not only did he found many new churches but personally baptized some twelve thousand Irish people as Christians.

Many of those who left the old Irish Druid religion and converted to Christianity still held to their ancient religious practices, some of which have survived to the present. As a result, many Christians around the world now use the holly tree for decoration at Christmastime and kiss one another beneath the mistletoe.

Patrick made popular at Easter the native Irish practice of lighting a fire to celebrate the coming of springtime. He himself would sometimes chant a prayer, asking for the personal help of Christ against the magical sayings of his continuing rivals, the Druids.

Patrick's eventual victory over the Druids may have led to a famous legend. According to the story, he drove out of Ireland all that country's snakes and frogs and toads. He is supposed to have done it by causing them to leap into the sea as he rang a "sweet-voice" bell. For whatever the scientific reason, Ireland remains without snakes, frogs, and toads, while the triumph of Christianity there is a matter of history,

something in which Patrick undoubtedly played a crucial role.

Another story relates to the Irish shamrock, that country's national flower. Patrick supposedly told an unbeliever that there could be a Holy Trinity—Father, Son, and Holy Ghost—in the same way that the shamrock has three leaves and a single stalk. Today, the shamrock appears virtually everywhere across Ireland on March 17, Saint Patrick's Day, the date set aside for remembering the deeds of Patrick.

March 17 is also the day on which Patrick is supposed to have died. The year of his death, like that of his birth and many details of his life, remains uncertain.

What is certain, however, is Patrick's place in history. As an Irish historian, Seumas MacManus, once put it, "What Confucius was to the Orient, Moses to the Israelite, Muhammad to the Arab, Patrick was to the Gaelic race."

Hence, when considering the coming of Christianity to their land, the Irish continue to think primarily of one man: Patrick.

Thomas Aquinas

(1225?–1274) Educated as a Benedictine, became a Dominican monk and an outstanding medieval scholar, one who wrote both of science and religion

Most historians of religion agree that Thomas Aquinas deserves to be ranked with the greatest of all Western philosophers and champions of Christianity. Yet, surprisingly, his life was extremely simple, marked by little travel and devoted almost entirely to study and to teaching in such cities as Paris, Rome, and Naples.

His writings, however, address problems that still stand at the very heart of issues facing Christianity in the modern world. The works of few other Christians have proven so helpful to defenders of the faith. If for no other reason, he clearly deserves the title of saint given to him by the church.

Probably in the year 1225 Thomas was born in a castle located near Naples and owned by his family. When he was three years old an electrical storm struck the castle, a bolt of lightning killing one of his younger sisters. Thinking their son had been spared by God, his parents placed him in a Benedictine monastery for education when he reached the age of five. They hoped that he later would choose to follow a holy life, becoming a priest and serving the Lord who spared him.

For seven years, until he reached the age of twelve, young Thomas remained in the monastery, studying much about religion but also about ancient Greek and Roman history and philosophy. Seldom encouraged to play games, he spent most of his time as a child in reading and prayer.

Then suddenly, because of warfare between Pope Gregory IX and Emperor Frederick II, Thomas was forced to flee from the monastery, returning to live with his parents in their new castle at Loreto.

There he found himself facing instead of prayer a social life filled with music and drinking and competition in games of knightly combat. For Thomas Aquinas, the experience proved a shock, but one he accepted with smiles, along with considerable prayer. Legends have survived about how he often made a special point of giving vast amounts of food, along with flowers, to poor people near the castle.

Before very long, the father of so generous a boy decided to enroll him at the University of Naples for religious study. Despite the well-known wildness of the young people there, Thomas continued to give himself almost totally to learning. According to one story, he once repeated for his class the entire lecture of a professor, actually improving on the teacher's presentation.

It was at the University of Naples, at the age of sixteen, that Thomas decided to turn away from the Benedictine Order and join the Order of Saint Dominic—the Dominicans. To him, the Benedictines were people of wealth who stayed to themselves. The Dominicans, by contrast, actually went out to work among the people, trying to feed the poor while relying on begging to support themselves. They also were known as scholars, especially involved with the ideas of the ancient Greek philosopher Aristotle.

Learning of her son's decision to leave the Benedictines and join the Dominicans, Thomas's mother, Theodora, was furious. Rushing to Naples, she learned that he already had left for Rome. She then sent for two other sons, who caught up with Thomas, holding him until their mother arrived.

In tears she pleaded with him to change his mind, return to the prosperous Benedictine Order, and one day become an abbot, as she always had hoped he would. Thomas refused. Two of his sisters also tried to persuade him but, to everyone's surprise, he convinced both of them to become followers of the Dominicans.

Thomas's brothers tried once again to win him back to the Benedictines, actually cursing at him, threatening him, even ripping away his clothing. When those tactics failed, they placed in his room while he was away a beautiful young prostitute.

On returning to the room, Thomas immediately chased the woman away with a burning stick, vowing afterward never to have sex with any woman in his entire lifetime.

After all other methods failed, Thomas's mother finally appealed directly to the pope for help. But young Thomas insisted to the pontiff that what he wanted most of all was to live the simple life of a Dominican friar. He would not change his mind, no matter what the pressure upon him.

At the age of seventeen Thomas traveled to Cologne to study under Albertus Magnus, then known as one of Europe's outstanding scholars, not only of religion but of science and the arts. By the time he first met Albertus Magnus it is said that Thomas Aquinas already had managed to memorize much of the Bible. Still, he came to admire his teacher deeply, sitting in awesome silence at the great man's feet.

By then, Thomas, who rarely exercised, had grown heavy. His classmates thus took to teasing the quiet, overweight student, calling him "the dumb ox." One day, however, Albertus Magnus had Thomas speak in class, defending a difficult position. The result was a presentation so impressive that the famous teacher was amazed, declaring afterward that if the young man truly was a dumb ox, he was destined one day to fill the world with his animal voice.

In the summer of 1245 Albertus Magnus took Thomas Aquinas with him to Paris. For three years Thomas stayed in the French city as assistant to the scholar he so deeply admired. Much of his time was spent studying the philosophy of Aristotle and giving lectures on that subject.

Then, when Albertus Magnus returned to Cologne in 1248, Thomas joined him there, serving as a teacher as well as a preacher. Still young, he was accepted and highly praised by his audiences. By then he eagerly presented his own ideas about philosophy and religion.

In 1252 Thomas Aquinas found himself in Paris once again, formally receiving a bachelor's degree and shortly afterward the master of theology degree. By 1256 he had become a doctor of divinity, teaching theology in a Dominican school included as part of the University of Paris.

Larger and larger crowds gathered to hear him speak. They consistently found him to be an original person, creative in his thinking. As in his early youth, he continued to have a passionate desire to help the poor, to feed the hungry. When he was not reading or writing or standing at a speaker's platform, he kept himself in constant motion, pacing from place to place at considerable speed, expressing his thoughts as he walked.

In the years that followed, Thomas Aquinas found himself deeply engaged in a struggle between forces favoring the use of reason and those supporting faith alone. Aquinas declared that the two could work together—that people could use their minds fully, completely, without giving up a deeply emotional belief in God.

In many ways the very same quarrel continues among religious figures today, the writings of Thomas Aquinas serving as a means for bringing the two sides into harmony. His major teaching was that outstanding human intelligence was itself the result of God's creative power. Therefore, instead of being in conflict, faith and reason should work together through a belief in God.

The final years in the life of Thomas Aquinas were spent in Naples, close to his childhood home. It was there that he continued to work on his massive study, the *Summa Theologica*. Then, after a mass one day, he suddenly stopped writing, stopped teaching. He declared that all he had done seemed like "so much straw compared to . . . what has been revealed to me." Increasingly, he grew ill.

In 1274 Pope Gregory X asked that he attend a major meeting of the church to be held in Lyons, France. On his way there Thomas, already weak, suffered a serious injury, hitting his head on a tree branch hanging over the roadway.

Early in the morning, on March 7, 1274, he was given the last rites of the

A painting of Saint Thomas Aquinas, scholar and writer. *Brown Brothers.*

Church and prepared himself to meet with God. Soon afterward, he died.

At the time of his death, Thomas Aquinas had not yet reached the age of fifty. Still, he had already produced thirty-four volumes of writings. Usually he arranged for three or four scribes to copy down remarks he made to them or that he delivered to audiences. In his professional career, just as in his childhood and early youth, he worked away constantly at study and correspondence, only rarely taking time for pleasure.

Sometimes he beat himself with an iron chain in penance or personal sorrow for what he considered to be his sins. It was then that he often would imagine himself in conversation with his favorite sisters, both of whom had already died.

Despite the health problems Thomas Aquinas experienced in the final stages of his life, the works he produced then live on today. His *Summa Theologica* and *Summa contra Gentiles* have been basic documents of the Catholic Church for the last seven hundred years. The *Summa Theologica* in particular is an attempt to introduce people to holy writings in as simple a manner as possible.

In the year 1323 Thomas Aquinas was raised to sainthood. Then, in 1567, Pope Pius V chose him as one of the Doctors of the Church, in company with such leading personalities as Jerome, Ambrose, Augustine, and Gregory I. Today he is celebrated, too, as the special supporter, or "patron saint," of Roman Catholic educational activities.

Many of Thomas's ideas have fallen out of favor, including his attention to whether angels know one another or how angels move from place to place. In recent years, however, popes repeatedly have used his writing, faced as they are by a rise in purely "earthly" concerns among Catholics around the world. Writing in 1974, Pope Paul VI spoke of Thomas as a model of the way religious leaders should search after real truths in human existence.

Much has changed on our planet, of course, since the time of Thomas Aquinas. Yet philosophers and learned figures in the field of religion still turn to him for guidance on what life is all about—and how best to live it.

PART VI

CHRISTIANITY SINCE THE REFORMATION

Martin Luther

(1483–1546) Leader of the Protestant movement, he intended to reform the Christian religion by giving greater attention to life's immediate problems

Many Christians in America consider themselves Catholics. Even more of them, however, say they are Protestants—members of a Christian faith formed in Europe nearly five hundred years ago in a sharp breakaway from some practices of Catholicism.

The principal leader of that religious revolt was Dr. Martin Luther. In spite of certain glaring flaws in his character, he now stands out as one of the truly important personalities in the history of the human race. It was Luther, more than any other figure, who brought about the coming of the Protestant Reformation.

The child Martin was born on November 10, 1483, in the town of Eisleben, located in the German province of Saxony. Soon after his birth his parents, Hans and Margarethe Luther, moved to nearby Mansfeld, where Hans began laboring in the copper mines.

Although poor, with six other children, the Luthers worked hard to be certain that Martin was well educated. Always a good student, young Martin later remembered his childhood as a time of disciplined study and a deep commitment to the Catholic Church.

As a college student, he paid for some of his meals by singing in the streets, music always being of special interest to him. In 1502 he received a bachelor of arts degree from the University of Erfurt, followed by a master of arts degree in 1505, almost at the head of his class.

After such outstanding success he then followed his father's wishes and entered law school. Yet, just two months later, he dropped out of the law program and entered a monastery at Erfurt, declaring his intention to become a monk.

According to a story he later told, the decision came when he had been caught in a violent thunderstorm. To save himself, he pleaded to Saint Anne for help, promising to become a monk if he survived the storm. A few days afterward he began his formal career in religion as a member of the Order of Saint Augustine.

In 1507 Luther became a Catholic priest, an achievement his father greeted with deep disappointment. It was during young Martin's religious studies that he thought less and less about his father, the person he formerly had respected most. Instead, he came to admire greatly the thinking of Johann von Staupitz, a leader of the Augustinian order. Staupitz had chosen Martin in 1510 to visit Rome on a church-related mission.

For Luther, that trip proved crucial. Arriving in the Holy City with great faith in the Catholic Church, he at first was shocked and then deeply offended by what he saw there. Priests freely drank alcohol, and some of them even were involved with women. Catholic leaders, including the pope, received money for the granting of "indulgences," freedom from punishment for past sins. Private merchants also sold indulgences, sometimes receiving commissions from the church of as much as one-third of what "sinners" paid out.

After returning home, Luther received in 1512 the degree of doctor of theology from the newly formed university at Wittenberg. When Staupitz retired, the still-young Martin Luther took his place as a professor, teaching students about the Bible and its meaning, a task he was destined to perform for the rest of his life.

As a teacher, Luther soon became known for his sense of humor. Often he interrupted his lectures in Latin to speak seriously in German. Before long, other professors actually began to join with students to hear what he had to say. In time, Luther found himself increasingly unhappy with some of the teachings and practices of the Roman Catholic Church. He came to believe that people were following their religion through *fear* of God rather than the *love* of God.

Almost daily, Luther grew more convinced that truly "just" people—sincere believers—could serve God as Jesus himself had done: by *faith alone*. Thus, many years later, when Martin Luther did his own translation of the Bible into the German language, he carefully used the words *alone* or *only* when dealing

A portrait of Martin Luther by his friend, Lucas Cranach. *Culver Pictures, Inc.*

with how a person could achieve salvation through faith.

According to Luther, then, a person could be saved from punishment after death not by human accomplishments or, for example, by giving money to the church. Instead, salvation must come entirely because of the person's faith in the Lord. That idea was destined to become the central argument—the key point—in the formation of the Protestant religion.

As Luther's lectures became even better known to the general public, people began traveling great distances to hear him. They listened as he praised such ancient figures as Paul and Augustine, as well as the popular thinker of his own time, Erasmus. But young Luther did not limit himself to praise. He openly criticized such current personalities as Thomas Aquinas and the ancient Greek philosopher Aristotle, once describing Aristotle as a "damned heathen!"

Before long, Luther became a leader in calling for the direct and careful study of the Bible itself as a way to return Christianity to the original teachings of Jesus. He made it a special point to attack Pope Leo X for selling indulgences, forgiving people for wrongdoing in exchange for contributions of money. Luther pointed out that not only rich Christians but poor ones as well paid money to monks in exchange for forgiveness of past sins.

In the nearby town of Wittenberg, one priest, Johann Tetzel, raised a surprising amount of money in that way. As a result, Luther preached sermon after sermon against such practices. Still, Tetzel continued to sell his statements of forgiveness.

Then, on October 31, 1517, just before All Saints' Day, Dr. Luther acted dramatically. He nailed to the outside door of his church the so-called Ninety-five Theses: statements questioning the right of the Pope and his followers to forgive people for bad deeds in exchange for money. Christians, said Luther, did not need papal letters of pardon to win God's forgiveness. Nor could such letters actually guarantee to people that they would not be punished.

In earlier centuries the Ninety-five Theses probably would have remained only a matter of debate among members of the clergy, something to be fought out among themselves by religious leaders. But by 1517 a mechanical invention—the printing press—had made possible a dramatic change.

Printed copies of the statements soon were in the hands not only of such prominent figures as the archbishop of Mainz but of common people in locations throughout Europe. Therefore, the controversy became a matter of broad public interest, with opposition as well as support for Luther's message rising to a heated frenzy.

In April 1518 Luther appeared in Heidelberg at a meeting of the Augustinian Order and was told to apologize for his statements. Instead, he strongly defended those ideas and succeeded in winning over many supporters to his side.

The Pope then tried to have him come to Rome, but Luther refused. Instead, Cajetan, the Pope's representative in Germany, met with the defiant religious leader in a conference held at Augsburg. Once again, Luther stated that he would not take back the statements he had made. Because of that, rumors quickly began to spread that he would be taken to Rome in chains to stand trial. Instead, he returned once again to the safety of Wittenberg.

Slightly more than a year later, in the city of Leipzig, Luther found himself locked in open debate with the papal defender Johann Eck. Eck accused him of behaving much like Jan Hus, a reformer who, in 1418, had been burned to death at the stake for his protests.

In a fierce response, Luther went so far as to admit a major disagreement with Catholic religious authorities. It was the Bible, he declared, that must be followed closely, not just the opinions of leaders in the church.

When word of that debate reached the Pope, he ordered that many of Luther's writings be burned in the city of Rome. He also described forty-one sentences in Luther's writings as "heretical, offensive, erroneous, scandalous, . . . and corrupting." In no more than sixty days, declared the Pope, Luther must apologize for those statements.

On December 10, 1520, in a public ceremony in Wittenberg, Martin Luther formally burned the papal demand. With the flaming document in his hand, he spoke as if the Pope were actually there, declaring to him: "Because you have corrupted God's truth, may God destroy you in this fire."

Less than a month later, on January 3, 1521, the Pope formally declared Luther excommunicated from the Catholic Church—thrown out of membership in it.

Many German people became deeply upset by the Pope's action. As a result, it was agreed that Luther should appear personally in the city of Worms, speaking to the legislative group, or Diet, there. Although many of the Pope's followers in Germany objected to his presence, Luther set out eagerly for Worms. With German knights acting as his protectors, he arrived to tremendous cheers from crowds in the streets.

On April 17, 1521, Martin Luther appeared formally before a gathering of both religious and political figures at the Diet of Worms. On the next day he refused totally and absolutely to apologize for what he had been saying. He could not, he suggested in simple German, go against either his own conscience or against the Word of God.

There was little else that now could be done, declared Luther firmly. "Here I stand. I can do no other."

Eck shouted angrily at Luther, who replied to him in even greater anger. As the German emperor quickly declared

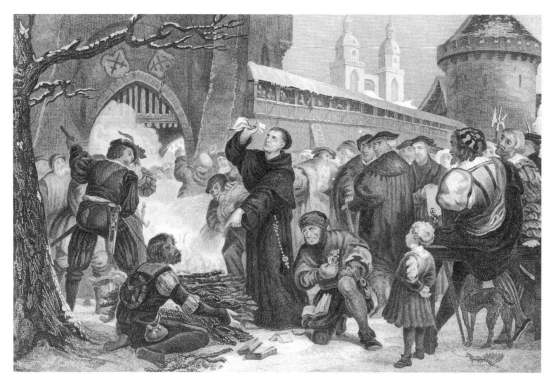

An engraving from Labouchère's painting shows Luther burning the papal document in front of the east gate of Wittenberg. *Culver Pictures, Inc.*

the proceedings closed, Martin Luther marched proudly through a crowd of friends and foes, his fist raised upward in triumph.

Few moments in history are so well known or so important. And few events have done so much to shape the directions of future generations. Dr. Martin Luther had openly defied the authority of the Catholic Church and many of the institution's leaders in his own country. From that time on, conflict was inevitable: it had to take place.

Following the departure of Luther and many of his supporters, the Diet proceeded to pass the now famous Edict of Worms. The edict formally removed him from his role as a priest in the Catholic Church. It also called him an outlaw and declared that all of his past writings were to be burned.

With the help of leaders who still favored him, Martin Luther made his way back to safety in Wittenberg. There he took refuge in a castle, the Wartburg, where he was removed almost completely from both enemies and friends.

For almost a year he busied himself with scholarship, much of that time spent in translating the New Testament from Greek into German. He also wrote for release to the public a series of sermons, some of which he considered among his very best. Alone much of the time, he grew a beard and, without exercise, gained weight. Often he was discouraged, even depressed.

In 1522 Luther found it necessary to return to public life in Wittenberg. Other German leaders protesting against the Catholic Church had begun demanding even more radical changes than he himself had supported. Some of them predicted the end of the world very soon and called for the actual killing of Catholic priests.

In response, Luther once again took to speaking in churches, calling for good sense and calm. Church reform should take place, he said, but in reasonable ways, not in the style of those leaders he described as "fanatics." Such men, declared Luther, cared little for common people in the streets but instead craved glory for themselves. In response, one of those he had attacked described Dr. Luther as Dr. Liar and accused him of "whoring and drinking."

In 1524 a rebellion of poor farmers, known as the Peasants' War, broke out in the Black Forest area, later including farmers from other parts of Germany. Luther reacted by saying that, although unfortunate, inequalities in wealth were bound to take place in human exis-

tence. Therefore it was wrong for the poor to use violence in order to make themselves richer.

To help prevent a complete breakdown in public order, he wrote a blistering pamphlet entitled "Against the Murdering and Thieving Hordes of Peasants." Just as he once had attacked the powerful figures of the Catholic Church, he showed remarkable boldness in striking at the seemingly victorious peasant revolt.

As a result, when the Peasants' War finally ended, many of the poor people chose to join other non-Catholic protest groups such as the Anabaptists instead of following Luther.

In 1525 the scholarly yet aggressive Dr. Luther found himself involved in another kind of conflict, a sharp disagreement with the brilliant theologian Erasmus. To Erasmus, Luther was not nearly liberal and "humanistic" enough, but too rigid and old-fashioned. In reply to such charges by the great freethinking scholar, Luther prepared an extremely angry paper entitled "Concerning the Bondage of the Will." His hard-hitting arguments in that declaration still are used today by many followers of his particular point of view about religion.

For Martin Luther, the year 1525 had its good side, too, in terms of relief from the Peasants' War and the bitter debate with Erasmus. It was in that year that Luther married Katherina von Bora, or "Katie," a former nun who was destined to serve him as devoted wife and companion.

She became a model for his future writings on how a married life should be lived. The couple had six children of their own while adopting eleven others. They also encouraged many students to live in their home.

In 1526 the Edict of Worms, which had sharply condemned Luther, was lifted by the German government. Still, many Catholics continued to express anger at what they considered an open rebellion against church authority. By 1529 the Catholic statements grew even more heated, causing followers of Luther to respond with a formal protest of their own.

Their message proved so strong that, ever since that time, such Christian protesters against Catholic Church doctrines have continued to be known as the "Protestants."

Yet, despite their agreement that Catholics were wrong in many ways, Protestants continued to disagree among themselves. The Swiss reformer Ulrich Zwingli, for example, declared that the body of Jesus is forever in heaven and will not appear again on earth. Luther, by contrast, argued that Christ not only could be in heaven but anywhere he willed himself to be, including an occasional return to earth.

The Protestants argued seriously about such matters. But faced with increasing violence by Catholics, they agreed to come together, at least for a time. To make closer cooperation possible, Luther gave more and more authority to the gentle Philip Melancthon (1497–1560), sometimes described as "the greatest teacher of the Reformation." Whereas Luther usually refused to compromise or to "make deals," Melancthon worked hard to bring together the opposing Protestant groups.

It was principally Melancthon who arranged the so-called Augsburg Confession, a vital agreement signed in 1530 by leaders who previously had been in competition. While Luther sometimes disagreed with Melancthon, he very much liked him and firmly resisted the many attempts of enemies to bring the two of them into conflict.

Only once did Luther completely reject his friend's work—when Melancthon spoke of the papacy in what Luther considered too favorable a way. Giving authority and power to a pope was wrong, according to Luther, since Christianity should always be a matter of faith, not of deeds or works.

Faith alone, he declared, was at the very heart of the Christian religion. And it was such faith that determined whether, after dying, a person would go to heaven or to hell. Nor should there be priests with any special authority, said Luther, but only "a priesthood of all believers."

In time, Luther's ideas spread widely. They were accepted not only in his native Germany but in Austria and Hungary, and with even less opposition in Norway, Sweden, and Denmark. A hymn that he wrote, "A Mighty Fortress Is Our God," became a cornerstone of religious observances across much of Europe and, before long, too, in the newly discovered lands of North America. Even today it is widely heard.

The final years of Luther's life were marked by serious illness, beginning in 1537. For almost a decade after that he suffered from a heart condition and a variety of medical disorders.

During those years, however, he remained strong in his opinions. He described one opponent as "a great big fool" for thinking that the earth moved around the sun instead of the sun around the earth. He spoke of his rival Erasmus as "an atheist" who was "bad through and through."

As he grew older, he continued to believe in a God of love, but also to believe in the Devil—and in the strength of evil forces. One of his final writings was particularly vicious in identifying his enemies with those forces. He called it *Against the Anabaptists, Against the Jews, Against the Papacy at Rome,*

Founded by the Devil. That study not only was searching but also angry and deeply bitter.

Through much of his life but particularly toward the end, Luther expressed strong feelings against the Jews. His followers in the religious body known to history as Lutherans often accepted those ideas, including even the German Lutherans of the twentieth century. After the brutal Adolf Hitler rose to power in Germany in 1933, some Lutherans opposed that dictator's increasingly bloody treatment of the Jewish people. But most members of the group remained silent or supported Hitler. They did so even when millions of Jews systematically were murdered.

Lutherans in countries such as Norway and Denmark refused to go along with such cruelty, but in Germany, where Hitler made it a special point to link his Nazi movement to Lutheranism, he won over large numbers of active supporters. Martin Luther's hatred of Jews quite possibly survives in that country even into the present.

In the United States, however, the situation has recently seen dramatic improvement. In April 1994, America's Evangelical Lutheran Church issued a "Declaration to the Jewish Community," expressing deep sorrow over Luther's anti-Jewish teachings and their terrible effects, particularly during the time of the Nazis.

The American Lutherans noted that some five hundred years ago their founder's statement, "On the Jews and Their Lies," had led to the homes and synagogues of Jews being set on fire and their prayer books being taken from them.

Luther had called for other action, too: taking money away from Jews; the establishment of camps where they would be imprisoned; and finally, the expulsion of all Jews from Europe.

Like Hitler, the Reverend Louis Farrakhan of the Black Muslim (Nation of Islam) movement in America had Luther's hateful words about the Jews reprinted and distributed to his followers. That action may well have played a strong part in the decision of American Lutherans to take a strong stand against their founder's anti-Semitism.

As already described, Luther's burning desire to see his view of Christianity rise in triumph led to still other problems. He openly and viciously criticized Catholics, particularly the popes. He spoke out strongly against brilliant liberals such as Erasmus, as well as against uneducated workers during the Peasants' War. It well may be that in launching such bitter attacks, Martin Luther limited the eventual success of the Protestant Reformation. Otherwise, Christianity might have been more completely transformed.

Still, there is little doubt that it was Luther who took the lead in changing the historical course of the Christian religion. Instead of subscribing to a religion that centered primarily on getting its believers to heaven, Luther and his followers concentrated on people's needs while still alive on earth. Those needs were to be met by acts of faith, along with service to others, not through payments to a priest.

Early in the winter of 1546, despite the deep concerns of his wife, Luther set out for Eisleben, the place of his birth. There he hoped to win agreement between two princes engaged in a bitter dispute. After working hard with them he wrote to his wife about his success in bringing the two men together. Then, only a few hours later, the exhausted Luther became ill.

On February 18, 1546, Martin Luther died.

His body then was removed to Wittenberg for formal burial. It was his close supporter and friend, Melancthon, who gave the funeral address there, recognizing Luther as a man who, in his lifetime, had helped shape the very direction of Christianity in modern times.

Now, more than five hundred years after Luther first appeared on earth, he stands out as one of human history's truly significant figures.

John Calvin

(1509–1564) Organized Protestant theology as a vigorous challenge to Catholicism

Martin Luther usually is considered the father of Protestantism—the movement that challenged the Roman Catholic leadership of Christianity. Luther's influence probably was greatest in such countries as Norway, Sweden, Denmark, and parts of Germany. The figure who perhaps contributed most to the Protestant movement in the rest of Europe and then in America was John Calvin.

It was Calvin's hope to reshape believers in Christ by turning their attention back to the Bible instead of focusing on the organized church. His followers, such as the American Puritans, often persecuted people who did not agree with them. Like Calvin himself, they sometimes were willing to deal with their opponents through the use of physical force.

Calvin was born to a middle-class family in Noyon, a town located in the province of Picardy, France. By the time he reached the age of twelve, he was described as brilliant, a hardworking student who learned quickly. Even that early in life he was known, too, for his seriousness of manner and, as some people said of him later, his "coldness."

While still in his early teens, Calvin enrolled at the University of Paris. He then entered law school and managed to complete it by the age of twenty-two. During those years he also made a special effort to study the Bible in Greek and Hebrew, as well as in the Latin version then used by the Catholic Church.

Upon the death of his father in 1531

young John Calvin felt free to give up a possible career in law. Instead, he devoted himself completely to the study of religion, even then a matter of his greatest passion.

The decision to concentrate on religion was destined almost immediately to change the course of his life. In 1533 he helped Nicholas Cop, an official of the University of Paris, to write a speech in support of Martin Luther's Protestant position.

So strong was the reaction to that address that Cop and Calvin were threatened with death. Both of them quickly fled from Paris, Calvin taking refuge in Basel, Switzerland. His religious studies there led him to become even more firmly convinced that Protestantism was the proper direction for Christianity to take.

Having made up his mind absolutely, Calvin at once began to write on behalf of the Protestant cause. In 1536 he completed *Institutes of the Christian Religion,* a book he was destined to change and republish many times during his life. Even today it is recognized as one of the most important works ever written about Christianity. Its first appearance caused Calvin to be recognized almost at once as a leader of the Protestant Reformation, the organized attempt to modify Christian practices.

After that book appeared, Calvin no longer could live only a scholarly life, devoting himself entirely to study and writing. While visiting the Swiss city of Geneva in 1536, he was approached by Guillaume Farel, a friend from his days in Paris who then was working vigorously to win Geneva over to Protestantism.

The fiery young Farel became furious when Calvin refused at first to remain in the city to help him. He declared that God himself would punish Calvin for leaving and would cause him to be cursed forever afterward.

Altogether apart from the threats, Calvin finally decided to stay on in Geneva. He began immediately to work for the transformation of the city into a model of the Protestant movement— a place with rigid social laws and strict regulations about people's behavior.

Almost overnight, the people of Geneva became examples of how Calvin believed Christians ought to live their lives. Yet to him it seemed that the changes had not gone far enough. In a sermon delivered in 1538 he declared that the inhabitants of the city still were acting too lightheartedly. It was the right of ministers, he said, to remove from church affairs the kinds of people who were too loose in their conduct.

So angry did some citizens become that on the very next day after the

A painting by Labouchère depicts John Calvin leading a meeting of reformers in Geneva. *Culver Pictures, Inc.*

sermon both Calvin and Farel were asked to leave Geneva.

For the next three years Calvin lived in the German city of Strasbourg. There he served as minister in a church and, often free to be alone, busied himself once again with writing.

While in Strasbourg he married Idelette de Bure, the widow of a man he himself had once won over from another Protestant branch. Although none of their children survived to adult-

hood, John Calvin and his wife found a close relationship in their marriage and much happiness together.

Meanwhile, Calvin's reputation as a Protestant leader began to spread widely. In 1541, with many apologies from political figures for what had happened three years earlier, he was asked to return to Geneva. Showing no signs of pride in his victory, he accepted.

In the years that followed, Calvin worked to transform Geneva into a model of how Protestantism should operate. He welcomed members of the faith who had been persecuted in other places by angry Catholics. He helped to establish the University of Geneva, using it as a center for the movement that, in time, had come to be known as Calvinism.

Almost certainly, his long-term goal was to use Geneva as a base for spreading a message throughout much of the world, the message being his very own view of the Protestant Reformation.

Before long, Calvin virtually became the ruler of the Swiss city. He scarcely hesitated at all to punish residents who took positions in opposition to his own view of Christianity. He had two ministers banished from the city for expressing religious ideas that he considered too liberal. One of them had refused to agree with him that people were destined from birth to go to heaven or hell, regardless of how well they behaved.

In 1553, when a minister, Servetus, refused to accept the idea of the Trinity (Father, Son, and Holy Spirit), Calvin helped to have him arrested. Then, although reluctantly, he agreed to have Servetus burned to death in a public ceremony—perhaps the cruelest act in all of Calvin's life.

Nevertheless, in spite of his cruelty, as the years went by, even many of those in Geneva who originally had

opposed John Calvin as a principal leader of the Protestant movement came to accept him. His ideas spread not only to the rest of Switzerland but to England, Scotland, and the Netherlands. In time, he gained firm support, too, in some of the British colonies in North America, particularly in New England.

One of his policies that proved especially important was that local religious officials—not the ministers—were to hold greatest authority in the church. Thus, even if a minister and other church leaders were arrested by government officials, new leaders immediately could take their places.

Members of each congregation soon began to realize, therefore, that it was they themselves, not just the ministers, who were responsible for the success of their cause.

Such practices, based on rule by the people, often go far in Western civilization in helping free institutions to survive. To Calvin, that kind of thinking was a crucial quality of the Protestant Reformation.

As a person, John Calvin was very different from the first great Protestant leader, Martin Luther. He often impressed observers as cold and distant, a shy man, reluctant to come forward, who only rarely spoke of himself as "I." Yet those who knew him well described his deep feelings both about religion and personal matters. On the death of his wife he is said to have been lost in passionate grief for an extended time.

According to friends, he often saw life as uncertain, confusing. Thus he felt that religion could help people only if it were strong and sure. That well may have been a reason for his willingness to support firmly the authority of the Bible, even when its meaning may have seemed unclear to some.

Although Calvin had an unusually fine mind, he still spoke of the human heart—which expressed feeling and emotion—as being more important than the head in shaping people's conduct.

To him, the feelings of faith in Christ and love of God were the truly important qualities in life.

At the same time, John Calvin was a practical person. He thought that people should read the Bible to answer real questions about real life. What kind of conduct is right? What is wrong? How should human beings behave toward one another? Reading the Bible and then following what it taught should be the proper path to good behavior. And to practice such use of the Bible on a daily basis, people had to rely on their good sense—their intelligence.

Today, many of those who criticize Calvin say that he saw human beings as basically more evil than good. And, in fact, his writings do deal quite often with human sinfulness. Yet Calvin also believed that people could repent for their sins—could regret what they had done—and then change their lives by following the example of Jesus.

Life, according to Calvin, is a struggle. And the way to survive in it, and then to triumph, is to be deeply serious: to look straight ahead along life's highway without giving too much attention to pleasures. Too much pleasure, he felt, prevents people from concentrating enough on God.

The more we know of God, said Calvin, "the more we increase in love." According to him, those human beings who are most faithful will be the ones to see "God's face, peaceful and calm and gracious toward us."

As John Calvin grew older, he had more and more duties to perform. Often he became very tired. After the death of his wife, there was nobody close to him that he could turn to.

Then, finally, on May 27, 1564, he died.

In the years that followed Calvin's death, his ideas spread widely. The Presbyterian and Congregational churches of England were organized on the basis of his teaching. In America, the Puritans of New England drew much from him. So, too, did Protestant groups in France, Germany, the Netherlands, Hungary, and Scotland. The

Anglican Church of England held to many of his beliefs.

Some recent scholars believe that his religious views were also important in politics and economics. Politically, he favored the idea of a free republic instead of rule by a monarch—a king or a queen. From an economic standpoint, students of capitalism have argued that Calvin supported the basic rights of people to achieve monetary rewards for their hard work.

Above all, however, historians describe John Calvin as a person who will be remembered for his religious beliefs. Of those, perhaps most important of all was his deep and continuing commitment to what human beings could learn from a thorough knowledge of religion. Such lessons were best to be gained, said Calvin, by studying carefully the life and teachings of one man—Jesus Christ.

Desiderius Erasmus

(1469?–1536) Defender of a humanistic approach to religion

Desiderius Erasmus was the illegitimate son of a Catholic priest. As an adult he was destined to become a scholar deeply involved in the critical period of the Protestant Reformation and the Catholic response.

His translation of the Greek version of the Bible into vivid, exciting Latin opened the way for Martin Luther and other reformers to work with the Holy Book in their own languages. Yet toward the end of his life he was condemned by both Catholics and Protestants for his failure to accept completely the position of either competing side.

Today, Erasmus is praised and honored by virtually all representatives of the Christian religion, as well as by academic leaders around the world. To some, he is ranked as the greatest of humanist scholars ever to live.

Erasmus was born in Rotterdam, Holland, probably in 1469, although the exact date is uncertain. His mother was a physician's daughter. As a schoolboy he succeeded in writing so well in the classical Latin language that his teachers marveled at his ability. Sometimes he even composed lengthy humorous verses in Latin.

After both of his parents died, he and his brother, also born out of wedlock, were sent to religious schools, both of them eventually entering monasteries. In 1492 he was ordained to the priesthood.

Even while a student, Erasmus felt that his teachers were too concerned with formal religion and not enough with scholarship, particularly the study of ancient civilizations. Soon after becoming a priest, he accepted a job helping a Catholic bishop with the study of nonreligious classics. It was at that time that he wrote, "All sound learning is secular learning," suggesting that there should be far less academic attention given to the study of religions.

Soon afterward the same bishop enrolled him at the University of Paris to learn more about religious subjects but also to teach about Greek and Roman classics. In 1499 Erasmus traveled to England with one of his students. There he met and became a close friend of the brilliant scholar Thomas More. Other travels took him to France and Italy for extended periods of study and teaching.

In Italy he wrote a particularly strong statement, declaring that people's personalities could be shaped by their formal education, especially by their readings. A person's good traits could thus be stimulated, while bad traits could be discouraged. To Erasmus, therefore, schooling was a crucial factor in shaping the human character.

Returning to England as a guest in the home of Thomas More, Erasmus composed what would become his most famous book, *Praise of Folly*. In it he ridiculed people's deep superstitions about their religions, particularly their eagerness for miracles and a willingness

to think of religious figures as holy saints. Monks, he pointed out, often became more immoral than did ordinary citizens. Another church abuse was the collection of vast amounts of money from people for the purchase of indulgences—the granting of freedom from punishment for their sins. Only a few years later, Martin Luther's attack on indulgences was destined to help break apart the Catholic religion.

Increasingly aware of problems within Christian society, Erasmus spoke of education as the solution. The teachings of Jesus Christ, he said, could restore the religion to its proper role in guiding human conduct. But to achieve that goal, religious leaders once again would have to preach what Jesus had taught and at the same time live good lives themselves.

In 1517 a turning point came both in the life of Erasmus and in the history of Christianity. That year marked the publication of Martin Luther's Ninety-five Theses, challenging the authority of the Catholic Church. Many of Luther's followers gave high praise to Erasmus for inspiring their leader.

Although Erasmus openly continued to applaud Martin Luther, he also worried deeply about a possible breakup of the entire Christian religion. To him, it was crucial to keep the faith united.

In order to achieve that goal Erasmus tried hard to bring the opposing sides in

Hans Holbein's portrait of Erasmus. *Brown Brothers.*

the dispute together. He pointed out that the great power held by church leaders lay at the very heart of the problem. Church services, he said, should begin to involve common people more directly, while priests should be brought closer to other people by being allowed to marry. If steps such as those were taken, declared Erasmus, the strength of Christianity would revive.

In the years that followed, Erasmus often found himself caught between the conflicting forces of the Catholic Church and the Protestant followers of Luther. Luther once attacked him strongly for his defense of various church actions. Catholic officials, on the other hand, sometimes spoke of him as a rebel against the church.

As the struggle continued between Catholics and Protestants, Erasmus worked to develop a view of religion that would be comfortable to ordinary people, regardless of the conflicts among theologians. Above all, he wanted Christians to follow the teachings of Christ—to live the "good life" by knowing about the Savior's personal beliefs and daily practices.

While Luther and his Protestant followers fought on against Catholics and their popes, Erasmus urged that all Christians live simple lives, without stormy battles over religious doctrines or codes of belief.

In 1529 the Protestant city of Basel, Switzerland, where Erasmus was living, passed a law against Catholic worship. As a result, Erasmus and several of his friends moved to nearby Freiburg, a Catholic university community. There he wrote on many topics, continuing to work for an end to religious conflict among Christians.

It was in July 1536 that Erasmus, having returned to Basel to supervise the publication of some of his new writings, fell ill.

With "dear God" as his final words, he died.

In the years following his death, the conflict between Catholics and Protestants grew more serious, often truly bloody. Yet to many scholars in Europe, the moderate ideas of Erasmus continued to hold strong appeal. In places such as the Netherlands his views were quoted in support of the more liberal treatment of religious dissenters.

Nevertheless, tough-minded religious leaders in several countries either had his works banned altogether or arranged for their censorship, removing portions they disliked.

Now, with the passage of centuries, the ideas of Erasmus have grown in acceptance and in popularity. Particularly in the twentieth century, it has become clear that he was a champion of those aspects of Christianity that defend personal liberty.

Like such thinkers as the French philosopher Voltaire, Erasmus stood firmly for the rights of every human being.

Indeed, to Erasmus, the central purpose of society, aided by the direct study of religious classics, was *to serve the people.* Hence, it no doubt is proper for us to remember the life of Erasmus, above all, as the life of a *humanist.*

John Wesley

(1703–1791) First founded and then championed the successful growth in England of Methodist Protestantism

One man, John Wesley, personally founded a major branch of the Protestant faith, its believers known as Methodists. Today that group numbers more than thirty million members, second only to Lutherans among all the branches of Protestantism in the world.

To Wesley, nothing was more important than the practice of religion, particularly a person's private prayers to God. To him, the experience of prayer gave meaning to existence. It turned uncertainty and lack of confidence into a way to deal with daily problems, a way to live one's life.

Wesley's mother, Susanna Annesley, the child of a British minister, was one of twenty-five children. She had made it a point to learn Latin, Greek, and French and to study theology carefully. Although she married Samuel Wesley at the age of nineteen and gave birth to nineteen children, she still continued to read about religion. She also taught it to her children.

Some historians have argued that Susanna probably came to know more about the Bible than either her father or her husband—both of them professionals in the religious field. She kept a careful diary and wrote many letters about religion and even conducted Sunday evening meetings about it in the family's barn.

John Wesley, born in 1703, was Susanna's fifteenth child and from the very beginning one of her special favorites. When he was six years old a fire broke out in the family's home, almost certainly set by neighboring farmers who considered Samuel Wesley a stubborn minister who too often was rude to them.

When Samuel discovered that all the Wesley children but John had escaped the fire, he knelt down to God in memory of his son. Neighbors suddenly caught a glimpse of the boy standing inside the house at a rear window. They then climbed onto each other's shoulders, making a human chain upward to rescue him just before the house collapsed.

According to John Wesley's mother, her son's rescue was an act of God— something the Lord had done with a divine purpose in mind for the boy's future.

John's father agreed, but declared that in saving the child's life, God actually had listened to his personal prayers as a minister. Because of that, Samuel Wesley decided that a religious career was indeed the right direction for his son to take.

When John was ten years old, he was enrolled at the prestigious Charterhouse School in London as a step on the way to Oxford University. Although not an outstanding student, he took time on his own to study Hebrew and to keep his body in good condition by running. Because older students at the school had a first option to eat meat at mealtime, John became a vegetarian, a habit that remained with him ever afterward.

In 1720 John Wesley was admitted to Oxford University, where he studied for five years. During those years he grew more and more serious about religion. He read many books on the subject. He prayed. Then, in September 1725, he officially became ordained as a deacon in the church.

In spring of the following year he was chosen for a fellowship at Lincoln College, Oxford University. There, he taught younger students as well as studying on his own. More than ever before in his life, he separated himself from other people, dealing entirely with religious readings as well as engaging in advanced scholarly studies. As the years went by he grew ever more intense, aware almost always of death and devoted to his mission in life.

One of his crucial activities at Oxford was to form, along with his brother Charles, a group known as the Holy Club. Members of that society would meet together for silent prayer. They would speak openly about their strengths and weaknesses. They would give away whatever money they had to poor people in slums and in prisons. Sometimes John Wesley even gave away his own food, leaving himself weak and ill.

John Wesley (standing) conducts a meeting of the Holy Club at Oxford. His brother Charles is seated third from left at the table. Engraved by Bellin after a painting by Marshall Claxton. *The Bettmann Archive.*

In 1735 John and Charles Wesley, along with two other members of the Holy Club, set sail for America, hoping to convert Indians in Georgia to Christianity. The Wesley brothers did so even though their mother, by then a widow, had barely enough money to meet her needs for food and shelter.

Along with the four Englishmen on their voyage to the New World were Moravian Germans, people who greatly impressed John Wesley for their courage in the face of terrible storms at sea. Because of that, he worked hard at learning German in order to speak directly with them.

Once in Georgia, Wesley became deeply disappointed with the Indians he had come to teach about Christ. To him, they were "gluttons, thieves . . . liars, and murderers." To please Colonel James Oglethorpe, the British leader of the colony, Wesley shifted his attention to the English colonists there, trying to work with them on religion. But to most of the colonists he seemed far too rigid, too intense, and too demanding of having things his own way.

A portrait of John Wesley by W. Hamilton. *The Bettmann Archive.*

An especially severe problem developed for Wesley because of his love for Sophia Hopkey, a young woman in Savannah, Georgia. Although the two cared deeply for each other, Wesley decided not to marry her, thinking that sexual involvement would cause him to lose much of his interest in religion.

Four days after he told Sophia of his decision, she married another British colonist, a man Wesley thought of as far from outstanding in looks, intelligence, or concern for religion. Young Wesley became particularly disappointed when Sophia refused to continue meeting him for the reading and discussion of religious books. In response, he declined to administer to her the Communion ceremony, a decision that deeply angered many of the Georgians.

For a time, Wesley argued his case, but in December 1737, seeing that he had become a person of controversy, he decided to return to England.

Writing in his diary on shipboard, he wondered whether he truly was living his life properly. He had worked to convert the Indians. Before departing for America he had tried to feed the poor. He had given his life to religion. But it seemed to him that perhaps he had been a failure.

Only a few days after arriving in London, Wesley's life dramatically changed. It was then that he met Peter Böhler, a Moravian missionary. Böhler convinced young Wesley that to live a good life and to succeed in it, he had to teach the idea of "faith alone." He had to go to God and teach other people to go directly to God. Such absolute faith was the only answer to the question of how to live a life. Faith!

John Wesley immediately began to preach and practice that doctrine. He spoke first to a prisoner who was about to be executed and was surprised to see that the man could then face death supported by confidence in eternal peace. In the weeks that followed, Wesley spoke to people attending services in churches as well as those he met on the streets, in taverns—anywhere.

To him, his new view of religion had been "an Awakening."

On the evening of May 24, 1738, at the age of thirty-five, Wesley reached a turning point in his career. On that night he addressed a group of people, many of them Moravians, in a service held on Aldersgate Street, in London. Before beginning to speak he had been reading Martin Luther's remarks on Paul's Epistle to the Romans.

For the first time in his life, that experience had made him feel at one with such church leaders of the past as Paul, Augustine, and Luther. He had concluded that, indeed, there was "good news" to be spread as widely as possible: the good news that salvation could come by faith alone.

Soon afterward he departed for Germany, intending to learn even more from the Moravians there. It was, to him, almost a new faith that he had acquired, one based on flaming enthusiasm, an almost electrical excitement, and hope for the future.

On returning to England, Wesley spoke in every church in London that would accept him.

Before long, however, problems began to arise. Many church leaders turned against his teachings and refused to let him address their congregations. Some people considered him too informal, too emotional, in his speeches. Before long he was prohibited from speaking to most of London's Protestant congregations. For him, the experience must have been deeply discouraging.

But then, unexpectedly, the tide began to turn in his favor. In part the reversal came because of Wesley's cooperation with George Whitefield, who also had been a member of the Holy Club at Oxford University. Whitefield, too, had gone to Georgia to preach and, unlike Wesley, had been received there with great enthusiasm.

Yet, after returning to London, he was greeted with the same kind of anger that Wesley encountered. Scarcely a single church in all of London would invite him to preach. Other cities also rejected him.

Wesley and Whitefield then decided to attempt a new course of action. Whitefield was to be first. Appearing outdoors in the open fields, he spoke to larger and larger crowds. Finally, as many as ten thousand people would come to hear him.

Wesley initially was concerned about such bold public demonstrations. But then he changed his mind. After delivering his own outdoor sermon before one enormous crowd, he happily declared, "The spirit of the Lord is upon me, because He hath anointed me to preach the gospel to the poor."

Wesley soon was speaking regularly to great audiences of people, many of them nonbelievers, in locations all across England, Scotland, Wales, and even in Catholic Ireland. Month followed month and year followed year. All the time, Wesley became more popular, more warmly accepted. Some of his listeners would even cast their bodies to the ground, writhing with emotion. Rowdies who came to riot against him would often be so deeply moved by his presence that they offered to protect him.

Not only did Wesley speak to audiences, he also wrote music, visited prisons, and helped to start schools and orphanages. Caring little for money, he ate only sparingly, owned no home, and used even his spare time in a Christ-like way, helping the poor.

In 1751 he married a widow who had nursed him when once he fell and hurt his ankle. Although they had no children, the two remained together for thirty years before her death once again left the great minister on his own.

Ten years later, in 1791, John Wesley himself died.

In his lifetime he had been the father of the enormously popular Methodist religion. He had written much. But per-haps most important of all, he had come to value the central importance of emotion in people's religious experience. It was feeling, far more than intellect—or so he believed—that could change human lives and that might even turn sinners into saints.

Over the last two centuries the Methodist approach to religion has undergone many changes, but what still underlies the faith of that body are the teachings of one man, its founder, John Wesley.

George Fox

(1624–1691) Founder of the Quaker religion

Visitors to church sessions of the Society of Friends—the Quakers— often are deeply moved. The group's meetings are simple, without the emotional leadership of a "fire-and-brimstone" preacher. Instead, members of the congregation break the opening silence by speaking as individuals. Services then are marked on most days by kind, sincere statements of religious belief and personal feeling.

Such practices grew directly from the religious views of George Fox, an Englishman who founded the Society of Friends, based on the teachings of Jesus. It was Fox, acting on his own, who broke even further from the Anglican faith than had the British Puritans. He came to feel that personal experience and personal belief in God truly should shape the way people live their lives.

Fox was born in a British village known today as Fenny Drayton, in the province of Leicestershire. As a child he tended sheep and worked as a cobbler, receiving only slight formal education. Still, he read much and made it a point to write as often as possible.

Fox's father, a weaver by trade, was himself a Puritan and introduced his son to that point of view. His mother may have been even more passionately devoted to the Puritan cause and was destined to be persecuted for her beliefs during the rule of Queen Mary. Not surprisingly, George grew up as a serious, highly religious child who played little.

Even before reaching the age of twenty, George expressed serious unhappiness

An undated lithograph of George Fox. *The Bettmann Archive.*

with the religious practices of his friends and neighbors. He felt that, despite sermons given in church, they drank too much, cheated one another in business dealings, and shot one another in civil wars. Discouraged with such behavior, he spent more and more time alone, fasting and reading the Bible.

Then, in 1647, he had an experience destined to transform his life. As he later described it, the Divine Spirit spoke directly to him. Despite the "darkness and death" he saw everywhere around him, he also saw love coming from God, something he thought could be shared by all people.

Soon he began meeting with people on the streets, drawing more and more converts to his position. Sometimes he spoke strongly to crowds attending services in their own churches, and for that act he briefly was thrown into prison.

In 1652 Fox addressed a group gathered at Pendle Hill, near Westmoreland and Lancashire in northern England. Followers joined him there by the hundreds. They are said to have seen him as a person of great sweetness and warmth, moderate and appealing in his approach but also deeply committed.

Not long after the Pendle Hill experience, George Fox visited with Judge Thomas Fell, who never converted to his movement but became a strong sup-porter. Fell's wife, Margaret, however, not only joined the newly formed Society of Friends, or Quakers, but became one of the group's most active members. Eleven years after Judge Fell died, Margaret and George Fox were married. From that point, she is said to have become "mother" of the Quaker religion.

Behaving dramatically as they wandered about in search of converts, the Quakers sometimes met with sharp opposition. Critics charged that they often interrupted church services, speaking out and even breaking glass bottles while ministers attempted to preach. They refused to swear oaths in courtrooms, arguing that people did not swear oaths during their usual daily activities—and often lied. They would not remove their hats before judges and other authority figures; to them, everyone was equal. Most of the men refused to serve in the army, declaring that warfare was not a Christian way of behavior.

In response to such controversial Quaker activities, British judges often took strong actions. It is said that by 1689 some fifteen thousand members of the Society of Friends had been imprisoned. Many believers were whipped in public, while others were branded or had their tongues pierced. During his life, George Fox himself was imprisoned eight times.

Faced with such actions by governmental authorities, Fox began organizing Quaker groups to meet regularly. Leaders of the young religion held formal business sessions every month, every quarter, and at the end of every year. That pattern continues to the very present in the governing activities of the church.

In 1672, following his release from a term in jail, Fox led a close-knit group of Quakers across the Atlantic Ocean to the New World for missionary purposes. They visited islands in the Caribbean, such as Jamaica, before traveling to British colonies in Virginia and in New England. Indian tribesmen guided them through New Jersey. Visits to Maryland and Rhode Island played an important role in strengthening the small Quaker settlements in those colonies.

In 1677, William Penn, a well-to-do Quaker and the founder of Pennsylvania, journeyed with George Fox to Holland and northern Germany. In those countries they met with small but deeply devoted groups of their religious followers.

As Fox grew older, the Quakers continued to be attacked from the outside but to draw closer together in their faith. In Great Britain they sometimes tried to win public attention to their cause, walking through the streets while wearing little or no clothing, as the Hebrew prophet Isaiah had done in biblical times.

Eventually, the Society of Friends became a far more balanced, moderate religious group. While allowing much freedom for individual members, they increasingly worked toward mutually shared goals.

As a result, Quaker membership grew steadily. New members might come, like George Fox himself, with only limited wealth and meager educational backgrounds. In time, however, people of prosperity and extensive education, such as William Penn, also were attracted to the Society. The new members joined with the old in their practices. They dressed in simple clothing. They spent little time with entertainment from art, music, or the theater. They used tobacco and alcohol seldom if at all. And male members made it standard policy to wear hats at all times except while praying.

At the same time, members of the Quaker religious body showed a joyousness about their religion—and about their futures—not common to other Protestant groups. With George Fox as their leader, they expressed faith in human goodness. They rejected the Puritan belief that most people could look forward only to an afterlife in hell. Although still persecuted, they lived with purpose and with hope.

Fox continued to believe, too, that God spoke to people directly with an

An 1815 engraving showing American Quakers going to religious services. *The Library of Congress.*

"inner light"—a voice that told them to do good things and to work for humanitarian goals. The Quakers stood out strongly against war, as well as against such practices as slavery in America. In their church services they still did not have a preacher but allowed men and women freely to state their opinions on social and religious issues.

Membership in the Quaker religion never became enormous. Yet the group gained great respect, not only in England but in America and other nations, too. Meanwhile, George Fox held firmly to his principles. In his own life he lived by ideals and held out those beliefs as models for other people.

In London, in January 1691, George Fox died.

William Penn declared in a statement given in Fox's memory that his friend had lived a life of great strength, but that his existence had meant even more. He had been "a new and heavenly-minded man and all of God-Almighty's making."

Such a model may indeed be what kind and merciful religious movements are all about. Quakers share one another's problems. They are sensitive to social issues. They work together to build a better and a happier world. And, like George Fox, they try to help people to walk through life with good cheer.

Mother Teresa

(1910–) Winner of the Nobel Peace Prize for help given to the poor both by herself and by the Catholic missionary order she organized

During this, the twentieth century since the birth of Jesus Christ, few personalities have stood out so vividly, or made such a great difference in the lives of people around the world as a Catholic nun, known to history as Mother Teresa.

She was born in the town of Skopje in the area known as Macedonia, then occupied by Turkish forces and later to become part of Yugoslavia. At the time of her birth in August 1910, the name she carried was Agnes Gonxha Bojaxhiu. Her father, Nikola (Kole) Bojaxhiu, and her mother, Drana, both were religious Catholics in a land where most people were Muslims rather than Christians.

When Agnes was nine years old her father died, causing her mother to try to make a living as a seamstress. Yet even though Drana had far less money than before, she still made an effort to help the poor as well as to give much of her time to people who were old and ill.

The practice of helping those who truly needed help was something that young Agnes watched carefully—and something she never would forget. Even as a child she began thinking about the possibility of caring for people less fortunate than herself, and doing so as a nun in the Catholic Church.

When she reached the age of nineteen, Agnes joined the Order of Loreto, a group dedicated to helping the poor people of India. To go ahead with that plan, she had to make hard choices: to say farewell to her mother and to the

Mother Teresa as a young nun. *SPCK.*

rest of her family in Skopje and to agree
that she never would marry or have children of her own. For the rest of her life
she would have to "live only for God."

It was a difficult decision, but she
determined to go ahead with it.

Saying goodbye to her friends and
family, she soon found herself bound
for the home of the Loreto Order,
located in Dublin, Ireland. There she
was taught English so she herself could
teach it to schoolchildren in India. She
also learned the ways of a nun: how to
dress, how to read aloud from the Bible,
and how to pray.

Finally, she took on a new name,
Mary Teresa of the Child Jesus. It was to
be the sign of change for a new career, a
new life she was about to begin.

For the first two years in India she
studied to become a Sister of Loreto,
learning the Hindi and Bengali languages while improving her English. At
last becoming Sister Teresa, she was
assigned to work with nurses in a medical center. Next, she began to teach history and geography to children of the
rich in a convent located in Calcutta.
Yet, as she knew, on the outside of the
convent were the poor and unhappy—
people in need of help.

It was in 1937 that Sister Teresa took
her final vows as a member of the Order
of Loreto. Not long afterward she was
appointed head (principal) of the school
where she taught, thus taking on for the
first time the name she later would raise
to glory, Mother Teresa.

For nine more years she served at the
convent school. Then, in September
1946, while riding a train toward a religious meeting, she thought she heard
the voice of God. As she later described
the experience, the Lord ordered her to
leave the convent where she had
worked for so long and go out to help
the poor.

To Mother Teresa, there was no choice
but to obey. She was summoned by the
"call" of God.

Mother Teresa at work in one of her hospitals. *AP/Wide World Photos. Photograph by Eddie Adams.*

At first, those in charge of the Loreto Order would not agree to let her go. But Mother Teresa continued to pray for the fulfillment of her wishes. Finally, she was permitted to go. Removing the formal clothing of her order and wearing a sari, the humble robe of a poor woman of India, she walked out alone into the streets of Calcutta.

In the weeks that followed, she gained skills in caring for the sick, the dying, and the newly born. Living with a Catholic order, the Little Sisters of the Poor, she gave special attention to chil-dren living in Calcutta's vast slums. She would sit outside with them, teaching them the alphabet and arithmetic. Then she would give them soap to clean themselves and milk to drink.

In the evenings she would walk the streets once again, trying to help anyone who needed her. Often she was followed by crowds of people, some of them grabbing at her clothing, even trying to kiss her feet in hope that she would do something for them.

As Mother Teresa later described it, when she helped a child or an old person she would pretend to be lendng personal help to Jesus himself. That thought would give her hope, would give her courage.

Before long, other nuns joined with her as she walked the streets. Soon, too, a wealthy Indian Catholic gave them all a place to live in his beautiful mansion. There they would begin the day in prayer before going out to serve the poor.

In 1950, Mother Teresa won approval from Rome for the establishment of a new group of nuns, the Order of Missionaries of Charity, an order that began with twelve members. She and the other nuns started at once to provide care for poor people who were dying on the streets of Calcutta.

Eventually she arranged shelter for the impoverished in the back rooms of an old temple where they, at the very least, could die in the care of people who were trying to help them. While alive they were given food and medical care. But most important of all, they were given love.

The missionary order soon moved to larger quarters as more and more sisters joined the group. Yet Mother Teresa herself, the leader of the Missionaries of Charity, continued to work like all the others. She scrubbed the toilets and, stooped on her hands and knees, washed the floors.

Before long, Mother Teresa began acting to help the newborn babies and older children so often in India left by their poor parents to die on the streets. In a new home called Shishu Bhavan she and her nuns fed them, cared for them, showed them affection. As the children grew older, Mother Teresa provided them with schooling. Still later she would arrange for them to be married in Shishu Bhavan, even giving cakes and sweets for the wedding ceremony.

One of Mother Teresa's special concerns was care for people suffering from the disease of leprosy. Since ancient times such people had been left alone by others, fearing that they, too, would become weak, even paralyzed, later to lose fingers and toes.

What Mother Teresa and her order did was to open Shanti Nagar, a home removed from the heart of Calcutta. There, lepers could learn marketable skills and become independent, even if they had already lost parts of their bodies.

When doctors uncovered a new way to treat leprosy, Mother Teresa and her order played an important role in spreading word to people about how they could be cured. For lepers who could not be saved, she and the other sisters offered gentle treatment along with a place to live until the victims finally met their fates.

Mother Teresa with Anglican Archbishop Desmond Tutu of Cape Town, South Africa. Both have received the Nobel Peace Prize. Mother Teresa used the cash award given with the prize to establish a home for lepers. *Reuters/Bettmann.*

As years passed by, the fame of Mother Teresa grew, eventually spreading around the globe. By 1990, she and the Missionaries of Charity had opened 430 homes to care for needy people in 95 countries, including even such prosperous lands as the United States.

Mother Teresa herself traveled from place to place, supervising the work of her order. Once without money to pay for a flight on Air India, she even offered to serve as a flight attendant. On hearing of that incident, Indira Gandhi, then the prime minister of India, made certain that ever afterward Air India would provide Mother Teresa with free flights to locations around the world.

Over the years, she received more and more honors and prizes. Once the Pope came personally to Calcutta to meet her. In 1979 she flew to Oslo, Norway, where she was presented perhaps the most honored of all awards, the Nobel Peace Prize.

Even in old age Mother Teresa did not forget her central mission in life—to help the poor. Such people, she knew, live not only in Calcutta but in the rich-est of lands. As she once put it, even if there was only one such person, "He is Jesus, he is the one that is hungry for love, for care."

Mother Teresa clearly understood that it would be impossible for her to end completely the problem of poverty on earth. But she promised, with the help of God, that she and her comrades would continue to do whatever they could.

Such high idealism may well be at the very heart of what religion is truly all about.

PART VII

RELIGIOUS LEADERS IN AMERICA

Roger Williams

(1603?–1683) Founder of Rhode Island; believer in separation of church and state and in absolute freedom of religion

Young people always have asked the question, "What will become of me in life?" Through much of human history, though, there were fewer possibilities than there are today. If a boy's father was a farmer, the chances were that he would be a farmer, too. And girls had even fewer choices.

Young Roger Williams, growing up in England nearly four hundred years ago, had something else to think about in planning for the future: religion. Religion was the burning issue of the day—the question that was tearing Western Europe apart. In the religious wars of the time, fought between Protestants and Catholics, nations carried out long and bloody battles. Neighbors came to hate and kill one another over matters of faith.

Both Protestants and Catholics agreed that the church played an important part, maybe even the *most* important part, in helping people to escape an afterlife of horrible punishment in hell and to gain the greatest reward of all, salvation—an eternal life after death in heaven. But which church? And how should it be set up?

Such ideas were argued bitterly by the most able, intelligent, and powerful people of the day. Thus it was only natural that young Roger Williams, a bright and ambitious lad growing up in London, England, would be fascinated by them. Even before reaching his teens, he had decided to study the Bible and become a Protestant minister, working in the service of God.

Williams probably was born in 1603,

although his exact date of birth is uncertain. His father owned a tailor shop on Cow Lane, displaying his wares, as most London merchants did, from street-level windows. The family room and kitchen extended to the rear of the store, with bedrooms ranged above the second floor.

Along with studying the Bible, young Roger Williams learned the newly developed art of shorthand. Sometimes he took down in shorthand the sermons of ministers at Saint Sepulchre's Church. It was there that he attracted the attention of Sir Edward Coke, a well-known and respected London lawyer.

Coke, impressed with Williams's intelligence, hired him as a secretary. Then, in 1621, he provided a scholarship for him at the Charterhouse School to prepare him for college. Often he spoke of Williams as a "son."

Williams liked to sit in Parliament, taking down in shorthand Coke's stirring speeches on the rights of the individual in society. It was Coke who, in 1628, drafted the famous Petition of Right and led Parliament in its successful struggle to force King Charles I to accept it. Many items in the Petition of Right later became part of America's own Bill of Rights, such as the idea that no person should be put in prison unless convicted of a specific charge.

Young Williams listened in awe as Coke championed the rights of the people. Later, the great lawyer's beliefs would play a crucial part in his own life.

In 1627 Roger Williams graduated with honors from Cambridge University, again on scholarship. Two years later he was ordained at Cambridge as a Protestant minister.

From the very beginning of his career, Williams became known as outspoken and abrasive. He publicly declared that the Church of England, although Protestant, was still too much like the Catholic Church. It should be made simpler, "purer," more like Christianity in the time of Jesus. People who held such beliefs were coming to be known in England as Puritans.

Many Puritans already had left England, settling in the Massachusetts Bay Colony in America. There they hoped to set up what they called "a Zion in the wilderness"—a place to worship God in their own way, "a new Heaven in a new Earth."

In December 1630, Roger Williams and his young wife, Mary, set sail aboard the ship *Lyon*. After a rough crossing in high seas and intense cold, they arrived near Boston on February 5, 1631. The Massachusetts General Court (the colony's assembly), pleased with the arrival of a new shipload of settlers, declared a Day of Thanksgiving.

Almost from his first day in Massachusetts Bay, Roger Williams found himself in trouble with the colony's leaders. Those men, familiar with his knowledge and his skill as a preacher, offered him a position as minister to the Boston congregation, the most important congregation in the colony. To their surprise, he refused.

The Boston church, he explained, did things too much like the Church of England. It also mixed religious matters too closely with matters of government. Church and state, declared Williams firmly, should always be kept separate. People who believed that were known at the time as Separatists.

As a result of his dispute with the colony's leaders, Williams spent his first two years in the New World not at Boston but at nearby Plymouth Colony. That settlement was made up of the Society of Pilgrims, led by governor William Bradford.

Yet even at Plymouth, a colony that welcomed free ideas, Williams was considered too advanced in his thinking. Bradford wrote of him as "unsettled in judgment. . . . He is to be pitied and prayed for."

Next, Williams became minister in the town of Salem, a part of Massachusetts Bay. Again and again he clashed with the colony's leaders, especially the shrewd and scholarly Puritan minister

John Cotton. In his sermons, Williams charged that it was wrong to think that only Puritans knew the truth about God. Scores of great cities and nations flourished in history, said Williams, without holding to Puritan beliefs. In his view there were many ways to understand the mysteries of God. Therefore all religions, not just one, should be tolerated. And *none* should be persecuted.

Another of Williams's positions offended John Cotton and the elders of the Bay Colony even more—his stand on the treatment of the Indians. Williams reminded the leaders of Boston that before sailing to New England, they had promised to convert "the savages" to Christianity. They had raised money for that purpose. Instead, they had taken the Indians' land and otherwise mistreated them. It was possible, charged Williams, that Massachusetts Bay did not even have proper legal title to the land on which the colony had been built.

Williams also continued to point out the danger in failing to separate church and state. People and governments, he said, were already "corrupt." If the church became corrupted, too, by contact with government, then there would be no way for people to be "saved"— no way for them to get to heaven. And after all, reasoned Williams, providing the machinery for getting to heaven was the principal reason for a church in the first place.

At last John Cotton and the Massachusetts General Court lost all patience with Williams. Finding him a nuisance to have around, they charged him with "divers opinions" that, said the assembly, were "erroneous and very dangerous." Infuriated, Williams refused to be silent. He defied the General Court, preaching stronger and stronger sermons, writing angry letters to the church leaders. They demanded that he stop. But he refused.

On October 9, 1635, the General Court found him guilty of preaching "new and dangerous opinions" and ordered him to leave Massachusetts within six weeks. But because he was ill and his wife was expecting a second child, he was permitted to remain until spring, on the condition that he would not meanwhile spread his beliefs among others.

Returning to Salem, Williams soon began preaching again. The General Court sent soldiers to seize him and place him on a ship that was about to sail for England.

Secretly, however, Governor John Winthrop, who, like Sir Edward Coke, treated Roger Williams like a son, warned him of the coming arrest. Just before the arrival of the soldiers in Salem, Williams and a few followers fled on foot into the wilderness, into the midwinter snows of New England.

Roger Williams survived the winter of 1636 only because of his friendship with the Indians. At Plymouth and Salem he had traded with the Wampanoags and the Narragansetts. He had slept in their wigwams, eaten the smoked bear meat dipped in maple syrup that they prized so highly. He had given them gifts. He had learned their languages. The Indians had saved his life when, as he later recalled, "I was sorely tossed for fourteen weeks in a bitter winter season not knowing what bread or bed did mean."

In the spring of 1636 he crossed the Seekonk River and, at a great spring of fresh water, pitched camp. It was on that spot that he established his colony, naming it Providence. The land was a gift of Canonicus, chief of the Narrangansett Indians.

In the summer, Williams's wife, Mary, joined him at Providence, along with their second daughter, whom they named Freeborn in defiant pride over their independence from the rule of Massachusetts.

Soon other settlers followed Williams to live among the Narragansetts. Among them was Anne Hutchinson, who also was banished from Massachusetts for daring to say that salvation—getting to Heaven—did not depend on obeying the laws of church and government.

An unknown artist depicted the Narragansetts aiding Roger Williams during the winter of 1636. *Brown Brothers.*

With the help of Williams, Mrs. Hutchinson and a band of her followers gained title to the islands of Prudence and Aquidneck (both part of Rhode Island). Williams purchased the islands for forty fathoms of white beads, ten coats, and twenty hoes. But those items were only token gifts to the Indian chiefs. For as Williams explained, "A thousand fathom would not have bought either [island] . . . and not a penny was demanded. . . . Rhode Island was a gift of love"—the love that the Indian chiefs Canonicus and Miantonomo had for Roger Williams.

By 1643 Rhode Island had grown to include four communities: Providence, Portsmouth, Newport, and Warwick. The tiny colony quickly became a haven for those who had suffered persecution for their beliefs. Often, as in the case of the Quakers, Williams disagreed with the ideas of the new settlers. Yet he always welcomed them to Rhode Island

and firmly defended their right to practice their religion. At that time no other place in the English-speaking world offered such complete freedom of conscience.

Williams himself was changing, too. In 1639 he declared himself a "Seeker," saying that there was no one, true religion. Never again was he a member or an official preacher of any church. Instead, for the rest of his life he gave himself over to seeking the truth about God, allowing others to make up their own minds.

Before long, Rhode Island became a place of refuge for the poor, as well as for those in other colonies eager for religious liberty. Since anyone in good character in need of a place of safety was admitted, the elders of Massachusetts sneered at Williams's colony. They referred to it as "Rogues' Island" or "the Sewer of New England." And because Roger Williams believed in equality, they called him a "Leveller."

Under attack, Williams stuck to his beliefs. In his book, *The Bloody Tenet of Persecution*, he argued that it was wrong to force people into one supposedly "true" belief. That, he said, was against the teaching of Jesus Christ. Christ, said Williams, was a prince of peace, not of persecution. Hence, in Rhode Island, Catholics, Jews, and even nonbelievers were given full citizenship.

Indeed the oldest Jewish synagogue in America is located in Newport, Rhode Island.

Beginning in 1647, an assembly of the colony's towns began meeting. That assembly passed a code of laws based on Roger Williams's statement that "the Soveraigne, originall, and foundation of civill power lies in the people" and that "a People may erect and establish what forme of Government seems to them most meete." More than 125 years would pass before similar words found their way into the Declaration of Independence. In politics, as in religion, Williams was ahead of his time.

In 1654 Williams was elected president of Rhode Island, a position he held for three terms. For the rest of his life he held some public office, always refusing to accept pay for his work. Twice he traveled to England to defend the colony's legal rights. He served as peacemaker between bickering groups within Rhode Island, usually on matters of land ownership.

Frequently he was called on, too, as the only person acceptable to both the Indians and the English to prevent war between the two sides. But when war came, like the brutal King Philip's War (1675–1676), he sided with the English, helping to plan the fortifications of Providence.

Even in old age Williams continued

farming, trading, taking part in public affairs. Then sometime early in 1683, at about the age of eighty, he died. At the simple burial ceremony beside his house, guns were sounded in a military salute.

All his life Roger Williams had believed in every person's right to think freely about religion and to share in the common good through a free government. Such ideas, drawn from the finest, bravest minds in England, were not original with him—but in Rhode Island he put them into actual practice and made them live.

Grudgingly, even Cotton Mather, the crusty old Puritan minister, agreed. In more than forty years of exile, wrote Mather, Williams "acquitted himself so laudably that many juditious persons judged him to have the root of the matter in him."

Since the time of Mather, other generations of Americans also have come to believe that Roger Williams "had the root of the matter in him." Stubborn and argumentative, he nevertheless trusted his fellows, whether Indians or Englishmen. And they returned his trust, even those like Governor John Winthrop who, in expelling him from Massachusetts into the harsh wilderness, had made him "the most outcast soul in America."

They respected him for his honesty, his generosity, his open-mindedness, but most of all for his desire to live a life in the cause of all humanity. To Roger Williams, that was what religion really was all about.

Anne Hutchinson

(1591–1643) Champion of religious liberty and the rights of women in colonial America

Anne Hutchinson's life seemed settled. In 1633, at the age of forty-two, she was living quietly and comfortably in the English countryside. The wife of a wealthy landowner, she was the mother of fourteen children.

Ten years later, in a wilderness cabin in North America, Anne Hutchinson lay dead in a pool of blood. Around her sprawled the butchered bodies of all but one of her children.

What brought her to such an end? Why had she come to America?

The story of Anne Hutchinson is one of great courage. A person of strong beliefs, she stuck to her ideas, finally at the cost of her life. As a result, those who live after her in America have greater freedom to think as they wish,

for she helped bring to America the idea of freedom of religion.

Anne Hutchinson and her husband, William, came to Boston in 1634. It was then a town of about a thousand persons in Massachusetts Bay Colony. Most of its citizens had left England hoping to find religious freedom in North America.

The Hutchinsons came for the sake of John Cotton, the minister whose church they attended in England. When Cotton decided to come to America, the Hutchinsons gave up their comfortable life to be with him. Anne was herself the daughter of a minister. Even as a child she was interested in religious discussions.

William Hutchinson soon became a leader in Boston. Anne, intelligent and kindly, became one of the most popular women in the community. She was also a skilled midwife, a person who helped women deliver their babies. In Boston it was not thought proper for a male doctor to be present at childbirth.

Before long, the women of Boston looked on Mistress Anne, as they called her, with respect and love. Some said that when she delivered a baby, she seemed almost a partner of God, helping Him to bring a soul into the world.

But Anne Hutchinson was not happy just taking care of children and doing laundry. She had a fine mind. She studied the Bible and took part in the religious life of Boston. That was not unusual, since everyone in Massachusetts Bay was interested in religion and concerned with what might happen to their souls after death.

Soon after arriving in America, Anne Hutchinson began holding meetings of women in her home. She would discuss with them the sermon preached in church the Sunday before. Church members sometimes did this, and certainly there was no law against discussion in Boston—even though there were laws against many other things people liked to do.

But Mistress Anne did not stop at just discussing the ministers' sermons. She talked about her own religious ideas.

According to Mistress Anne, the most important thing about religion was God's love. A person, she said, should speak directly to God. Just obeying the laws of the church and government was not enough to get into heaven. Good deeds were not enough, either. God was a mystery, said Anne Hutchinson. A minister might help people, but sooner or later each man and woman would have to talk to God in his or her own way in order to find a place in heaven. People could not get in by building up good credit for obeying the church. Instead they had to love God and believe in Him. That was not something just to think about; it was something a person had to feel.

These ideas at once stirred a storm. All of Massachusetts Bay was excited. If Anne Hutchinson were right, said her enemies, nobody would have to obey the laws. Each person would make up his or her own mind about what was right and wrong. And if everyone spoke directly to God, what need would there be for ministers? Ministers would lose their jobs. For that matter, what need would there be for the church?

John Winthrop, the governor of Massachusetts Bay, and John Wilson, a leading minister, were furious. They both said that Mistress Anne was putting all of Massachusetts Bay Colony in danger. Savage Indians were all around, they said, and if people did not obey the laws of the church and the government, the colony would fail. Men could refuse to serve in the army, could refuse to pay their taxes. People would believe different things. They would be divided against one another and would stop respecting government officers and the ministers. Moreover, if the church were hurt, then everyone's chances for getting to heaven would be endangered, too.

At first many people lined up on the side of Anne Hutchinson. The women of Boston sided with her. So did Sir Henry Vane, who was elected governor of Massachusetts in 1636. Her brother-in-law, the Reverend John Wheelwright, gave sermons using her ideas.

Anne Hutchinson's strongest friend was the Reverend John Cotton, whom Anne and her husband had followed to America. She thought he was the only minister in Massachusetts who spoke the truth about God.

All went well for a while, but then things changed. When Henry Vane lost the next election for governor to John Winthrop, Vane sailed for England. Next, John Wilson called a meeting of all churchmen in Massachusetts. Angry and afraid, they declared Anne Hutchinson's ideas to be both dangerous and wrong. The General Court, which made the laws for Massachusetts, banished the Reverend John Wheelwright for defending her.

That left only one powerful friend—John Cotton.

Perhaps Cotton feared that the people of Massachusetts would take sides, some for Anne Hutchinson, some against her. If that happened, the colony would not be united against its enemies, the Indians. Perhaps he just did not have as much courage as Mistress Anne. Whatever the reason, John Cotton changed his mind.

He said that Anne Hutchinson was a good woman, a just woman, but that her ideas were not right. He told Hutchinson to admit she was wrong, even if she did not believe it. She refused.

The General Court put Anne Hutchinson on trial. It was not a fair trial. Nobody tried to find out whether she was right. Instead, she would have been found guilty just for saying that people did not always have to obey the ministers, and she already had said that even before the trial began. "Mrs. Hutchinson," said Governor John Winthrop, "you have broken the Fifth Commandment, 'Honor thy father and mother.'"

"You are not my parents," said Anne Hutchinson, sensibly enough.

"'Father and mother' means all those who make the rules," Winthrop replied. "And when there are rules, they have to be obeyed."

"Not when those rules are against the word of God," said Anne Hutchinson.

A painting by Howard Pyle shows Anne Hutchinson preaching in her house in Boston. *The Bettmann Archive.*

A woodcut depicting the trial of Anne Hutchinson. *Culver Pictures, Inc.*

"Enough!" cried John Wilson. "She has thrown dirt in the judges' faces!"

Winthrop agreed. "Say no more," he commanded Mistress Anne. "The court is satisfied. You are no longer fit to live in this community. You must leave."

It was the dead of winter, snow covered the ground, and Mistress Anne was expecting another child. Not even the stern judges of Massachusetts could send a woman to wander in the forests of New England at that time. She was allowed to remain in Boston until spring.

Once again, John Cotton begged her to say she had been wrong. All would be forgiven, and she would be allowed to remain in Boston for the rest of her days.

But when Anne Hutchinson came before the church elders, she would not lie about her beliefs. The Reverend Wilson read the final sentence declaring Anne Hutchinson to be in the hands of the Devil. She was banished from Massachusetts forever.

Anne Hutchinson rose and left the church, never to return.

In the spring of 1638, she and her family packed their belongings and moved to Rhode Island. Roger Williams, who had been made to leave Massachusetts for trying to keep the church separate from the colony's government, was already there.

John Wheelwright, William Coddington, and others who believed in Anne Hutchinson's ideas joined her in Rhode Island. She helped Coddington start the town of Portsmouth. When her husband, William, died in 1642, she moved to Long Island. The next year she moved to Pelham Bay, close to what is now New York City.

There, in the wilderness, a band of Narragansett Indians attacked and burned her home. They killed Anne Hutchinson and all of her children but one, a daughter who later was bought back from them by Dutch settlers.

So, unhappily, ended the life of Anne Hutchinson. However one judges her ideas, there is no doubt that she was a woman of great courage. She believed in freedom of religion and was willing to stand by her beliefs.

Nor is she forgotten in Massachusetts. On Beacon Hill in Boston, where all can see it, stands a statue of Anne Hutchinson. She was among the first of many strong women who helped build a tradition of human freedom in the New World.

Jonathan Edwards

(1703–1758) Led emotional religious revival, the Great Awakening, in colonial New England; later became president of Princeton University

To some students of history, Jonathan Edwards stands out primarily as a preacher of fiery sermons. His "Sinners in the Hands of an Angry God" portrayed the torture forever into the future of people damned to life in hell. He spoke of children sometimes as "little vipers." And he was known to say from the pulpit to his listeners that God was holding them over a burning pit, as if they were terrible insects.

It is said that members of his congregation would at times become so frightened that they held on to supporting posts in the church to save themselves from falling into the raging fires he described. Not surprisingly, after such sermons, whole congregations were known to turn to him for support, becoming his followers for reasons of emotion as well as for his astonishing intellect.

The father of Jonathan Edwards was a minister, too. So were his grandfather and great-grandfather. Yet none of them had an impact on society equal to that of Jonathan, a leading force in the story of religion in America. He is recognized as the father of the dynamic revival movement known as the Great Awakening and, to some, is the greatest of all American Calvinists.

Jonathan Edwards was born in 1703, the only son in a family of eleven children. By the age of ten he already had written a learned essay on the human soul. Two years later he won high praise for a scientific essay on spiders. At the age of thirteen he entered Yale College and, before long, was able to read Latin, Greek, and Hebrew.

Sixteen years old when he graduated from Yale, Edwards remained on campus for two more years to study religion before becoming a pastor in Manhattan. He returned to Yale for a master's degree. Then, at the age of twenty-four, he became an assistant minister to his grandfather, Solomon Stoddard, at a Congregational church in Northampton, Massachusetts.

In 1727, Jonathan Edwards married Sarah Pierrepont, the daughter of a New Haven minister. At the time, she was seventeen years old and deeply devoted to God and to the teachings of Jesus. The two were destined to produce eleven children, some of them exceptionally bright.

It was especially to Sarah that Jonathan owed a growing sense of emotional love for God, along with continued respect for religion, something he had been taught since childhood. To Edwards, marriage proved a remarkably happy part of his life, an experience that strengthened his devotion to the practice of theology.

When Solomon Stoddard died in 1729, Ewards became head minister of the church in Northampton. He immediately began to preach against the growing attention being given in New England to "free will"—the right of people to use their own judgment on moral issues. In sermon after sermon Edwards declared that people had to surrender their total faith to God. Faith alone, he said, was the way to salvation.

Before long Edwards found himself leading a highly emotional religious revival movement in Massachusetts and Connecticut. Known as the Great Awakening, it eventually spread all through New England, involving most of the region's Protestant groups. To Jonathan Edwards, the Great Awakening was "a work of God," based on "holy love."

In the late 1740s, after many years in Northampton, Edwards began to experience growing opposition from his own congregation. Unlike his grandfather, Solomon Stoddard, Edwards refused to admit to Communion services in the church certain people: any who had not formally become Christians through a personal religious experience. In that sense, he asked more of his followers than most other ministers.

He also protested the widespread exposure of young people in his congregation to books he considered obscene. From the pulpit of his church he openly announced the names of the many families involved.

The result was fierce conflict between Edwards and the members of his community, as well as with ministers

An engraving of Jonathan Edwards by S. S. Jocelyn and S. B. Munson. *Culver Pictures, Inc.*

in surrounding towns. Finally, in July 1750, Edwards was formally dismissed from his position.

Leaving Northampton, he soon accepted a position in Stockbridge, a frontier community in western Massachusetts. There he had responsibility for only a few families of whites but large numbers of Indians to whom he tried to teach the Christian religion.

Despite problems relating to language, occasional military conflicts, and his own illnesses, he managed to remain in Stockbridge for several years. While there he wrote *The Freedom of the Will* (1754), described by some critics as one of the greatest works on theology ever produced in America. In it, Edwards declared that because people are free to make choices, God would hold them responsible for their deeds; thus a sinner eventually would be punished, if not on earth then afterward.

In a still later study, Edwards charged that although not every person actually commits sinful acts, all human beings actually are inclined to sin. In that sense, it was not just a matter of the biblical Adam sinning at the beginning of time, but a tendency shared by everyone ever afterward. All of humanity was guilty.

At the same time, said Edwards, God is good, even producing a son, Jesus, to save people for life after death.

According to Edwards, to achieve the goal of salvation—getting to heaven instead of going to hell—people had to use both their minds and their hearts.

They had to think good thoughts but also to reach out to God with proper feelings. Thus in facing life's problems, wrote Edwards, people should think less of their own happiness and more about their love of God. They should spend their time in worship, prayer, and reading the Bible.

Jonathan Edwards used his years in Stockbridge for further developing and writing about his religious beliefs. Then, in the autumn of 1757, he was offered the presidency of a newly formed Presbyterian institution, the College of New Jersey, known since then as Princeton. Although he actually preferred to continue writing and preaching, he eventually accepted the appointment.

Arriving in New Jersey in February 1758, he began serving as the college's president. Early in his term he was given an inoculation to protect him from smallpox. Shortly afterward, however, he became a victim of that disease.

It was an event that led very soon to his death. During the century after the passing of Jonathan Edwards, his reputation soared. One of his followers, Samuel Hopkins, described him as standing among the greatest theologians of recent centuries. His written works were published again and again. That was true even during the Enlightenment in America, a period given over to belief in reason and balance rather than to deep emotional feeling about religion.

Following the Civil War in the United States (1861–1865), Edwards's reputation declined sharply. He was considered too passionate in his beliefs, too carried away with thoughts about terrible punishment in hell for human beings. Even religious leaders who praised his enormous skills in using logic tended to speak out against him, describing him as overly involved with the tragic elements in human existence.

Then, beginning in the late 1930s, the memory of Jonathan Edwards was reborn. University scholars dealing with the history of ideas in America began to describe his contribution as extremely important. Not only was he seen as a person of deep moral and religious involvement but as someone highly skilled in his use of complicated ideas—matters of the intellect.

In the second half of the twentieth century, Edwards became a hero to newly revived groups of conservative Protestants in America. They admired his emotionally strong support of *faith* in the church along with a passionate *love* of God.

To some, he was the very model of an evangelist: a Protestant minister teaching that the essence of the Gospel lay in people's sinfulness and that the possibility of personal salvation came through belief in Jesus Christ and faith in God.

Today, scholars and religious leaders still turn often to the teachings of Jonathan Edwards. He remains a major figure to historians of the American experience, as well as to people intent on finding meaning in human existence.

Joseph Smith

(1805–1844) Founder of the Mormon approach to Christianity

June 27, 1844. On that day a mob of angry foes of Joseph Smith stormed the jail where he was a prisoner and mercilessly shot him to death. So ended the life of a man remembered as founder of a religious movement— Mormonism—that today is highly respected in America and plays a central role in the prosperous state of Utah.

According to a book written by Joseph Smith's mother, both her father and her husband (Joseph's father) were fanatics about religion. They believed in faith healers, in demons, and in witchcraft. Western New York state, where Joseph was raised, then was the home of numerous Christian cults, small groups seeking original pathways to salvation.

Joseph Smith later wrote about the experience he had while a fourteen-year-old boy. All alone in a quiet grove of trees, he closed his eyes and prayed. Suddenly he saw before him two "glorious personages"—figures he later claimed to be God and Jesus.

As he described the experience, the two heavenly beings informed him that all of the current religions were incomplete and that sometime later they personally would lead him to the ultimate truth.

Three years later another vision is supposed to have come to him, this time in a setting marked by flames. An angel of God, he said, promised that one day he would come upon a sacred book, pointing the way to his leadership of a faith. For seven more years, according to Smith, still more visions continued to appear.

Then, "on the morning of the twenty-second of September A.D. 1827," as he put it, a book was mystically presented to him, written in an ancient language on golden plates. With the help of transparent stones he found alongside the plates, he translated the message of what later would be called the Book of Mormon. That volume supposedly was written by Mormon, father of the angel of God who previously had visited Joseph Smith.

Smith is said to have learned from the book that Jews from Jerusalem's ten Lost Tribes actually had settled in the New World. Even though Jesus soon appeared to guide them, they lost their lives after turning to acts of sin. Replacing them, said Smith, were the American Indians.

Several non-Mormon scholars have since suggested that Smith skillfully put the book together himself. He drew on Indian legends, on matters of controversy among Protestant subgroups, and on his own vivid imagination. Some historians say he also had the help of his young wife, Emma Hale Smith.

In 1830 the Book of Mormon finally was published. In that year, too, there first appeared the new church of Joseph Smith's creation, the Church of Jesus Christ of Latter-day Saints, known popularly as the Mormon Church.

Claiming that God had told him to move westward, Smith and his small group of followers settled in Kirtland, Ohio. Before long, his congregation included nearly two thousand members.

During the first months after arriving in Ohio, Smith spent much of his time in writing. His ideas drew heavily upon the Old Testament, especially in calling for a strong leadership group made up of religious figures such as himself.

The book that he wrote in 1833, known today as *Doctrine and Covenants*, asked that people join with one another in communities of faith, held together as nearly as possible by economic equality. Nevertheless, a business that Joseph Smith and two of his followers soon organized for personal profit cast serious doubts about his honesty.

Partly because of controversy over that business, Smith led his group westward to Independence, Missouri, a site he described as a "future Zion." There, too, however, he met with opposition, causing him, along with his followers, to leave in 1838.

The Mormons settled next in Nauvoo, Illinois, a town along the Mississippi River. That location proved enormously successful for the group, soon grown to eleven thousand people, making

A portrait of Joseph Smith. *Latter-day Saints Historical Department.*

Nauvoo the largest city in the state. Joseph Smith served both as its religious leader and its mayor, making the community the center of all Mormon activities.

In 1842 eight ships brought clusters of English citizens to America to convert to the Mormon faith. Thousands of Americans also joined.

Joseph Smith grew ever more pleased with the success of his religion. Before long he claimed leadership of the Mormon military force, wearing the formal uniform of a lieutenant general.

A crowd of forty thousand Mormons gathers in 1892 to watch the capstone placed on the newly constructed temple in Salt Lake City, Utah. The temple was completed the following year. *Utah State Historical Society.*

In 1844 he announced his candidacy for the presidency of the United States, claiming that it was "the will of God." Although he of course stood no chance of winning, he clearly had gone far from a childhood marked by poverty and only modest education.

One Mormon practice, however, that caused serious trouble within the group was polygamy—marriage to more than one wife at the same time. Smith himself had more than forty wives. Other Mormon leaders also took part in multi-ple marriages, claiming that no woman could be admitted to heaven without a marital relationship to a member of the faith.

The issue of multiple marriages was destined to have disastrous conse-quences for Joseph Smith. A small group of Mormons opposed to the prac-tice of polygamy banded together to organize a newspaper in protest against the practice. After the first issue of the paper appeared, Smith and his support-ers stormed the editorial headquarters, destroying the printing press and burning down the building.

Although the building's owners soon had Smith arrested, a Mormon political official quickly arranged for his release. At that point many of the non-Mormons in the area determined to take action against him. Since he had called out Nauvoo's public militia forces to protect the town, the angry dissenters had him arrested again, along with his brother, Hyrum, charging the two with "treason." When they were placed in the Carthage, Illinois, jail, the governor of the state promised to protect them there.

But then, on June 27, 1844, a mob of anti-Mormon rioters, their faces blackened to disguise them, stormed the prison. First they shot Hyrum to death. Then they angrily stormed at Joseph Smith, filling his body with bullets.

Still in his thirties, the founder of the Mormon faith had been brutally murdered.

In the months that followed, Illinois authorities took the Mormon Charter away from the believers. The group's new leader, Brigham Young, responded by organizing a departure from that state, moving far to the west. The result was one of history's great migrations. Hundreds of wagons traveled together in caravan after caravan, eventually settling in what today is the state of Utah.

Because of the Mormon practice of multiple marriages, the United States Congress at first delayed the admission of Utah to the Union. In 1896 it was at last agreed to accept the new state, but only under the expressly stated condition that such marriages would be declared illegal forever.

Today, Mormons are to be found not only in Utah and surrounding western states, but all across America and in places around the world. Many of them have been highly successful in business and in academics. Perhaps most surprising of all, they have been especially praised for their steadiness, regularity, and predictability—qualities in marked contrast to the character of their founder, Joseph Smith.

Yet it also is clear to observers that without the dramatic, attractive, and remarkably powerful personality of Smith—along with the strength and satisfaction accompanying his message—the Mormon religion would never have survived.

Joseph Smith unquestionably had been the shaper of his faith.

Isaac Mayer Wise

(1819–1900) Pioneer of Reform Judaism in America

When the year 2000 arrives in the Christian world, the year on the Jewish calendar will be 5760. Thus early Hebrew leaders, including Abraham, Moses, and Jeremiah, practiced their faith long before such vital religious figures as Jesus and Muhammad. Yet through all those many centuries of change, the habits and ceremonies of ancient Judaism continued to survive.

Even after the discovery and settlement of America, the old ways were carried on in the New World almost exactly as before. Then came industrialism and a need felt by many Jews in America to mix more comfortably with other people. It was at that time that a new branch of the ancient religion was born.

Known as Reform Judaism, its leading organizer was Isaac Mayer Wise.

Wise was born in 1819 in Steingrub, Bohemia (now a part of Czechoslovakia). His father, a teacher with very little money, died while Isaac still was a child. Young Isaac began studying the Talmud at age six. As he grew older he also studied Greek classics and other formal scholarly subjects, finally spending a year at the University of Vienna.

Despite his academic successes, he was aware that life for Jews probably would remain far from easy under the Habsburg monarchy that was ruling Bohemia. Hence, after becoming a rabbi and serving for a year in a Bohemian town, Wise decided to leave for the United States. In 1846 he and his wife,

Therese, and their baby arrived in New York City.

America opened exciting new possibilities for the young rabbi. It especially offered him freedom to practice the ancient Jewish religion in new ways. Serving with a small congregation in Albany, New York, he introduced his members to the idea of men and women actually sitting together in the synagogue instead of apart. A chorus was organized to sing religious songs. Finally, in place of the usual bar mitzvah, the ceremony by which boys were admitted to manhood at age thirteen, both boys and girls of about that age formally were admitted to the religion in a "confirmation" ceremony.

Although still new to the United States, Rabbi Wise next tried to press the idea of a single temple ceremony to be used by all of the nation's Jews. It was an effort, however, that met with almost no acceptance. Another of his plans also failed, one proposing to bring together the entire range of America's Jewish congregations into one organization.

Quite clearly, Wise's overall aim was to create a new form of Judaism, one especially right for the nation he already had begun to love.

In 1850 sharp disagreements began to break out among members of the young rabbi's own temple over his daring new practices. Before long, the controversy led to a demand for his removal. As a result, Wise and those followers who still supported him decided to form their own congregation, holding firmly to the principles of religious change popularly known by then as Reform Judaism.

In 1854 Wise moved to Cincinnati, becoming a rabbi of Congregation B'nai Jeshurun. In the years to come, Cincinnati was to become the base for his many highly innovative religious practices. Soon after arriving there, he organized a newspaper, the *American Israelite*, a national publication still popular today. He also began a German-language paper, *Die Deborah*, directed especially at Jewish women.

Wise established and for a time tried to operate what he called Zion College, teaching not only about Jewish subjects and the Hebrew language but about broader matters in American society.

When that project failed, he worked toward organizing a synod, or council, that would unite all American Jews. At a conference held in Cleveland, he actively led in producing the so-called Cleveland platform. Orthodox rabbis at first favored the statement, pleased that a Reform leader, Wise, would praise so highly the positions of the ancient Talmud. But soon they became suspicious, believing he was only suggesting

Isaac Mayer Wise as a young rabbi shortly after he settled in Cincinnati. *American Jewish Archives, Cincinnati Campus, Hebrew Union College, Jewish Institute of Religion.*

the use of such documents to win their support.

Meanwhile, several Reform rabbis angrily accused him of compromising too much with the old-fashioned practices. As a result, Wise's attempt to bring all American Jews together in unity went down to failure.

Another question then facing American Jews was slavery. Rabbi Wise strongly disliked slavery, but he feared that armed conflict between North and South possibly might destroy the United States, to him an extraordinary nation. Even after the Civil War broke out, he sided with President Lincoln's "Copperhead" opponents, finally launching a campaign for election to political office. But faced with the objection of his own congregation, he decided to withdraw from candidacy.

With the end of the Civil War, he began once more to work toward uniting American Jews, hoping personally to lead such a movement. His opponents, however, greeted him with fierce opposition, Reform rabbis from the East playing a central role in crushing his efforts.

Reform rabbis other than Wise managed in 1873 to form the Union of American Hebrew Congregations, with headquarters in Cincinnati. That group made no attempt to claim authority over member temples, hoping only to bring them together. Yet one of its early acts was to authorize the creation of a new institution, the Hebrew Union College, for the training of Reform rabbis.

When the college opened in 1875, its first president was Isaac Mayer Wise.

Known today as the Hebrew Union College–Jewish Institute of Religion, its campus is located within easy walking distance of the University of Cincinnati. Professors from both colleges in fields such as history cooperate frequently, while students use one another's libraries.

From the time Rabbi Wise took over the presidency, he used Hebrew Union College to help further his broader goals for the advancement of Reform Judaism. Remaining president until his death, he managed to ordain more than sixty rabbis. His own writings continued to spread across the country while students at the institution regarded him both with respect and with affection. In 1889 he became president of the Central Conference of American Rabbis, another position he would hold for the rest of his life.

Isaac Wise and his first wife, Therese, eventually became parents of ten children. After Therese died in 1874, Wise remarried, fathering four more children, including one boy who later became a rabbi and wrote a book about him.

The dream of Rabbi Wise that Reform Judaism soon would triumph in America never came to pass. At the turn of the century, large numbers of Eastern European Jews arrived in the United States, hoping for prosperity and freedom or fleeing from increasingly bloody acts of prejudice. Most of those immigrants, however, remained loyal to practices of Orthodox Judaism rather than joining the new Reform temples.

Much that Isaac Mayer Wise hoped for in his lifetime remained unrealized. Judaism in America was not united in the Reform movement. Wise's own prayer book, *Minhag America (American Usage)*, lost out to a competing volume, the *Union Prayer Book*. Finally, believing that Judaism should spread throughout the world, Wise opposed the creation of a Jewish nation in Palestine. It was a position still adhered to by many of his Reform followers when, in 1948, the state of Israel actually came into being.

Despite all of the disappointments that Rabbi Wise experienced, not many of the world's religious leaders have met with equal success. Reform Judaism attracted to membership some of the great figures of late-nineteenth- and early-twentieth-century life. Today it still flourishes, even serving as a model for leaders of other religions.

The person most responsible for the direction of the Reform movement in America was Isaac Mayer Wise. And although many of his goals were not directly realized, Judaism in America has largely taken on the character that he dreamed of during his productive lifetime.

Mary Baker Eddy

(1821–1910) Founder of Christian Science, teaching that spiritual health can cure physical ills

Mary Baker Eddy believed that God had called upon her to give new strength to Christianity. She tried to do that by founding a religious movement, Christian Science, dedicated to helping people control the health of their bodies through prayer and faith.

To her, it seemed that Jesus had healed people without using medicines, so that Christianity, if properly practiced, could heal without medicines in the present day world, too. Hence, the Church of Christ, Scientist, she established was based on a belief in God's goodness and love applied to the lives of human beings.

Mary Baker was born in 1821 to a farming family in New Hampshire. She was the youngest of six children.

Almost from the beginning she experienced problems with her health. As a result, her brothers and sisters, as well as her parents, treated her with special tenderness. Mary's grandmother read poetry to her, while her mother often would read aloud from the Bible.

By the time Mary was eight years old, she was certain that God was speaking directly to her. Although raised in a strict religious atmosphere, she decided early that the God she knew was a God not of anger but of love. Apart from her regular work in school, she independently studied moral science, logic, and philosophy, as well as such ancient languages as Greek, Latin, and Hebrew. As a teenager she taught a class of children in her Sunday school.

In 1843 she married, only to have her

husband soon die of yellow fever. Shortly afterward, Mary gave birth to a boy. She was in such poor health, however, that she could not care for her child, and he was sent away to be brought up by a foster family.

For three years after her husband's death, Mary herself lived with her older sister, Abigail. Through much of that time she suffered from a spinal problem and could scarcely walk, often needing to be carried from place to place.

Although still not well, in 1853 she married a dentist, Dr. Daniel Patterson. In the years that followed Mary was often confined to bed. Her husband, meanwhile, became interested in other women. During the Civil War, while on a mission for the North, he was captured and imprisoned by the Confederates. He finally escaped.

Alone once again, Mary read of the healing techniques practiced by Dr. Phineas P. Quimby of Portland, Maine. Quimby believed it possible to cure his patients without medicines but, instead, with faith and prayer.

Mary Baker Patterson visited Quimby and experienced temporary improvement in her health. Quimby's method, she soon came to believe, could help other people to better health and to religious satisfaction.

In 1866 Phineas Quimby died. By then the Civil War had ended and Mary had moved with her husband to Swampscott, a suburb of Lynn, Massachusetts. One evening she fell on an icy street there and badly injured her spine. She was carried to the home of a friend. The physician caring for her considered her spinal condition serious.

Then, while alone several days later, Mary Patterson read in her Bible the incident of Jesus' curing a paralyzed man by using personal prayer. Suddenly, she believed that God had healed her. Leaving her bed, she dressed and walked outside her room, startling a group of friends who thought her close to death.

The incident proved to be a turning point in her life, the moment she later described as the beginning of the Christian Science religion.

Not long afterward, her husband left her for another woman, the couple finally divorcing in 1873. For Mary there increasingly were other things—more important things—on her mind. She began to meet with people who were ill, claiming to cure some of them with mental and religious treatment.

The years that followed were, for her, a busy, productive time. In 1875 she saw published the first edition of her now famous book, *Science and Health,* known today as *Science and Health with Key to the Scriptures.* For a course she taught on Christian Science

Mary Baker Eddy addresses a crowd of Christian Scientists at Concord, New Hampshire, in 1901. *The Bettmann Archive. Photograph by W. Kimball.*

she increased tuition from one hundred dollars to three hundred dollars. In the city of Boston, she gave regular lectures about her beliefs. Then, in January 1877 she married Asa Gilbert Eddy, her third husband.

As time went on Mary Baker Eddy grew even busier. In 1879 she took the first steps in organizing the Church of Christ, Scientist. She then established the Massachusetts Metaphysical College, teaching about the proper treatment of diseases. New editions of *Science and Health* began to appear. Particularly in Boston, she found herself surrounded by enthusiastic, admiring followers of her faith.

In her older years, Mary Baker Eddy took still greater pride in her accomplishments. She once identified her

A photograph of Mary Baker Eddy in her later years. *Brown Brothers*.

book on Christian Science with a section of the Bible during church services and even arranged to have the book placed next to the Bible. Sometimes she spoke of herself as "Mother Mary" and described methods included in her teachings as similar to those used by Jesus.

Thousands of Christian Scientists joined in praise of Mary Baker Eddy for changing their lives. In Boston, over the years, the main church building of her faith was replaced by larger and more beautiful structures. Members sometimes came to visit there from locations around the globe. Copies of Mary Baker Eddy's book sold in larger and larger numbers.

Christian Science remained to her always a religion dedicated to belief in Jesus Christ. The cross on the cover of *Science and Health* meant to her a cross of suffering. But, in her mind, the suffering could be eased—through faith. That belief became the true meaning of what she preached.

As the time of her death approached, Mary Baker Eddy arranged in her will for the distribution of a personal fortune worth more than two million dollars, in those days a fabulous fortune. Yet even on the day before her death, she remained actively involved in her religious work.

On December 3, 1910, Mary Baker Eddy died. The medical examiner who visited her at the time described her remains as characterized by extraordinary beauty. "I do not recall," he said, "ever seeing in death before a face which bore such a beautiful, tranquil expression."

Modern Christian Scientists sometimes deny the charges of such respected figures as Mark Twain that Mary Baker Eddy borrowed much of her faith from the teachings of Phineas Quimby. Also, a writer who did not believe in her religious practices contributed greatly to the stylistic improvement of *Science and Health with Key to the Scriptures*.

Still, in Christian Science churches around the world today her ideals live on. Her own life and the practices she championed were crucial factors in the success of her faith. Mary Baker Eddy rightfully deserves to be considered alongside other truly great figures in the history of the world's religions.

Dorothy Day

(1897–1980) Radical Catholic journalist and upholder of women's rights who lived a life of voluntary poverty on behalf of those victimized by society

Dorothy Day was pregnant. She was not married.

When she told the father of her unborn child that she expected to have the baby baptized as a Catholic and to become a Catholic herself, he told her that if she did, he would leave her. "You can't be a radical and a Catholic, too," he said. "That's the church of the rich. . . . People are starving, and they put money into elegant buildings and fancy robes for the priests."

Dorothy knew that he meant it. If she had the baby baptized as a Catholic, he would abandon her.

And he did.

But that did not stop Dorothy Day. "To become a Catholic," she later wrote, "meant for me to give up a mate with whom it was the simple question of whether I chose God or man."

For the rest of her life she tried to combine the ideas of the Catholic Church with her political beliefs. She tried to live exactly as the Bible said that people should live—caring for the poor and the sick and working for peace. The result was one of the truly remarkable stories in the history of the human rights movement in America.

Dorothy Day, the third of five children, was born in Brooklyn in 1897. Neither of her parents was Catholic, or for that matter very much concerned with religion. Her father, a sportswriter who specialized in horse racing, actually disliked organized religions, often ridiculing them.

Until the San Francisco earthquake

of 1906, the Days lived in Oakland, California. Dorothy later remembered the earthquake and the great fear she felt in the face of powers of nature, as well as her own feeling of helplessness. "If I fell asleep, God became in my ears a great noise that became louder and louder, and approached nearer and nearer to me until I woke up sweating with fear and shrieking for my mother."

By the time Dorothy reached adolescence, she had become deeply involved in reading. Works by the scientists Darwin and Huxley intrigued her, as did the complicated ideas of such philosophers as Spencer, Kant, and Spinoza. Finally she discovered the classics of religion—the Bible, the *Confessions* of Saint Augustine, the Anglican prayer book, and the sermons of Jonathan Edwards.

At age twelve she visited an Episcopal church in Chicago with a friend, and from that time began learning prayers by heart. In her autobiography she says, "I had never heard anything so beautiful as the *Benedicite* and the *Te Deum*. . . . The Psalms were an outlet for the enthusiasm of joy and grief."

Her parents, hostile or at best indifferent to religion, found her fascination with the subject puzzling. For Dorothy Day, the world of religion offered a way to show her independence. Also, growing up in a home where it was considered improper to let one's feelings show, she found religion a way to express herself.

Not only did Dorothy read, she also enjoyed writing. Often alone, she began to keep a diary at an early age, even though her brothers sometimes found it and teased her by reading parts of it aloud. At twelve she helped start a neighborhood newspaper, writing stories and poems for it. In school she often wrote about the poverty she saw around her. Writing about people's suffering, she discovered, made her feel that perhaps she could do something about the situation.

By the time she graduated from high school, Dorothy Day had decided to become a writer. But what would she write about? At first she wrote about God, who she said spoke directly to her.

More and more, however, she wrote about the poverty she saw around her. It was the age of progressivism in America, the beginning of the twentieth century. Writers such as Jack London, Upton Sinclair, and Frank Harris were introducing Americans to the darker side of the nation's life—the slums, the hopeless search for jobs, the scandals in the packaging of meats and other food products, the breadlines.

By the age of sixteen Dorothy had come to believe that things could be different, that society could be

Dorothy Day at the age of nineteen. *UPI/Bettmann.*

changed—reformed. It was at that age that she entered a scholarship contest and won it, entering the University of Illinois as a freshman.

In college, however, she turned against religion. Like many of her friends, she came to see religion as a tool of the rich to keep poor people "in their place." She started to swear, perhaps cursing God as a way of pushing religion out of her life.

Jesus, she pointed out, had said, "Blessed are the meek." But, declared Dorothy Day, "I could not be meek at the thought of injustice. For me Christ no longer walked the streets of the world. He was two thousand years dead and new prophets had risen up in his place."

After two years of college Dorothy dropped out. She moved to New York's Greenwich Village, a section of Manhattan that attracted many freethinking artists and writers. There she joined with a whole generation of young men and women, idealists rebelling against what they considered an outdated set of middle-class moral standards.

That group demanded that the capitalist goal of making more and more money be replaced with greater freedom for individuals: freedom to experiment in literature and art and freedom from repression in relations with the opposite sex. In place of Jesus Christ, young people then drawn to Greenwich Village substituted Karl Marx, whose *Communist Manifesto* had cried out, "Workers of the world, unite! You have nothing to lose but your chains!"

To help the radical cause, Dorothy wrote articles for left-wing newspapers and magazines such as the *New York Call* and *The Masses*. She opposed America's participation in World War I. Finally, she was arrested in Washington, D.C., after joining in a protest march demanding the right of women to vote in elections.

Later, while still living in the wild, rebellious atmosphere of New York's Greenwich Village, she came to know such outstanding literary personalities as Eugene O'Neill, the playwright, and prominent political figures including Max Eastman, Elizabeth Gurley Flynn, and John Reed. Still seeking meaning in her life, she moved to Chicago. There she fell in love with a communist writer, an affair that led to the abortion of an unwanted child. Next she married a literary agent—a marriage that lasted less than a year and left her deeply depressed.

Returning to Manhattan, Dorothy walked the streets, seriously considering suicide. Instead, she threw herself into writing. The result was a novel, the thinly disguised story of her own unhappy life. To her surprise, a Hollywood film studio liked the book and paid her five thousand dollars for it.

With that money she bought a small beach cottage on Staten Island. There she entertained some of her old friends, including writers who soon would become well known—John Dos Passos, Hart Crane, Malcolm Cowley.

One of her friends who came to her cottage was Forster Batterham. Batterham, an anarchist, distrusted all governments, all churches. But he did like Dorothy. Daily they fished, talked, and studied species of sea life they found while walking together on the beach.

In the summer of 1925 Dorothy Day discovered that once again she was pregnant. Remembering her unhappiness after aborting her earlier child, she was overjoyed at the news. She decided to go ahead with the birth no matter what Forster Batterham said.

At the same time, she had been finding increasing comfort in the Bible. She had begun to attend church services regularly. Like most of her radical friends, she believed that churches had done too little to help poor people win equal justice in society. Churches, she thought, had convinced people not to struggle but to accept inequality and wait for a reward in heaven after death. Or as the communists put it sarcastically, "There'll be pie in the sky by and by!"

Dorothy Day had tried the life of Greenwich Village and found it unsatisfying. Now, at the age of thirty-five, she decided to find a deeper understanding, a more profound meaning in her life.

In March 1927, she gave birth to a daughter, Tamar Teresa. With the help of a nun she had met on the beach, she had the baby baptized in the Catholic Church. She, too, was baptized and became a Catholic.

At that point Forster Batterham left her. Dorothy's own father angrily stormed at her for joining the church of "Irish cops and washerwomen." Her Greenwich Village friends laughed at her; some thought she had gone crazy.

Dorothy shrugged off the criticism. In the Catholic Church she finally discovered the sense of order and certainty that always before had eluded her. She found a mystical—that is, a direct—relationship with God.

Still unsure of how to make a living, Dorothy Day returned to newspaper work. With the coming of the Great Depression of the 1930s, she described what she saw everywhere around her. She wrote about the struggles of the poor to survive. For her newspaper columns she covered strikes, protest meetings, conferences of intellectuals.

In December 1932, she reported on a hunger march of the unemployed in Washington, D.C. Afterward, she went to pray at the National Shrine of the

Dorothy Day (center) and two other protesters against the entry of the United States into World War I. *UPI/Bettmann.*

Immaculate Conception at Catholic University. "There," she later wrote, "I offered up a special prayer, a prayer which came with tears and with anguish, that some way would open up for me to use what talents I possessed for my fellow workers, for the poor."

Returning to New York, Dorothy Day found waiting on her doorstep a short, shabbily dressed man who spoke to her in a thick French accent, scarcely giving her time to reply. He preached to her about his ideas, developed over many years of working, thinking, talking. His name was Peter Maurin. And what she must do, he told her, was to start a Catholic newspaper to educate the public about the situation of the poor and the unemployed.

To Dorothy, it seemed that her prayer in Washington had been answered. From Maurin's idea grew a newspaper—the *Catholic Worker*—that projected her onto the national scene. From Maurin, too, came the overall solution she had been looking for, the answer to her problem of how to be a religious Catholic and also a worker for social change in America.

Dorothy Day was not a communist. It is true that, like Peter Maurin, she believed that the capitalist system—a society based on getting and spending money—was a dead end. Being rich, as she and Peter Maurin already had learned, did not make people happy.

Still, she did not think that the answer to humanity's problems lay in destroying the system of private property and then building something new on the ashes.

The solution that Dorothy Day worked out, with Peter Maurin's help, was highly personal. It was based on changing society by changing the lives of individuals. To succeed, she would have to teach people to cooperate instead of compete. She would have to help people to search out the spirit of God in their daily lives. It was that Holy Spirit, not some notion of "class struggle," that had rescued her from the emptiness, the meaninglessness of her earlier life.

God, she now was sure, could be found among the poor: in the breadlines, in the jails, in the hopeless lives of white tenant farmers in the South and of blacks suffering in the slums of Northern cities. Dorothy now made it her mission—her pilgrimage—to help the poor, and by doing that, to change society.

On May 1 (May Day, celebrated as a workers' holiday in many countries), 1933, Dorothy distributed the first issue of the *Catholic Worker*. The first press run was 2,500 copies. Within two years the paper's circulation had grown to 150,000. Its price always remained one cent.

The *Catholic Worker* had as one of its main goals the establishment of Houses of Hospitality. These were places where poor, homeless men and women could go to get help. Dorothy, as usual more practical than Peter Maurin, started by renting an apartment on Charles Street in Manhattan. There, hundreds of people lined up each day for a place to sleep or a meal of soup, bread, and coffee.

Swiftly the idea spread across the country. Within ten years more than forty Houses of Hospitality were being operated to feed and shelter the poor. When people applied for help, they underwent no test of race or religious belief. Anyone who came to the door was welcomed. Later, Dorothy Day and Peter Maurin established six farming communes. They were aimed at doing in the countryside what the Hospitality Houses accomplished in the city.

The beginning of World War II posed a serious dilemma for Dorothy Day. Always before, the *Catholic Worker* had spoken out firmly against war. As Dorothy Day pointed out, Jesus loved even his enemies, and had preached against violence. Therefore, Christians were obliged to believe that *all* wars were bad, not just some wars.

Yet she could not just stand by and accept the horrible deeds of Adolf Hitler, including the mass murder of Europe's Jews. The *Catholic Worker*

Dorothy Day in 1965. *AP/Wide World Photos.*

condemned Hitler's acts. Dorothy Day personally challenged the vicious anti-Jewish statements of an American priest, Father Coughlin. She worked ceaselessly to save Jews by having them admitted to the United States. She also reminded her Catholic readers that Jesus himself had been a Jew.

Nevertheless, Dorothy insisted that a war to defeat Hitler and his Japanese allies would, in the long run, bring terrible results to humanity. Later she cited as proof the deaths of thousands of civilians in air raids on Hamburg,

Dresden, and Tokyo. America's dropping of atomic bombs on Hiroshima and Nagasaki represented to her only the beginning of still greater horrors if people did not turn against wars as a way of settling disputes.

As she grew older, Dorothy Day still insisted on living the kind of life she suggested for others—one of "sacrifice, worship, a sense of reverence." Part of her worship was the voluntary choice of poverty. Traveling around the country, she stayed in the communities of the Catholic Worker movement. She ate the humble food her "guests" ate and, like them, wore cast-off clothing. True, she continued to read good books, enjoy classical music, and go to the theater. That was another side of her life, the private side. It was just as much a part of her as the Dorothy Day who gave her strength to build a humane community.

As she grew older and older, tributes to her came poring in from around the world. *Life* and *Newsweek* magazines produced flattering biographical sketches of her. In a cover story, *Time* referred to her as "a living saint."

Men and women she had encouraged continued to show their gratitude. From the slums of Calcutta, Mother Teresa sent greetings. So did the great writer and priest Thomas Merton. In 1973 Dorothy had gone to prison for the last time, having been arrested while picketing on behalf of the nonviolent action of Cesar Chavez and his United Farm Workers union. Chavez considered her, along with Gandhi, his greatest source of inspiration.

Dorothy Day died in November 1980, shortly after her eighty-third birthday. Her grave is on Staten Island, overlooking the ocean. It lies very close to the place where her daughter was born— the place where she took on her new faith and made her fateful decision to live a life devoted to healing and hope.

Martin Luther King, Jr.

(1929–1968) Martyred leader of the nonviolent wing of the American civil rights movement; recipient of the Nobel Peace Prize

Christmas was coming. Rosa Parks had been shopping all day. She was tired and her feet hurt. She climbed onto a big orange bus, paid her fare, and took a seat.

Then something happened that changed the course of American history. The bus stopped and four passengers, all white people, got on. There were no more seats. In Montgomery, Alabama, it was the law that blacks had to give up their seats to whites if the bus driver told them to. Rosa Parks was black.

The driver ordered three other blacks to give up their seats. Without a word, they stood. They were used to that kind of thing. It happened all the time in Montgomery. Besides, in 1955, it was the law.

But this time, when the driver told Rosa Parks to stand, she simply said, "No!" She would not give up her seat. She was tired. She had paid her fare—just like the white people. Why should she have to stand?

The driver called a policeman. He arrested Rosa Parks. At the city jail, she was fingerprinted. Her picture was taken, showing her holding a prison number—as if she were a common criminal. Then, after paying a few dollars in bail, she was allowed to leave. Her trial would come later.

The word spread quickly through Montgomery. A black woman had been arrested for not giving up her seat on a bus. It had happened many times before. But this time in the black part of town people buzzed excitedly. They were angry. "What can we do? This can't go on any longer!"

It had been nearly a hundred years since the Civil War, and black people still did not have the rights of other Americans. In America's South—and in other parts of the country, too—blacks ate in separate restaurants from whites, went to separate schools, drank from separate drinking fountains in public places, even swore oaths on separate Bibles in the courtroom. Few of them were allowed to vote in elections. Before voting, they had to pass difficult reading tests and pay a tax called a poll tax. They could not get good jobs or good housing. In small ways and in large ways, black people were made to feel all the time that they were not as good as whites.

For a long time, the blacks had accepted mistreatment without fighting back. They did not think anything could be done. But in 1954, something important happened: the Supreme Court of the United States said that blacks could not be given separate schooling from whites.

Why? Because in schools for blacks, the children did not receive as good an education. In America, education is critical in deciding how successful a person will be in life. If schools for blacks were not good, black youngsters would have less of a chance for success than would whites.

After the Supreme Court ruling, black people had new hope. Perhaps, at last, they would have the same chance as other Americans for a good life.

That is why, in 1955, the black people of Montgomery, Alabama, were so angry when Rosa Parks was arrested. Their hopes had been high, and now it looked as if nothing really had changed. They decided that this time they would stand up for their rights. But what should they do? And who would lead them?

The new minister of the Dexter Avenue Baptist Church in Montgomery was the twenty-seven-year-old Reverend Dr. Martin Luther King, Jr. Born in Atlanta, Georgia, he was only one of six blacks at Crozer Theological Seminary, where he went to study religion. Yet he graduated with the highest grades in his class and was also student body president. After that, he studied for a doctorate in philosophy at Boston University.

The night Rosa Parks was arrested, Martin Luther King and other Montgomery ministers met to decide on a course of action. They agreed that for one day, December 5, blacks should not ride the buses. That would show how they felt. Nearly three-fourths of all the bus riders in Montgomery were black. If they did not use the buses, the company

Dr. Martin Luther King, Jr., and his wife, Coretta Scott King, in his office in 1962. *Brown Brothers.*

would lose business. This strategy, called a boycott, is a peaceful way to bring about change.

Leaflets were quickly printed. They said, "Don't ride the bus to work, to town, to school, or any place Monday, December 5. . . . Come to a Mass Meeting, Monday at 7:00 P.M., at the Holt Street Baptist Church for further instruction."

On the morning of December 5, Martin Luther King and his wife, Coretta,

awoke early. They were eager to see how many people were on the buses. If half of the city's blacks stayed off the buses, King would have been pleased. At six o'clock the first bus passed near the Kings' house. It was empty! The second bus was almost empty, and so was the third.

To Martin Luther King it was a miracle. He jumped into his car and drove around Montgomery. The buses were almost all empty. Black people walked. They rode horses and even mules. They shared rides in cars with their friends. But they did not take buses.

The boycott did not last just one day. It continued for 382 days. King and the other ministers held meetings. They urged the city's blacks to be peaceful and calm. But they should not pay a penny in bus fare until the owners of the bus company agreed to give blacks the same right to seats as whites had.

The owners of the company were furious. Every day the boycott continued they lost money. Many of Montgomery's other whites were angry, too. They were not accustomed to blacks standing up for their rights. Sometimes whites threw rocks at the drivers who were sharing their cars with other blacks. They shouted and called the blacks names.

Martin Luther King told his followers not to fight back. He believed in love, not violence. In college he had studied much about Jesus, who said, "Love your enemies, bless them that curse you." He also had learned about Mahatma Gandhi of India. Gandhi had helped India win freedom from Great Britain by refusing to obey British laws. Even when he was imprisoned, Gandhi would not allow himself to hate the English or advise Indians to use violence against

them. Gandhi first had learned about nonviolence from the works of an American, Henry David Thoreau.

King, like Gandhi and Thoreau, believed that an unjust law should not be obeyed. Not obeying—known as civil disobedience—might mean going to jail. But if that was the price for doing what a person thought was right, Martin Luther King believed that the price should be paid.

He also believed that even if people did evil to you, you should do good to them. You should not hate them. As the great black educator Booker T. Washington once had said, "Let no man pull you so low as to make you hate him." King agreed. He wrote that no matter how badly blacks were treated, they should not hate their white brothers. To become a truly great people they must learn to "turn the other cheek"— not hit back if they were hit.

But they must never stop trying to win their rights. Most Americans, King thought, believed in fair play. They needed only to be shown that blacks were not being treated fairly. Then they would understand. They would help black people achieve equal rights.

The story of the Montgomery bus boycott spread quickly around the world. Money poured in from Latin America, Asia, and Europe, as well as from many parts of the United States, to help King in his fight. Almost overnight, King became an internationally known figure.

Seeing his picture on television and in the newspapers made some whites even more bitter. One evening a bomb exploded on the front porch of King's home. Nobody was hurt. A crowd of more than a thousand blacks gathered. Many shook their fists in anger. Others carried guns, knives, rocks, and broken bottles. In vain, the police chief tried to quiet them. So did the mayor of Montgomery. But the shouting crowd refused to listen. Someone had tried to kill their leader—and they demanded revenge. Nothing, it seemed, could block the onset of a bloody riot.

Finally Martin Luther King himself stepped out onto the smoking ruins of his front porch. He raised his arms and began to speak. At once the crowd grew silent.

"Don't get panicky," he said. "Don't get panicky at all. Don't get your weapons. Please be peaceful," he pleaded. "I want you to love your enemies. Be good to them. Love them and let them know you love them."

Then King, who, along with his wife and children, had just barely escaped death, concluded, "I want America to know that even if I am stopped, this movement will not stop, our work will not stop, for what we are doing is right.

What we are doing is just—and God is with us."

Slowly, peacefully, the angry blacks began to disperse to their homes. The police relaxed. There was no riot. King's words were repeated on television and in newspapers across the country. Americans saw that he meant what he said about nonviolence, even when his own life was in danger. "The strong man," he said, "is the man who can stand up for his rights and not hit back."

The bus boycott went on. It lasted until 1956, when the United States Supreme Court ruled that segregation of blacks and whites on vehicles engaged in interstate commerce is illegal.

At last the fight was over. Dr. King and his followers had won a tremendous victory. Now blacks could sit where they chose on buses and trains. Never again would they be required to give up their seats to whites.

When King next spoke to his people, he urged them not to boast about their victory. "I would be terribly disappointed," he said, "if any of you go back to the buses bragging that 'We, the Negroes, won a great victory over the white people.'" He wanted them to join together with whites to make Montgomery a better place—and he wanted them to remain nonviolent.

The bus boycott was only the first

step in King's struggle to help blacks get their rights. The fight spread all over the South and then to the North. But always King urged black people to use gentleness and kindness, not force—just as Jesus had taught.

Sometimes, even for him, it was not easy. Whites cursed him and spat on him. They threw rocks and tomatoes at him. They kicked and hit him. They threatened his life. They threatened his wife and four children. They burned crosses on his front lawn. Often he was thrown in jail.

In spite of everything, King kept on fighting for the rights of blacks. He showed his followers how to stay still even when they were being beaten or when mobs called them names and threw things at them. He led peaceful marches against all-white schools, restaurants, and movie theaters. He tried to get the names of blacks on voter registration lists so they could vote in primary and general elections.

In Birmingham, Alabama, King was met by snarling, sharp-fanged German shepherd dogs, held on leashes by policemen. The police turned fire hoses on the crowd of black marchers, even on the women and children. All across the country, people saw pictures on their television screens of the police dogs. They saw policemen clubbing people who would not fight back—

blacks who wanted nothing more than the same rights that most Americans already had.

More and more, King began to emerge as a new kind of American hero. Every time he was put in jail or beaten, he won followers to his ideas. Before long, white people joined in his marches. Together with blacks, they sang the most famous of all civil rights songs, "We Shall Overcome." The words of the song speak of a time when blacks and whites will live together in peace and happiness.

Martin Luther King believed that such a time really would come—someday.

In Washington, D.C., on August 28, 1963, he told more about his hopes for the future. That day he made one of the great speeches in all of American history.

More than a quarter of a million people—both black and white—gathered in front of the Lincoln Memorial. They had come to ask Congress to pass the civil rights bill, then being considered by Congress. If adopted, it would give blacks many of the rights that King and his supporters had fought for so valiantly.

"I have a dream today," declared King. "I have a dream that one day this nation will rise up and live out the true meaning of . . . 'all men are created equal.'

"I have a dream that one day on the red hills of Georgia, the sons of former

Dr. King making his "I Have a Dream" speech. *AP/Wide World Photos.*

Dr. Martin Luther King (first row, left) walks in Medgar Evers's funeral procession. *Culver Pictures, Inc.*

slaves and the sons of former slave owners will be able to sit down together at the table of brotherhood."

"I have a dream," said King again and again. Each time he told of his hope that the promises made for all Americans in the Declaration of Independence and the Constitution would someday come true.

"Let freedom ring," he cried out. "Let it ring until the day when all of God's children, black men and white men, Jews and Gentiles, Protestants and Catholics, will be able to join hands and sing in the words of that old Negro spiritual, 'Free at last! Free at last! Thank God almighty, we are free at last!'"

When King finished, men and women openly wept. His words were carried swiftly around the world by radio and television. Newspapers printed his entire speech. Now, unquestionably, he had become the foremost leader of America's blacks.

In 1964 King was presented the Nobel Peace Prize, an international award given to those who make outstanding contributions to the cause of peace.

When King won the prize he was only thirty-five years old—the youngest person ever to receive it. In accepting the award, he suggested humbly that it really was not his. Rather, it belonged to many people, black and white, still working with high courage toward an era of nonviolence and love in the United States.

Not all blacks agreed with King. Some argued that nonviolence was too slow. They pointed out that love, so far, was not winning equal rights for blacks. In Birmingham, Alabama, six children were killed when whites bombed a black church. In Mississippi, Medgar Evers, a black civil rights leader, was ambushed and killed in the driveway of his house. In Mississippi, three young people trying to help blacks register to vote were beaten and shot to death, their bodies found several weeks later buried near a dam. Who could love white people who did things like that?

New black leaders began to emerge. One of them, Malcolm X, called himself a Black Muslim, a believer in the Islamic religion. Malcolm said—at least early in his public career—that blacks

never would be able to live with whites. Instead, he said, they should rule a separate country of their own, made up of one of the states of the United States. There they would live their lives completely apart from whites.

Among other black leaders who disagreed with King were Stokely Carmichael and H. Rap Brown. Carmichael demanded that blacks should no longer try to love whites who beat them and insulted them. Instead they should fight back. "What we need," he said, "is Black Power!" H. Rap Brown did not mind violence either. "Violence," he once said, "is as American as cherry pie."

Many blacks believed that Malcolm X, Stokely Carmichael, and H. Rap Brown were right and that King was wrong. And, of course, some blacks understandably reacted angrily to white racism. In city after city, riots erupted—Watts (Los Angeles) in 1965, Cleveland, Chicago, Detroit, New York, and Newark in the following years. Buildings were burned and stores looted. Whites and blacks shot and stabbed one another.

By 1968 the battle for civil rights had become a nightmare. To some it appeared that America was on the verge of widespread racial warfare.

King would not change his mind. He believed that violence was wrong. He also knew that in America it was whites who had both the weapons and the numerical advantage. A war between blacks and whites would end in death—the death of the Negro race in the United States. Meanwhile, he remained convinced that most blacks still followed his ideas. What he needed was time to lead them away from violence and back to loving kindness. He needed time to prove that nonviolence really could work.

But he did not have that time. On April 4, 1968, in Memphis, Tennessee, Martin Luther King was shot and killed from ambush by a white assassin.

The day after he died, angry blacks began riots across the United States. In Washington, D.C., smoke and flames rose high in the sky within sight of the White House. Machine guns guarded the steps of the Capitol building. Violence, it seemed, was everywhere.

But violence was not the way of Martin Luther King. He did not want to be remembered that way. He wanted to be remembered with Jesus and Gandhi. They were men of peace who gave their own lives to make the lives of others better. King, too, gave his life to help build what he hoped would be a better world, a world of right and of justice.

Now Americans have had an opportunity to view their racial situation more clearly. In the years since Dr. King's death, most of his foes—both black and white—have faded into history. Meanwhile, the name Martin Luther King has earned a hallowed place in the annals of human freedom. Streets and schools in the United States and abroad have been named after him. College scholarships have been established in his memory. A national holiday—Martin Luther King Day—has been set aside by Congress to honor his achievements, thus placing him in the front rank of American heroes, along with George Washington and Abraham Lincoln.

What has happened, then, is that time has proven King far more right than wrong. The American people, in honoring him, have affirmed what Lincoln called "the better angel" of our natures. It is not violence and hatred that America has celebrated, but rather, the ideals of peace and love and the brotherhood of humankind.

And those, of course, are the ideals represented in the life—and the sacrifice—of Martin Luther King.

CONCLUSION
Religion in the Future:
The Coming of a Worldwide Faith?

This book has examined the lives of past religious leaders, the people who shaped such faiths as Hinduism, Buddhism, Jainism, Sikhism, Judaism, Christianity, and Islam.

But what of the future?

Will the world's religions of past and present join somehow in the centuries to come and give birth to a single "world religion"—a worldwide faith bringing together everyone who inhabits planet Earth?

In the beginning of human history people largely lived their lives as part of nature. They were surrounded all the time by the sun and moon and stars, by lightning and thunder, by wind and rain, and by changing seasons. No wonder, then, that they turned first of all to the worship of nature.

Next, they moved to idol worship. They showed their faith in statues of various animals and gods—powerful images admired by families and tribes and, eventually, by people across broad stretches of territory.

In time, the belief in idols gave way to religions we now know well, the great faiths of the last six thousand years. Leaders around the globe expressed their views and managed to attract followers. Akhenaten, Zoroaster, Mahavira, the Buddha, Confucius—all won deep admiration from those who reached out for guidance about the meaning of life and how best to live it.

Still other people depended on different kinds of leaders, different kinds of faiths. Their models came to be Moses, Jesus, and Muhammad, along with such later figures as Martin Luther, John Calvin, and Mary Baker Eddy.

Recent centuries have been marked by thinkers eager for tolerance and for compromise. Unitarians, Mormons, and Reform Jews have been willing to achieve their goals without resorting to warfare, but rather with an emotional feeling that religion sometimes can suggest—the sense of love and belonging.

In our own time, of course, we have observed the deeds of radical figures such as the Ayatollah Ruholla Khomeini. Leaders like these often use religion to achieve their political goals. Recent leaders in the United States, including Louis Farrakhan, openly have expressed religious hatred in order to win followers to their side.

Such examples raise serious doubts as to whether humanity will ever see a world religion—a universal faith. Many defenders of competing faiths still claim today that theirs is the only true pathway to salvation. This is their belief even though the strongest of past religious movements eventually have given way to change. Nor does it seem likely that any one dynamic new personality in the field of religion will somehow manage to triumph completely. That, too, has never happened.

Yet the hope of religious harmony in the future is not altogether impossible. People always have been drawn together. The largest part of the Christian Bible is made up of the Old Testament of the Jews. Japanese Shintoists have included in their faith many contributions from Confucian and Taoist religions. Hindus work toward ever greater fellowship, even using ideas of the Buddha and of Christ. Sikhs managed to merge the Hindu and Muslim traditions. Such modern groups as the Bahá'ís and the Unitarians consciously make it a point to work the ideas of other religions into their regular services.

The unification of the world into one religious faith may never happen. Still, people could, in time, gain greater understanding of other forms of belief. That knowledge could lead to a breakdown of ongoing prejudice and hatred. It could lead to a willingness to listen to people with different viewpoints. And by hearing what others say it is possible to respect them, even to love them.

Times have changed. Jet planes now can bring together people from the farthest reaches of the world in less time than was necessary for ancient Christians and Jews to walk between Nazareth and Jerusalem. In the period since World War II rockets have carried people to the moon and transmitted knowledge to us about the planets.

In such an era of dramatic change, people of different nationalities may well come closer together in a political sense. They could also move on to new religious views, drawing on older ones held by past prophets.

If that occurs, future generations may well gain a broader and a fresher sense of what life on earth really is all about.

Further Reading

Since the most ancient of times, people have asked the truly essential questions of life. Why am I here? What is life all about? How did I come to be? What will happen to me after I die?

Religious leaders have had to face those issues in their very own lives. They have had to deal with matters of right and wrong, good and evil. Sometimes they themselves have written down their thoughts. Sometimes followers have joined with them in recording important stories and beliefs.

The result has been a wealth of materials concerning the great religions of history and those personalities who preached the faiths in humanity's past years.

In preparing this volume in the Great Lives series it has been particularly helpful to have access to the writings of scholars in the field. Special thanks are due to the perspectives provided by Charles Francis Potter in his insightful volume, *The Great Religious Leaders* (Simon and Schuster, 1958).

Also significant were two works by Joseph Gaer, *How the Great Religions Began* (Dodd, Mead, 1956) and *What the Great Religions Believe* (Dodd, Mead, 1963). For general background, the classic contribution by William James, *The Varieties of Religious Experience*, rev. ed. (Collier-Macmillan, 1963), provided highly useful insights. So, too, did Huston Smith's *The Religions of Man* (Harper and Row, 1958).

Finally, no study of religious leaders would be complete without the joy of direct and frequent reference to the holy books of various faiths, including for example the Bhagavad Gita of the Hindus, the Dhamapada of the Buddhists, the Koran of the Muslims, and differing versions of the Bible used by the Christians and Jews.

The study of religion remains, of course, a major topic in the academic world. If, therefore, you wish to learn more about the personalities included in *Great Lives: World Religions*, it might prove helpful to examine some of the historical works that have played a part in making this book possible.

As you do, you may also wish to remember the words of the biblical prophet Isaiah, for, like so many great figures in the history of religion, Isaiah believed that religious leaders have a special responsibility to their followers. Or as he once put it:

> The spirit of the Lord God is upon me, because the Lord has anointed me to bring good things to the humble. He has sent me to bind up the brokenhearted, to proclaim liberty to the captives, to open gates for those who are imprisoned, to comfort all who mourn, and to give the mourners in Zion beauty instead of ashes.

Part I: Faiths of Ancient Egypt and Persia

AKHENATEN (AMENHOTEP IV)
Aldred, Cyril. *Akhenaten: King of Egypt.* London: Thames and Hudson, 1988.
Montet, Pierre. *Lives of the Pharaohs.* Cleveland, Ohio: World Publishing Company, 1968.

ZOROASTER (ZARATHUSTRA)
Campbell, Joseph. *The Masks of God: Occidental Mythology.* New York: Viking, 1964.
Pangborn, Cyrus R. *Zoroastrianism: A Beleaguered Faith.* New York: Advent Books, 1983.

Part II: Asian Religions

CONFUCIUS
Creel, H. G. *Chinese Thought from Confucius to Mao Tse-Tung.* Chicago: University of Chicago Press, 1960.
Ware, James R. *The Sayings of Confucius.* New York: New American Library, 1955.

BUDDHA (SIDDHĀRTHA GAUTAMA)
Marshall, George N. *Buddha, the Quest for Serenity: A Biography.* Boston: Beacon Press, 1978.
Percheron, Maurice. *The Marvelous Life of the Buddha.* Translated by Adrienne Foulke. New York: St. Martin's Press, 1960.
Suzuki, D. T. *Zen Buddhism.* Garden City, N.Y.: Doubleday Anchor, 1962.

MAHAVIRA
Schweitzer, Albert. *Indian Thought and Its Development.* New York: Holt, 1936.

NĀNAK
MacAuliffe, Max A. *The Sikh Religion: Its Gurus, Sacred Writings, and Authors.* New Delhi: S. Chand, 1985.

MOHANDAS K. (MAHATMA) GANDHI

Erikson, Erik H. *Gandhi's Truth*. New York: Norton, 1969.

Fischer, Louis. *Gandhi: His Life and Message for the World*. New York: New American Library, 1954.

Part III: Islam and Its Descendants

MUHAMMAD

Roberts, D. S. *Islam*. New York: Harper, 1982.

Rodinson, Maxime. *Mohammed*. New York: Pantheon, 1971.

BAHÁ'U'LLÁH

Esslemont, J. E. *Bahá'u'lláh and the New Era: An Introduction to the Bahá'í Faith*. Wilmette, Ill.: Bahá'í Publishing Trust, 1970.

Hatcher, William S., and Martin J. Douglas, *The Bahá'í Faith: The Emerging Global Religion*. San Francisco: Harper and Row, 1985.

AYATOLLAH RUHOLLA KHOMEINI

Rajaee, Farhang. *Islamic Values and World View: Khomeini on Man, the State, and International Politics*. Lanham, Md.: University Press of America, 1983.

Wright, Robin. *In the Name of God: The Khomeini Decade*. New York: Simon and Schuster, 1989.

Part IV: Judaism

MOSES

Goldstein, David. *Jewish Legends*. New York: Peter Bedrick Books, 1987.

Wiesel, Elie. *Messengers of God: Biblical Portraits and Legends*. New York: Random House, 1976.

JEREMIAH

Blank, Sheldon H. *Jeremiah: Man and Prophet*. Cincinnati, Ohio: Hebrew Union Press, 1961.

Skinner, John. *Prophecy and Religion: Studies in the Life of Jeremiah*. Cambridge: Cambridge University Press, 1922.

GOLDA MEIR

Martin, Ralph G. *Golda: Golda Meir, the Romantic Years*. New York: Scribners, 1988.

Meir, Golda. *My Life*. New York: Putnam, 1975.

Part V: Jesus and the Christian Experience

JESUS

Mauriac, François. *Life of Jesus*. Chicago: Thomas More Press, 1936.

Renan, Ernest. *The Life of Jesus*. 1863. Reprint. New York: Modern Library, 1927.

PAUL

Mitchell, William M. *St. Paul the Traveller and the Roman Citizen*. New York: Putnam, 1903.

Speer, Robert E. *Studies of the Man Paul*. New York: Fleming H. Revell, 1900.

AUGUSTINE

D'Arcy, M., ed. *Monument to St. Augustine*. New York: Sheed, 1931.

Pope, Hugh. *St. Augustine of Hippo*. Garden City, N.Y.: Image Books, 1961.

PATRICK

Hanson, Richard Patrick Crossland. *Saint Patrick: His Origins and Career*. New York: Oxford University Press, 1968.

Thompson, E. A. *Who Was Saint Patrick?* New York: St. Martin's Press, 1986.

THOMAS AQUINAS

Chesterton, G. K. *Saint Thomas Aquinas: "The Dumb Ox."* New York: Doubleday, 1956.

Maritain, Jacques. *St. Thomas Aquinas.* New York: Meridian Books, 1958.

Part VI: Christianity Since the Reformation

MARTIN LUTHER

Bainton, Roland H. *Here I Stand: A Life of Martin Luther.* New York: Abingdon-Cokesbury Press, 1950.

Todd, John M. *Luther: A Life.* New York: Crossroad, 1982.

JOHN CALVIN

Daniel-Rops, Henry. *The Protestant Reformation.* London: J. M. Dent, 1961.

McNeill, John T. *The History and Character of Calvinism.* London: Oxford University Press, 1954.

DESIDERIUS ERASMUS

Bainton, Roland H. *Erasmus of Christendom.* New York: Scribners, 1969.

Huizinga, Johann. *Erasmus of Rotterdam.* London: Phaidon Press, 1952.

JOHN WESLEY

McConnell, Frances J. *John Wesley.* New York: Abingdon Press, 1939.

Rauschenbusch, Walter. *A Theology for the Social Gospel.* New York: Macmillan, 1917.

GEORGE FOX

Trueblood, D. Elton. *The People Called Quakers.* New York: Harper and Row, 1966.

Van Etten, Henry. *George Fox and the Quakers.* New York: Harper and Row, 1959.

MOTHER TERESA

Serrov, Robert. *Teresa of Calcutta.* New York: McGraw-Hill, 1981.

Mother Teresa. *My Life for the Poor.* New York: Harper and Row, 1985.

Part VII: Religious Leaders In America

ROGER WILLIAMS

Jacobs, William Jay. *Roger Williams.* New York: Franklin Watts, 1975.

Winslow, Ola Elizabeth. *Master Roger Williams.* New York: Macmillan, 1957.

ANNE HUTCHINSON

Battis, Emery John. *Saints and Secretaries: Anne Hutchinson and the Antinomian Controversy in the Massachusetts Bay Colony.* Chapel Hill: University of North Carolina Press, 1962.

Rugg, Winifred King. *Unafraid: A Life of Anne Hutchinson.* Boston: Houghton Mifflin, 1930.

JONATHAN EDWARDS

Levin, David, ed. *Jonathan Edwards.* New York: Hill and Wang, 1969.

Miller, Perry. *Jonathan Edwards.* New York: W. Sloane Associates, 1949.

JOSEPH SMITH

Brodie, Fawn M. *No Man Knows My History: The Life of Joseph Smith, the Mormon Prophet.* New York: Knopf, 1945.

Hill, Donna. *Joseph Smith: The First Mormon.* Garden City, N.Y.: Doubleday, 1977.

ISAAC MAYER WISE

Heller, James G. *Issac M. Wise.* New York: Union of American Hebrew Congregations, 1965.

Philipson, David. *The Reform Movement in Judaism*. New York: Macmillan, 1931.

MARY BAKER EDDY

Eddy, Mary Baker. *Science and Health with Key to the Scriptures*. Boston: Christian Scientist Publishing Co., 1875. Now published by The First Church of Christ, Scientist.

Gardner, Martin. *The Healing Revelations of Mary Baker Eddy: The Rise and Fall of Christian Science*. Buffalo, N.Y.: Prometheus Books, 1993.

DOROTHY DAY

Coles, Robert. *Dorothy Day: A Radical Devotion*. Reading, Mass.: Addison-Wesley, 1987.

Miller, William D. *Dorothy Day: A Biography*. New York: Harper and Row, 1982.

MARTIN LUTHER KING, JR.

King, Martin Luther, Jr. *Stride Toward Freedom*. New York: Harper and Row, 1958.

O'Neill, William L. *Coming Apart: An Informal History of America in the 1960s*. Chicago: Quadrangle, 1971.

Index

C1

j 922 Jac

6/97

Jacobs, William Jay.
Great lives: world relig
ions /
23.00   05/08/97 AFW-8382

JOHNSTOWN
PUBLIC LIBRARY